PATHWAYS

CAMILLE PETERS

Camille Peters ☺

PATHWAYS

By: Rosewood Publications

Copyright © 2019 by Camille Peters

Rosewood Publications

Salt Lake City, Utah

United States of America

www.camillepeters.com

Cover Design by Karri Klawiter

To my beloved Mother, Lareen Peters,
whose constant love, support, and belief in me have been the means
for me to achieve my dreams.

CHAPTER 1

*T*he Forest had always had a mind of its own; whenever I stepped within the trees, I never quite knew where its constantly shifting pathways would lead. Many legends about the mischievous Forest roamed the village of Arador. It was said that the trees acted as the guardians of the countless stories carefully preserved within their limbs.

My family's cottage bordered the Forest, shaded by its overhanging branches. No one knew the Forest as well as I did. Over the years I'd become familiar with its language, spoken not in words but in the whispers of its rustling branches. I would never forget the first time the Forest had gently lured me inside with its promise of adventure. The branches swayed, an invitation within the rippling leaves, beckoning me to enter.

I tentatively stepped into the woods. Trees stretched out in all directions, twisting above me to form a cocoon. The pine-scented air felt different, heavy with mystery and secrets, all containing discoveries just waiting to be made.

My heart immediately connected with this vast being—love at first sight. I soon realized that the Forest felt the same way about me.

There were no paths...at first. Leaves crackled beneath my feet as I carefully maneuvered around trees, fallen logs, and overgrown vines as the Forest tugged me deeper and deeper inside. The trees grew thicker and their branches scraped my skin the farther I ventured in, following the Forest's guidance, whispers in the dancing wind.

Midst the foliage, a path suddenly appeared where one hadn't existed before. As I stared, the path *shuddered* before shifting and twisting itself until it stilled, veering off to disappear in a thicket of trees. Curiosity tickled my senses. How had the path magically appeared? More importantly, where did it lead?

Tree sap stuck to my skin as I rested my palm on the bark of a nearby pine. "You won't let me become lost, will you?"

The branches swayed gently, the Forest's assurance. Splendid.

Since that day several years ago, I'd become an avid explorer of wherever the Forest decided to lead me, never repeating the same destination twice. I carried my sketchbook and pencils so I could draw each of my new discoveries. The Forest stretched for miles, but no matter how the pathways changed or how far I traveled, the Forest kept its promise and I never lost my way.

I spent hours within the trees, trying to uncover each of its mysteries. I discovered meadows dotted with wildflowers, clearings with twisting streams that may or may not have been enchanted, a lily-pad-dotted lake, rocks with messages scrawled in an unknown language, and trees that not only transformed into other species when the mood arose, but which were perfect for climbing.

Even if I didn't find anything new, I'd sit beneath the clustered branches for hours, my sketchbook propped against my knees, either to draw, to slowly turn the pages to revisit past drawings—each a treasured memory—or simply to bask in the tranquil stillness: just me, the Forest, and my pencils to keep me occupied.

I slowly emerged from today's enchanted drawing stupor and glanced up at the sky. The sun was no longer directly overhead, signifying the hours that had melted away without my noticing. Oh dear, Rosie wouldn't be pleased to have been kept waiting. Again.

I scrambled to my feet, brushed dirt and leaves off my patched dress, and shoved my sketchbook into my satchel before picking my way along the overgrown path that snaked through the Forest. Normally, the paths twisted and moved every few steps until it decided on a direction, but they were being uncannily still. I glanced imploringly up at the towering trees.

"Could you show me a shortcut? Rosie is waiting."

Like a loyal friend, the Forest heeded my plea. The path before me quivered. I watched it rearrange itself to curve northeast before I followed it as quickly as I dared without risking tripping over any protruding roots, stealing only a single glance behind me to see the path wriggle back to its original position.

The path ahead meandered to the Forest's edge, where dear Rosie waited, arms crossed and wearing an exaggerated pout.

"It's about time you showed up. I was running out of stories to explain your absence."

Doubtful; Rosie never ran out of stories. I offered a repentant smile. "Did you come up with any good ones?" Asking Rosie about her stories did wonders for her ill humor.

A thoughtful pucker lined her brow as she pressed her

thumb to her lips. "Plenty, each more fantastic than the last. Shall I share my favorite?" She looped her arm through mine and we strolled along the Forest's border. "I imagined you'd met a dark and handsome stranger in the woods and fallen madly in love."

I snorted. "Please no."

"Don't you dare protest how I choose to write my stories," she said. "When you play the heroine in Rosie's tales, even *you* long for true love rather than continuing to stubbornly entertain your delusions that you want a future devoid of romance."

"They're not delusions; I don't *want* to fall in love."

Even though we'd had this conversation dozens of times, my words were still lost on Rosie, the ultimate romantic. She heaved a rather dramatic sigh. "I just don't understand it. Every heroine wants to find their true love."

"Not me—and before you argue, you know perfectly well why."

"Not all men leave like your father, Eileen."

I flinched at her mention of him, but as always I buried the pain from his abandonment deep before it could take root. "That's what my mother believed, and look what happened to her."

Rosie pursed her lips but she dropped the subject—for now. No doubt before our visit was over she'd broach her favorite topic yet again; she just couldn't imagine my future not containing a prince and a happily ever after like she'd always imagined for herself.

We wandered to our favorite area, tucked several paces within the Forest, a charming clearing awash in wildflowers, shady hemlock trees, and thickets of strawberries whose plump, sun-kissed fruit grew no matter the season.

We settled in the grass and Rosie held up her picnic

basket, filled to the brim with day-old leftovers from her family's bakery. "No excursion is complete without a picnic, a picnic we almost lost the opportunity of having when Ferris tried to steal these. Thankfully, I managed to avoid his usual older-brother antics." She handed me a chocolate pastry before taking one herself.

I frowned at mine suspiciously. "This isn't one of your enchanted treats, is it?"

"Certainly not." Rosie took an exaggerated bite from her pastry. "See? Perfectly safe."

I watched her closely for any signs of magic at work before I took a tentative bite of my own. *Mmm...*moist, fluffy, chocolatey. "I never know with you."

She giggled unrepentantly. "I do like to experiment, but I'd never give my best friend something spelled without telling her first...unless it was a love spell."

She gave me a pointed look that made me fear she actually planned to concoct a scheme such as that sometime in the future. She indelicately shoved the remainder of her pastry in her mouth and licked her fingers.

"Unfortunately, I haven't had a chance to bake from *Enchanted Sweets and Delights* for ages. Mother has suspected I've been sneaking peeks at it and now locks the book away. So far, my quest to steal it back has been unsuccessful."

"You're rather obsessed with that book."

She waved that accusation away. "I don't bake from it enough. Life could use more magic. It's found in abundance in storybooks." She sighed. "Unfortunately, today's scene in *The Tale of Rosalina* has been rather dull, considering I've spent so much of it waiting and we have yet to do anything to fill this chapter with adventure." She gave me a sharp, accusing glare.

I shifted guiltily. "I'm sorry I kept you waiting."

"I may be appeased if you tell me of your own adventures within the Forest."

"I was sketching."

She rolled her eyes as she snatched another pastry. "Unsurprising and dull. Your story is always the same."

"Not with the Forest's constantly shifting pathways always leading me to a new drawing spot."

I pulled out my sketchbook and turned to today's picture, tipping it to show her. Rosie's ill humor vanished as her expression brightened with appreciation. She eagerly took my sketchbook to examine it more closely.

"Oh, it's exquisite. You're so talented." She admired it a minute more before returning my sketchbook. "I suppose I must forgive you for keeping me waiting. Now, do you want to hear the latest delicious tale I heard from a customer at the bakery about the Dark Prince?"

I cocked an eyebrow. While few in Sortileya had actually seen Prince Deidric, our monarchy's heir to the throne, everyone knew the many whispered rumors surrounding him, all of which painted a rather unflattering image of him: dark, foreboding, and sinister. I doubted most—if any—of the rumors held any truth. Rosie naturally believed every word.

"What's the story this time?"

"Something positively wicked." Rosie leaned closer, eyes bright. "He's been poisoning his betrothed, Princess Rheanna of Draceria, drop by drop into her goblet with every visit."

I frowned skeptically. "He's *poisoning* her?"

Rosie nodded. "Isn't it dreadful?"

"Last I heard, the entire Dracerian family were all in perfect health." Not that I heard much about the neighboring kingdom's monarchy, but surely news of a poisoning would spread rapidly.

"That's the *claim*," Rosie said with a shiver of excitement.

"They're trying to keep the Princess's declining health hushed up, but naturally it's all a ruse. Princess Rheanna's health is rapidly deteriorating. Soon the Dark Prince will be in need of a new betrothed."

She trailed off, her gaze far away as she lost herself in her story—whether the one she was telling me or another she'd just thought of to tell herself. Lips twitching, I snagged another pastry to keep myself occupied until Rosie emerged from her stupor, blinking rapidly.

"Are you attending tomorrow's dance?"

I groaned. Predictably, we couldn't stay away from the topic of romance for long. "You know I never attend the dances."

"But I keep hoping you'll change your mind. At least one of us needs to find her prince charming, and I've long been convinced that meeting him at a dance is the proper way to do it; it's the usual method employed in stories."

She twirled her golden hair around her finger, her blue eyes bright and wistful. She truly looked like a heroine straight from a fairy tale, a fact that had always given her great satisfaction. It was one of her multitude of reasons she believed she was destined for a happily ever after.

Yet apparently her tale currently wasn't going well, for she sighed dejectedly. "I, of course, dance beautifully, but my skills are utterly wasted on the village boys, none of whom seem to be my heart's match. A stranger who attended the last dance showed some promise, but his hands were clammy, naturally disqualifying him from being my prince."

"Well, with so many clammy-handed dance partners, there are slim odds of my finding the one, meaning there's no reason for me to attend the dance."

"Perhaps you'll have better luck than I have, but we won't know unless you attend."

CAMILLE PETERS

I sighed. "For the umpteenth time, I don't *want* to fall in love."

She pouted momentarily before brightening. "Then come for the sole purpose of helping me hunt."

That sounded nearly as torturous. I was finished with this conversation. I picked up Rosie's now-empty basket and went to the thicket of berries to pick some for mother. Not so easily foiled, Rosie followed me, continuing her monologue about the essential traits her true love must possess, as well as the latest news from the court provided by her cousin. I desperately tried to tune her out, for each word of her recitation chipped away at the defenses I'd built over the years to protect myself.

"Can you read out loud from our current book?" I asked when Rosie finally paused to take a breath. Her eyes widened with guilt. She lowered her gaze to her hands, which were now wringing together in her lap.

"Now, don't be cross, Eileen, but I had to do *something* while waiting for you like the loyal best friend that I am. But today's reading was most delicious, so of course I don't mind reading it again." She removed the book from her own satchel and turned to our bookmarked place. "Pay close attention, for this chapter is filled with a lot of adorable romance."

I bit my lip to suppress a sigh. Perhaps having Rosie read out loud wasn't such a good idea.

But despite my reservations, I quickly became immersed in the tale spun in Rosie's smooth storytelling voice. It was admittedly a rather sweet portrayal of all I'd determined never to allow myself to have. But I forced myself to push those rebellious thoughts away in order to strengthen the defenses around my heart.

No matter what Rosie said or how beautiful the fairy tales we read together were, I'd determined years ago that love wasn't in my future. No matter what twists and turns my own story took, I would not be swayed from that predetermined course. Ever.

~

AN HOUR LATER, I said goodbye to Rosie and returned home, my basket of berries dangling from my arm and my mind swirling with unwanted but unsuppressed visions of adoring gazes, stolen kisses, and sacrificing everything for true love, all of which had been featured in abundance in this afternoon's story.

I unhooked the gate and walked up the path to our cottage, nearly swallowed up by twisting vines of honeysuckles freshly in bloom. Their sweet perfume mingled with the scent of baking bread drifting through the open window.

Inside, Mother perched anxiously at her weaving stool in the front room, her attention riveted not on the colorful pattern she was creating but on the front door, her eyes clouded with worry. She relaxed as I entered.

"Eileen, dear, thank goodness you've returned. You've been gone such a long time."

Remorse for my tardiness filled me as I glanced at the clock on the mantle. Between my delay in the Forest and becoming extra engrossed in Rosie's story—despite its mushy content—I'd been gone longer than I'd promised.

I bent down to sweep a kiss across her cheek. "I'm sorry, Mother. I lost track of time. I hate the thought I worried you."

She smiled her forgiveness as she cupped my chin. "I know it's silly for me to worry. Just because you're late doesn't mean you'll never return…"

I instinctively stiffened as memories I'd fought to suppress invaded my mind. Ten years had passed, feeling at times like only a few months and at others like a thousand lifetimes. Cheerful, fun-loving, adventurous Father had told us he was traveling through the Forest to the capital to make some trades. He'd promised to return in a fortnight. Only he never had. Search parties yielded no information about what might have happened to him.

First days passed, then weeks, then months, and eventually years. My childhood self hadn't fully understood what had happened. How could my dear father have vanished, despite his assurances he'd return to us? I'd spent endless days waiting for him on the front step until winter arrived, forcing me indoors, where I spent countless hours pressing my face against the front window, waiting and hoping for an arrival that never came.

Mother changed after that, her cheerfulness gone, replaced by grief and heartache. She often clutched Father's portrait against her heart and sobbed. As I watched her, quenching my own tears, the realization slowly settled over me:

Mother loved Father. Fiercely. He'd seemed to have loved her, too, but that obviously hadn't been enough to satisfy his restless spirit and prevent him from coming home to us. Now Mother was left with nothing but a broken heart.

Without Father we had no livelihood, but despite the long, harsh years that followed, we managed to get by. Mother wove, I gathered berries to make jam, and we took in laundry. Many villagers helped, but nothing could fill the void Father's absence had created. The worst part about his abandonment was that to this day we still had no idea why he'd left.

Perhaps I'd done something wrong.

Mother's smile—for she always managed to have one for me—softened into a concerned frown puckering her brow. "Are you alright, dear?"

I shook my head to clear it from the painful swirl of memories and forced my own smile. "I'm fine." It was my most frequent lie. I turned around and carried the basket of fruit to the table. "Shall I mash these to make jam?"

"Eileen?"

I heard Mother approach but didn't turn around. I couldn't risk her seeing the tears that had come uninvited to my eyes, tears I'd told myself years ago never to shed. Crying would create cracks in my protective walls and allow me to reexperience the emotions I no longer wanted to feel. It was less painful this way.

"Perhaps we can bake the berries into a pie," I continued, still not turning around. "We can bake two and trade one for some supplies—"

Mother rested a light hand on my back. I flinched at her touch. "I miss him, too."

I bit the inside of my lip until I tasted blood, hoping the pain would stave off the tears now flowing down my cheeks. "I don't miss him." My voice cracked, betraying my second-most-frequently-told lie.

"Something must have happened to him. He'd never just *leave* us."

"But he *did* leave us."

Mother was silent a moment, a silence filled with her own pain. I inwardly cursed myself for being the cause of it, but sometimes I couldn't help it; even after all this time, my emotions were still too raw and too close to the surface for me to always successfully suppress them before they leaked out.

"He loved us," Mother finally murmured.

I snorted. *Love.* I hated that word. If Father leaving was what love was, then I wanted no part of it. No matter how beautiful Rosie's stories about romance were, they were all make-believe. Thus, I'd never give another man the opportunity to hurt me the way Father had.

The day I'd first discovered Mother crying over Father, I'd chosen to lock my heart away forever. Love wasn't worth the pain it inflicted, especially not when the fickle emotion was too fleeting to ever last.

CHAPTER 2

The Forest practically pushed me down an unfolding path thick with foliage the moment I stepped inside. I looked curiously at the trees but didn't question them. The winding trail made many jagged twists and turns, each change deliberate and purposeful; it was unlike the Forest to be so selective in its guidance.

I'd never questioned the Forest before, but I paused now in order to peer inquisitively at a rosemary pine. "Where are you taking me?"

The branches rustled but otherwise made no reply.

I nibbled my lip as I peered down this path as far as I could see. It was thick and overgrown, as if it were part of the Forest itself rather than a trail weaving through it. With the shadowy light and its twists and turns, it was impossible to see where it led, but I trusted the Forest; it had never led me astray.

I continued down the path, picking my way through the vegetation. The trees grew in closely intertwined clumps and the minty air felt different, heavy with mystery and discoveries just waiting to be made. I was probably the first to walk this course in years.

After several minutes, the path widened into a large clearing, which the trees surrounded like a halo. I tipped my head back to stare up at the artistic pattern the canopy of branches formed above me. Lovely, to be sure, but almost disappointing after such a strenuous journey. I studied the clearing more closely, searching for something to justify the Forest's insistence on leading me here.

The hemlock trees grew in an unusual pattern: the way the branches twisted made them resemble a person. Inspiration tickled my senses as the beginnings of a story formed in my mind, one I needed to capture with my pencils.

The story Rosie and I had been reading was the legend of a princess who, abandoned in the woods, grew up within the trees and became a ruler amongst all who lived in the Forest. Upon her death, her spirit became part of the Forest, giving it both life and a mind of its own.

Today's project would be an imaginative portrait of this Forest princess. After silently admiring my most recent treasured sketches, I opened to a fresh page in my sketchbook and studied the hemlocks' branches. My hand caressed the page as I reproduced this legend with fluid strokes...

A twig snapped, piercing my sketching revery. I gasped and twisted around. The shadowy trees were completely still, their dark, budding limbs stretching endlessly towards the sky. Heart pounding, I slowly scanned the entire clearing. Empty.

No one was here. I released my pent-up breath and returned to my sketch, but my white-knuckled hand remained frozen, hovering over the page. Something—or *someone*—had to have made that noise.

I held my breath and listened intently. The Forest's previous symphony of twittering birds had ceased, leaving nothing but thick, tense silence. It was unlike the Forest to be so quiet.

The back of my neck prickled and I felt as if a heated gaze bore into me to scrutinize my every move. I glanced over my shoulder, expecting to see a mysterious intruder watching from the trees. No one was there.

Some of the darker tales of the Forest the villagers often exchanged in warning whispers invaded my mind: *There are tales of many who lost their way amidst the trees after the Forest's paths led them astray, for they say the blood of its victims is what gives it life.*

I'd never believed those stories; my Forest was anything but sinister. I'd explored it for years and had never encountered another living soul, let alone a dangerous one. Thus the pathways wouldn't have led me to this clearing if the Forest sensed any danger...would it? Whatever I thought I'd heard was merely my mind playing mischievous tricks. No one was here except for me and the trees...trees which were being uncannily quiet, as if they'd fallen into a deep slumber.

My assurances did little to calm me. I fought for breath—each sharp and painful in my fear—and hunched back over my sketchbook to focus on drawing the tree's budding leaves in a way that made them resemble the princess's tresses, desperate for a distraction. But my hand remained frozen over the page.

The Forest had been unusually particular today about which pathways it led me down. Was there a purpose to its guidance?

Another twig snapped. I straightened rapidly, my heart hammering as I listened intently, trembling.

"Is someone else here, Forest?" I whispered. The trees remained completely still. My fear escalated as the sensation I was being watched intensified.

I shivered. Imagination or not, I couldn't stay here a

moment longer. I snapped my sketchbook shut and scampered towards the edge of the clearing. The moment I moved, footsteps—their sound nearly lost to the deafening pounding of my heart—sounded behind me.

I froze and listened; they paused when I did. I crept a few steps more, and so did the intruder. No mistake about it: I wasn't alone. I clutched my sketchbook like a protective shield as I wound my body behind a trunk and huddled there, trying to control my frantic pants of breath.

Silence.

I listened to every sound of the Forest as I waited, trying to detect a human heartbeat within the trees. All seemed quiet, but I *sensed* something; the Forest felt different, on edge, as if it could sense an intruder, too.

I remained hidden for several minutes before I slowly released my pent-up breath. Huddling here wasn't leading me any closer to the Forest's border, which was where I now desperately wanted to be. I slowly stepped away from the tree and gasped sharply, my sketchbook slipping from my hand.

A man stood in front of me, blocking my path.

My heart skittered to a stop. So there *had* been someone following me, a stranger dressed in red velvet trimmed with gold to showcase his noble rank and who wore a hardened, rather sinister expression, as if he meant to hurt me.

He leaned leisurely against an aspen, staring at me with large, ebony eyes, which widened when he saw my face. For a moment, neither of us spoke as we warily surveyed the other. A foreign, pleasant warmth loosened the fear tightening my chest as I studied the stranger's face, lingering on the chestnut curl dangling across his forehead.

He stirred first, blinking rapidly, before he snapped his gaping mouth shut. His expression hardened again. "What are you doing in my Forest?"

Chills rippled over me as my mind scrambled to find an explanation for this man's presence. I warily eyed the sword strapped to his waist. The treacherous Forest had betrayed me by luring me into this stranger's snare. This clearing would undoubtedly be my gravesite, and the story of my demise would become another cautionary tale parents whispered to their children about what happened to those who wandered in places they weren't supposed to.

Those overdramatic thoughts were exactly what Rosie would think in this situation. I shook my head to clear it. I couldn't think about that now. Escape. I needed to escape, but the man's eyes held me captive as if they were chains, binding me to him. He straightened and slowly approached. I backed into a tree and pressed myself against the trunk until its bark embedded into my back.

He loomed over me. "Who are you?"

I didn't answer. I couldn't. My voice had been swallowed up by the fear pounding through my bloodstream with every frantic beat of my heart.

The man's jaw tightened. "Answer me. I expect a response when I ask a question."

His hand hovered over his gold sword encrusted with blood-red rubies. My breath caught. Did he mean to murder me? Fear seized my pounding heart in a tight clamp, but thankfully he made no move to draw his sword.

Instead, he frowned. "Ah, you're afraid I might use this? You believe me a man capable of hurting an innocent maiden? It appears I'm making a rather poor first impression." He studied my features, the hardened lines of his own softening with his perusal.

I finally found my voice. "Please don't hurt me."

He stroked the hilt of his sword with long, slender fingers. "Who said anything about hurting you? I would, however, appreciate an introduction."

I tightened my jaw and shook my head. Disappointment filled his eyes, as if I'd denied him something precious. He continued to stare, his gaze lingering on my hair. He reached out a hesitant hand to stroke a loose strand.

My hair slipped from his fingers as I jerked back, glaring. "Don't touch me."

He blinked, as if emerging from a stupor. "I meant no harm. If you won't tell me your name, can you at least grant me a token to remember our meeting? It's not every day I encounter such a fair maiden in the woods."

He drew a dagger and carefully placed it against the same strand of hair resting against my neck. My breath hitched. I jolted away and the blade nicked my flesh. I winced at the sharp, biting pain. Blood trickled down my neck, staining my pale skin with dark splotches.

The stranger flinched, as if my pain had been his own, and watched the blood dribble down, seeming unsure what to do. Crimson stained his cheeks as he yanked his gaze away. I gingerly touched my neck and withdrew my fingers, gaping at the blood staining them.

"You cut me."

He cleared his throat, shifting awkwardly as he determinedly looked at his feet. "My apologies, I didn't mean to hurt you." He bit his lip in remorse.

I stared at him in disbelief. I could still feel the shadow of his cold blade as I stroked the wound on my neck, sticky with blood. How could I have met such a hardened man in my beloved Forest, a place I'd believed harbored safety? The betrayal was sharp.

"I only wanted a lock of your hair." He withdrew a handkerchief and held it out to me. I made no move to take it. "I'm sorry. I just—I'm sorry." He made another attempt to hand me his handkerchief. When I still refused it, he dabbed at my cut himself and sighed when I flinched away. "Won't you allow me to play the part of a gentleman?"

"Do you see a gentleman here?"

Despite the blush still staining his cheeks, his lips quirked into a smile. He tilted his head to study me, as if I were a complicated riddle he was desperate to solve. "You're unlike anyone I've ever met. I must have your name."

"I don't share my identity with sadistic strangers."

His eyebrows rose. "What did I do to deserve such an insult when we've only just met and I'm attempting to tend to your wound?"

"A wound *you* inflicted," I snapped. "You don't appreciate it when your prey bites back? Perhaps you thought you'd caught a sheep when, in reality, I'm a fierce cobra."

"Undoubtedly, with a venomous tongue like yours."

Amusement had replaced the fierceness previously filling his eyes. Great, I'd stumbled onto a predator who enjoyed playing with his food. I folded my arms and gave him my most skewering glare; by the way his lips twitched, it didn't seem very effective. His black gaze searched mine as if looking for an answer to a great secret.

"Won't you tell me your name?"

"Do you honestly believe you can convince me after I've already adamantly refused?"

"Considering I outrank you and I asked nicely, yes, I do."

I rolled my eyes. "I'm sure that, as a noble, you're used to everyone groveling at your feet, but I refuse to obey you."

His jaw tightened. "Is this the game you want to play? Because if so, it's only fair to warn you that in every game I participate in, there's only one outcome: I *always* get my way."

"Except for now, because I'm not inclined to give it to you, no matter how much you try to persuade me."

He frowned. "Stubborn, aren't you? But I refuse to

concede until I've obtained my objective." He glanced around the clearing, as if searching for something. "The Forest led me to this area for a particular reason, and I need to know why. If it was to meet you, then I cannot leave without your name. Will you tell me if I say please?"

"No."

The stranger's brows furrowed. "Why not?"

"You truly expect my cooperation after the friendly reception you've given me?"

He closed the distance between us. "Despite your resistances in giving me what I want, I find your spunk thoroughly enchanting."

For some inexplicable reason, I found myself lost in his ebony gaze. "Is this how you toy with all your victims?"

"No, this honor befalls only you." He leaned closer and I turned my head, shuddering as his breath caressed my skin. "Please tell me your name."

I shook my head, unable to speak through the strange sensations I was feeling. It pushed against my fear—warm, fluttery, and strangely appealing. What *was* this emotion?

"Please." Longing filled his voice. "You don't understand. I have to know."

"Then brace yourself for disappointment, because I refuse to give you my name after the way you've treated me."

He sighed as he withdrew. "Seems fair."

I raised my eyebrows and he smirked.

"Despite your belief to the contrary, I won't force you to do anything…although I do hope to persuade you. I find the longer our interaction goes, the more anxious I am to know your identity."

I sighed. "Why are you so desperate to learn it?"

He tilted his head to study me once more. "You're like no one I've ever met before. I can't quite put my finger on what it is that's…"

"…getting beneath your skin?"

He smiled wryly. "Something like that."

I smirked, satisfied that I'd riled him, my revenge for his sinister presence invading my sanctuary. "Good, then you've gotten what you deserve."

He frowned. "You believe I'm a bad person?"

"I believe you're choosing to be something sinister for the sole purpose of your amusement."

His frown deepened and once more he studied me closely. "Why do you think that?"

I didn't answer. He waited patiently for a moment before his lips twitched.

"Uncooperative. It makes me even more curious as to what brings you to my Forest."

His Forest? "The Forest belongs to no one, but if my presence bothers you, I'll happily humor you by leaving."

He bowed and motioned towards the edge of the clearing. "Be my guest. There's no need for you to linger if you don't want to. However, there is one small problem…"

His dark eyes lit up and my stomach knotted. Whatever idea had just occurred to him, it probably wouldn't be one I liked.

"What's the problem?"

He raised an eyebrow. "Problem? There's no problem. It'd be impolite for me to keep you here longer than you desire to remain."

I narrowed my eyes. "You claim to have the power to keep me here? This Forest doesn't belong to you; thus, you can't entrap me in it like some prisoner."

I spun on my heels and stomped towards the edge of the clearing, but the stranger darted in front of me, blocking me. "Please don't leave yet."

My glare sharpened. "Excuse me? Do you need to toy with me further in order to stroke your inflated ego?"

His lips twitched again and amusement danced in his dark eyes. It made him seem almost human, and I didn't like it. "I really want to know your name."

"There's no reason for you to know it, not when we're never going to see one another again."

"I wouldn't be so sure of that."

I tightened my jaw and attempted to dart around him, but he was too quick for me. I took another step forward but he didn't get out of my way; he took a step back, matching my movements with his in order to keep me in his line of sight. My gradually abating fear returned, clawing at my heart.

"Whatever game you're playing, please stop."

"A game? Is that what this is?" He stroked his chin before nodding to himself. "If it's a game you want, then allow me to enlighten you on how this particular one is played."

A shiver rippled over me. I wrapped my arms around myself to try to mask it. "What's the game?"

"A riddle." He offered a boyish grin. "I enjoy riddles. If you can solve mine, I'll tell you which path will lead you back to Arador."

"How do you know which village I live in?"

He smirked up at the Forest's swaying branches, as if he and the trees were sharing a private joke. "A lucky guess."

I eyed his smirk. "You think you're so clever, but you're not the only one. I know these trees and thus don't need your help finding my way out of—" My words became trapped in my throat as I glanced around the clearing. *No...*I slowly turned in a circle, searching, my heartbeat escalating when I couldn't find what I was looking for. "Where did the pathways go?"

"Ah, that's the problem I mentioned earlier."

I stared at the lack of pathways in disbelief, unable to comprehend what I was seeing. No matter where the Forest had led me in the past, a path had always existed to guide me back home. It was part of the Forest's promise it'd given me when I first breached its trees.

Heart in my throat, I spun on the stranger, who watched my reaction with far too much amusement for my liking. "What did you do?"

"You believe I'm responsible for the Forest's tendency to shift its pathways?"

My heart pounded in my ears, making it difficult to think. "You keep calling this Forest *yours*; if you're conceited enough to assert ownership of it, you must claim responsibility for its mischief."

"I make no such claims. The Forest is its own master; I'm simply on excellent terms with it."

"As am I."

"Apparently, your relationship with it isn't as good as mine, else it'd be listening to you now rather than me."

Obviously. *Curses.* I gritted my teeth. "What did you do with the pathways?"

The stranger lazily examined the tip of his blade with too innocent of an air. "I may or may not have told them to disappear for a bit."

"And the Forest listened to you?"

"Rank has its advantages."

"But the Forest listens to no one."

He shrugged. "Believe that if you will, but even you can see that the pathways have vanished, just as I hoped for our little game."

I scanned the thicket of trees again, feebly hoping for the path that had led me here to reappear. It didn't. "Where did it go?"

"Not to worry, it's not completely gone; there's always a path, even if it's merely hidden. Oh look, there are two now."

As if the Forest was the silent servant of this mysterious man, two paths appeared several yards away, each snaking off in opposite directions. He rested his chin on a fist, studying them a bit too theatrically.

"But now you have a new problem: there are two. Which one is the correct one?"

I scowled. "You know, don't you?" Somehow he did, even though his knowledge should have been impossible.

"You seem to have a habit of making mistaken assumptions, don't you? No, I haven't the faintest idea which path you need to take. But the Forest does. If you answer my riddle correctly, it'll lead you to where you need to go."

Which was as far away from this man as possible. "I don't believe I trust the Forest anymore; it seemed overly eager to lead me to you today."

His eyes widened at that. "Interesting. As I mentioned earlier, it led me to you today, too. Perhaps it thought I could use some humbling from having a feisty commoner put me in my place."

I smirked at that success. "Assuming the Forest reveals a path, how will I know it's the right one?"

"I suppose you won't until you reach the end of it, but I don't think you need to worry; it seems to like you."

"Not as well as you, obviously."

He chuckled—a surprisingly warm sound—and reached out to give the nearest tree an affectionate pat. "Everyone likes me."

"Well, not me."

"Unsurprising. You and everyone else seem not to."

My forehead furrowed at that complete contradiction. A challenging look glistened in his eyes, as if he desired me to call him out on it, but since he wanted it, I naturally wouldn't humor him.

I folded my arms across my chest as if the gesture could protect me from whatever came next. "As thrilling as this unpleasant exchange is, I very much want to leave. What's the riddle?"

"Before I give it to you, might we discuss payment?"

I sighed impatiently. "Payment?"

He raised an eyebrow. "Surprised? Everything comes at a price, and this is no exception. So in exchange for helping you find the correct path, I want your name."

This elaborate scheme was all for my name? My identity truly meant so much to him? "Will you uphold your end of the bargain if I give it to you?"

"I'm a man of honor." And he bowed.

I searched his eyes for any sign of deceit, but they were like dark, endless tunnels, stretching too deep for me to detect any emotion. I sighed. There seemed to be no other choice but to trust him, even though he obviously didn't deserve it.

"Very well, I'll share my name in exchange for this riddle of yours."

He leaned closer, his previously emotionless eyes now undeniably eager.

I took a deep, steadying breath. "My name is Eileen."

"*Eileen.*"

A strange thrill rippled over me as he said it in his honey-smooth voice. He studied me a moment before smiling. It completely transformed his face and caused my stomach to give the strangest flip-flop.

"Your name fits you."

"And what's yours?"

"Ah, my identity wasn't part of our bargain. Now, are you ready for your riddle?" At my nod, he motioned towards the two paths disappearing into the woods. "As you can see, you're standing at a fork with two paths—one that leads towards the unknown, the other towards your desired destination of home. Because you cannot distinguish between the two paths, you must seek guidance. Luckily for you, the two trees heading them will offer the solution; unfortunately, you can only appeal to one for help. But beware: one tree only tells truths and the other only lies. You only have a single question to ask one of the trees and must therefore carefully determine which question will guarantee you discover the path you seek."

For the first time in our encounter, I smiled. "A clever puzzle."

"Indeed. It's a favorite of mine."

Despite his still-hardened countenance, light filled his eyes. He was getting far too much amusement from this.

"Are you like one of the trees in the riddle? Do you always tell truths or do you always tell lies?"

"A bit of both," he said.

"Then tell me: now that you have your desired payment, will you let me go whether or not I answer your riddle correctly?"

He offered a small smile, my answer. Perhaps this man wasn't as sinister as I'd initially believed.

"So this riddle is unnecessary," I said. "You'll let me go regardless of whether or not I solve it. But I'll still humor you and play." I turned to the two paths, nibbling my lip in thought. "I'd simply ask one tree what the other would say."

"And how would that help you?"

"If I asked the lying tree what answer the other would give me, it would naturally tell me the opposite of the truth. If the correct pathway is the one on the right, it would know the honest tree would tell me so and thus say it's the left one. If I asked the honest tree what the lying one would say, knowing the other tree would lie, its honesty would give me the same answer— to take the left. Whether the tree I ask is lying or telling the truth, the answer is the same, and thus I would know the left path is the wrong one and would take the right."

Admiration glistened in his eyes. "Surprisingly clever... and rather fun, especially considering I got what I wanted. Let's see if the Forest likes your answer."

Together we watched the paths merge into one, which I had no doubt would take me to my desired destination. "That one leads to Arador," I said confidently.

"Perhaps it does, perhaps it doesn't. That's the funny thing about paths; you can't see where they lead unless you walk them." He bowed with a flourish and motioned towards the single pathway, which twisted into the dense trees.

I frowned at the stranger. "Where's your path?"

"Unfortunately, it's different from yours, but I'm hoping our paths cross again some day."

Well, *I* didn't hope for such a thing. "You're not going to follow me, are you?"

"Only if you want me to."

I most certainly didn't. I warily eyed the single path. Although it was currently being deceptively obedient by not moving, it'd already breached my trust enough that I wouldn't discount the possibility of it becoming rebellious the moment I set foot on it.

I glared back at the stranger, needing to make one thing clear before departing. "We're never going to see one another ever again."

With that, I turned and bolted. Branches scratched my flesh as I crashed through the trees, going wherever the Forest led me despite now being unsure it'd really guide me to safety, not after its suspicious obedience to the bidding of that mysterious man. I strained my ears for his pursuit, but the only sounds were my crashing through the trees, my sharp breaths, and my heartbeat throbbing in my ears.

Thunder shook the sky, and after several toying rumbles,

a tumult of rain broke from the heavens, soaking me to the skin and filling the trail with mud. I struggled to lift my feet, and twice I tripped.

Through the torrents of rain, I finally glimpsed the edge of the woods just up ahead. Moments later, I burst from the trees and collapsed in a panting heap, waiting...for surely the stranger would emerge, his eyes bright from the thrill of watching my flight.

Any moment now...

But the Forest remained still, the trees solemn sentries harboring the dark stranger within.

CHAPTER 3

I lay in the mud, my heart pulsing beneath my fingertips, each thud a rhythmic message: I'd escaped the Forest and the stranger within. Even now, I could still feel his presence extending from the trees, taunting me.

How could I have met such a sinister person in *my* Forest? The Forest and I had an understanding. I'd trusted it. Would I ever be able to return? I tipped my head back to glare accusingly at the trees. Save for the wind gently swaying its branches, the Forest was completely still, as if too ashamed of itself to talk to me.

When the light began to fade, the thought of Mother's worry finally compelled me to stand and hurry home. Through the thick sheets of rain I could barely make out the glowing lantern in our front window, beckoning me to safety. I stumbled up the garden path and collapsed, exhausted, in the front room.

"Eileen, is that you?" Mother's voice, taut with panic, drifted closer towards where I lay sprawled on the ground. She gasped sharply. "Eileen! Thank goodness."

She was beside me in an instant. Completely disregarding my soaked and muddy state, she pulled me into a suffocating embrace, burying her teary face against my head as she stroked my hair and murmured my name over and over.

Eventually, she pulled away and frantically scanned my body for potential injuries. She took in my frazzled appearance and my torn dress caked with mud. "What happened?"

I couldn't answer. I allowed her to lead me to the hearth and set me in front of the roaring fire, where she draped a blanket over my shoulders. I wrapped it tightly around my shivering frame as Mother pulled up a chair and sat across from me, staring intently.

"Something's obviously happened. When you didn't return, I thought…"

Guilt gnawed at my heart that I'd made her worry. "I've been in the Forest."

She sighed and pressed her fingers to her temples. "I know you love the Forest, but you know how I feel about your frequent visits there. One day you're going to get lost and never return to me." She took my hand and squeezed it.

"I can't help but visit; I love the Forest, and I'm never lost when I'm within it. It calls to me." But now I was no longer sure whether I trusted it enough to return.

"You shouldn't be listening to trees, you should be listening to me. Now, I want answers. What happened in the Forest? You went deep into the woods, didn't you?"

I shifted guiltily. My silence only confirmed her fears. She sighed wearily.

"Oh Eileen, you promised you wouldn't go far." She stroked my hair, pushing it over my shoulder to expose my neck. Her face paled further as her frantic gaze took in the gash sliced along my collarbone from the stranger's blade, nearly camouflaged in all the mud. "What happened? Who gave you that cut?"

"A nobleman's dagger."

Mother gasped sharply. "A *nobleman's* dagger? Whose? Tell me."

The memory of his black, seemingly soulless eyes filled my mind and I shivered. "I don't know. He didn't tell me his name."

Though I'd foolishly given him my own—an unfair exchange. The thought of that dark stranger now possessing my identity knotted my stomach.

"What do you mean you don't know his name?"

I shrugged. "I just met him in the Forest. It was strange; I've never met another person in there before..."

I trailed off, my brow furrowing. The entire meeting and the Forest's motives behind it were a total mystery. Why would the Forest lead me to someone who'd cause me harm?

"Why did he hurt you? Did he attack you? Are you harmed anywhere else?" Her gaze frantically combed over me, searching for further injuries she may have missed.

"No..." How could I explain a situation I found perplexing myself?

"Then how did you get that cut?" Her hands stroked me uselessly, as if the gesture could wipe away the stranger's inexplicable actions.

"He claimed he was trying to take a strand of my hair."

Mother stared at me blankly. "What?"

I shrugged again. "He gave no other explanation."

Mother looked like she was going to launch into another round of questions, seeking answers I didn't have. Hoping to stave off the onslaught, I gave an exaggerated wince. "Ow, it stings..."

Mother's expression twisted. "You poor dear..." She lightly prodded my wound with her fingers. "It's not as deep as it looks, but it'll likely scar. *Oh...*"

She muffled her breathless sob as she stood and bustled

to the cupboard for her herbal remedy. She returned and cleaned the mud off my neck, paying careful attention to the locket I always wore, Father's last gift to me before he left. Then she gently lathered the spicy-scented salve along my cut, each massage causing the stinging pain to gradually cool.

"You know I don't like you wandering that Forest. If you'd only listened to me, this would never have happened." She pursed her lips as she dabbed another layer on my wound.

"I was just drawing and—" Horror pierced my heart. I jerked to my feet, severing Mother's touch. "My sketchbook!"

I scrambled outside, where the rain had become a thunderous roar. Lightning flashed across the dusky sky, illuminating the gathering puddles, puddles that now filled the Forest floor, destroying my lost sketchbook. My heart sank at the realization. I needed to find it. I headed towards the gate, but Mother grabbed my wrist and yanked me to a stop.

"Where are you going?"

"My sketchbook—" I tugged desperately on Mother's grip, but her hold was firm.

"It's too dark and stormy. You'll never find it."

She was right. My heart tightened even as it tried to tug me towards the Forest and my lost drawings.

Dazed, I allowed Mother to lead me back inside and sit me in front of the fire. I stared unseeing into the dancing flames. Several years ago after a particularly cozy evening spent with Father in front of the hearth, I'd drawn a picture of this very fireplace. I'd spent hours capturing the movement of its popping embers and the blended dance of its colors. Now that drawing was gone. They all were, lost in the rain. Tears trickled down my cheeks.

Mother stroked my dripping hair. "I'm so sorry, dear. I know how much your sketchbook meant to you."

I buried my tear-streaked face against her lap. Her soothing touch moved to rub my back.

"Have you told me everything that happened?"

There was so much still left unsaid—the foreign way the stranger had made me feel, his riddle, his fierce need for my name. But none of that mattered now. My encounter with the mysterious man felt part of another lifetime, the acute aching loss of my sketchbook eclipsing everything else. Years of work, memories, and captured snippets of my imagination —all gone, destroyed in the storm. My heart twisted at the thought.

"I can't believe it's gone."

"I know your pictures meant a lot to you," Mother murmured. "Perhaps you can duplicate some of them. I have a little bit of coin saved. We'll go into the village tomorrow and buy you a new book."

I shook my head. Not only could we not afford such a luxury, but I didn't want a new sketchbook—one that was blank and empty of all my precious drawings—I wanted *mine*. Was there any hope of finding it and salvaging it?

Outside, rain lashed against the windowpanes, no sign of the storm relenting anytime soon. But as soon as it did… "I'm going to look for it tomorrow."

"But it's inevitably destroyed."

My heart cracked at the thought, but I couldn't give up hope. The Forest knew how much my drawings meant to me. Perhaps it had somehow protected my sketchbook. "You don't understand, I *need* to go back for it. It's my greatest treasure."

Mother shook her head. "What if you encounter that man again who attacked you? It's too dangerous to go back."

My most prized possession was still in the Forest. No matter its current state, no matter the potential risks, I couldn't leave it there. "I have to find it. Please, Mother."

"No, Eileen, you can't return to the Forest. I can't bear the thought of you wandering those trees after what just happened." Mother's eyes became glassy with worry. "I'm sorry you lost something so precious to you, but surely you realize your life is worth more than the tattered remains of your sketchbook."

Any tattered remains of my life's work was better than nothing at all. My sketchbook and all it contained could very well be destroyed—a thought which sent piercing grief through me, as if I'd lost a dear friend rather than mere parchment and charcoal.

I released a strangled sob. *"Please."*

"Absolutely not." Mother's tone was firm. "I haven't the faintest idea why that stranger tormented you, but I won't risk losing you. You're all I have left. Never enter that Forest again."

Her eyes were so wild and desperate that I pursed my lips and nodded, an agreement that was nothing more than a lie to appease her, for no matter what Mother said, I *needed* to get my sketchbook back. Its absence had taken a piece of my locked-away heart with it.

ROSIE WAS WAITING with wriggly impatience when I arrived at the village library the next day. Despite the continuous rain, she'd summoned me early in the afternoon, instinctively knowing I had a fantastic story to share and unable to wait to hear it. Naturally, she wanted the recitation to occur in one of our favorite places—the single-room library consisting solely of a few tables surrounded by shelves containing every book in Arador, most of which we'd read, several multiple times.

The moment I arrived, she pounced on me, squeezing me

in a suffocating hug. "Are you alright? I've been hearing the most ghastly rumors. I've been worried sick at the thought that I almost lost my best friend." Her hug tightened.

How had she heard anything about it? "I'm alright," I managed breathlessly. She pulled away to scan me from head to toe, her gaze lingering on the cut on my neck, parting my dark hair to better examine it.

"While you certainly seem fine now, you're not entirely unscathed." She led me to a table tucked away from the other villagers, as if my injury had rendered me incapable of walking on my own. "You must have had quite the adventure. Tell me every detail. I cannot bear to be in suspense any longer."

"But one of the aspects of enjoying a good tale is to tell it gradually in order to build up the suspense."

She sighed. "Normally, I'm the biggest advocate for proper story conventions, but really, Eileen, I can't bear it today. Cheat this once by beginning with the climax and working your way backwards."

"What have you already heard?" For this being Rosie, she'd somehow heard *something*, but I had no idea what or from whom. Had my mother talked to hers that morning?

She clutched my hands and leaned closer, lowering her voice to a whisper. "I heard you encountered a mysterious stranger in the Forest and narrowly escaped with your life. Is it true? Please tell me that it is."

"He didn't nearly murder me," I corrected, unsurprised that Rosie had already added her own dramatic spin to my tale.

"I heard he had a sword, meaning he *could* have. Oh Eileen, it's positively dreadful." She shivered, doe-eyed, both with fear on my behalf and excitement for my adventure. "Tell me everything at once."

Considering Rosie already seemed to know the climax, I

began at the beginning with the Forest's strange urgency to lead me to a destination that didn't seem particularly special, save for it being the first place I'd ever encountered another person. Before I could even continue, Rosie held up her hand to stop me.

"Wait, the Forest lured you to where you met this stranger?"

I studied her warily. "Yes. Why? Is that important?"

She nodded. "Extremely. Please continue."

She listened with rapt attention as I recounted the rest of the tale: the stranger, the cut, and his cryptic riddle. When I finished, Rosie stared at me for a moment with her typical "lost in a story" expression before she beamed.

"That was the most perfect of all stories; it was positively thrilling."

"*Thrilling?* Rosie, my story could have ended in countless tragic ways."

"But thankfully it didn't," she said brightly. "Goodness, you're so lucky, Eileen. If I wasn't afraid of getting lost, perhaps I'd venture into the Forest in hopes something like that would happen to me. The only adventures I experience are in books—unless you count surviving dances with clammy-handed dance partners."

I leaned back in my seat with a frown. "I fail to see what's so wonderful about my experience." For there were plenty of things I found awful about it—my Forest's betrayal, the gash on my neck that would undoubtedly scar, losing my sketchbook, and the unnamed emotion that filled me at merely thinking about the man I'd encountered. Though strangely, that wasn't entirely unpleasant.

Rosie began pouring the tea she'd brought with her and handed me my steaming cup; I warily eyed the nearby librarian busy dusting the shelves before accepting it.

"I can't believe you fail to see your incredible good

fortune, for the Forest guided you not to a stranger, but to your true love." Her eyes widened with wonder.

I choked on my sip of tea. "My *what?*"

"Your true love." Rosie clasped her hands, doe-eyed once more. "I must have a gift, for remember I imagined the entire scenario for you just days before it happened: you encountering a handsome man while wandering the Forest. But I prefer the version of the story that actually occurred; having its pathways lead you to your heart's match is so much more romantic." She clutched her heart at the thought and sighed.

I wrinkled my nose. "He's *not* my heart's match. The man was as irritating as they come." Not to mention a nobleman would never be interested in someone like *me*.

Rosie waved my words away and scooted her chair closer. "He was handsome, wasn't he?"

"*Handsome?*"

"Certainly." Rosie stirred cream into her own tea and took a dainty sip. "Whenever heroines meet mysterious men, they're always handsome. Always." She pursed her lips in thought. "I'm not sure *why* exactly, but that's how it is in books, so naturally that's how it will be for us as well. Thus your mysterious stranger must have possessed the physical characteristics essential for your true love: tall, dreamy, and definitely handsome. He was, wasn't he?"

"No," I lied, but heat dotted my cheeks, giving me away.

Rosie squealed—earning her several glares from the nearby reading patrons—and leaned closer, splotching tea on her dress in her excitement. "Oh, I knew he was good looking. One doesn't meet dark, mysterious strangers in the Forest without them being dashingly handsome. It's definitely true love."

I rolled my eyes. "How? The man's nothing more than a stranger. I don't even know his name."

Once again she brushed that thought away. "Technicalities. Just because you two are barely acquainted now doesn't mean he's not *the one*. Despite your fierce resistance to the contrary, I've always known your heart had a match. Every heart does. Oh look, you're blushing. You know I'm right, don't you?"

I refused to allow her to win this ridiculous argument. "Attraction is not the same thing as love," I protested. "Even you know that, else you'd have been in love with most of the boys in the village."

"Yes, but attraction is certainly a start." Rosie stirred three spoonfuls of sugar into her second cup of tea, expression thoughtful. "You can't dismiss an initial attraction; it's what draws two individuals together in order for them to explore one another's hearts and discern whether they're a perfect match or not."

"The man's conceit and odious manner are both clear indicators that we most definitely *aren't* a match."

Rosie sighed impatiently. "Must you be so doubting? You told me the Forest led you to him. Why would it do that if he wasn't your prince?"

"I don't know the Forest's motivations, but I do know I've long since determined I have no prince."

"Everyone has a prince."

I rolled my eyes. "You read too many stories."

Naturally, Rosie chose to ignore this particular comment. Her expression softened. "I know your father leaving was difficult for you, but you've allowed your pain to hold you back long enough. I just want you to be happy. What better way to heal than to move forward?" Eyes bright, she leaned closer. "You must return to the Forest and ask it to lead you back to him."

"After its recent behavior, I'm not sure I trust it any longer. The only request I'll make of the Forest is for it to take me to my lost sketchbook."

Rosie's eyes widened. "You lost it?"

My heart wrenched as I nodded. "Hence my story isn't a romance but a tragedy, for my cut isn't the only casualty from the encounter; with yesterday's rain, my sketchbook is likely lost forever." I blinked rapidly to stave off my tears.

She rested her hand on top of mine. "I'm so sorry."

For a moment we sat in silence as she gazed unseeing at the walls of books enclosing us like a cocoon, as if appealing to her beloved stories for inspiration. Then she straightened, expression determined.

"You must return to the Forest and look for it."

I frowned. "Mother wants me to stay away. She's convinced I'll encounter that man again."

"That's exactly what I'm desperately hoping will happen," Rosie said. "Especially if he's your true love like I believe."

"How many times do I have to tell you—I don't want love. I only want my sketchbook."

"You do want love; you just don't realize it yet. Return to the Forest to find your sketchbook, and if you're meant to see that mysterious man again, I'm sure the Forest will lead you to him. It did so once…" She trailed off with a knowing smirk, as if she'd already read the end of my tale and discovered it played out exactly as she envisioned it would; when Rosie wanted a story to go a certain way, there was no dissuading her.

I caressed the rim of my now-empty cup with my fingertip. "My ruined sketchbook could be anywhere in that vast Forest."

"Heroines shouldn't give up merely because a few obstacles arise. The Forest has always taken a liking to you…as much as a bunch of trees can like anyone. Thus it's sure to help you." Rosie considered the matter further before giving a firm nod. "This is exactly how your next chapter must go: you must return for your sketchbook and see whether or not the Forest leads you to something far more spectacular...like that dashing stranger again."

Her case made, she sat back in her seat as if she considered the entire matter settled. Despite my doubts, one thing was certain: I wouldn't be appeased until I'd searched for my beloved sketchbook. Even though it was currently lost in the woods that harbored that dark stranger, as soon as the rain let up, I'd return.

CHAPTER 4

I walked alongside the Forest's border, brushing against the branches still wet from the recent rain. It had been three days since I'd last entered, and despite the trees rustling beckoningly, I hesitated.

I could still feel the sinister stranger's presence emanating from the woods, especially since I'd been dreaming of him. In my dreams I was trapped in the Forest, forced to walk a continuously changing pathway that twisted and turned so rapidly I could scarcely keep up. As I struggled, the stranger watched with a smirk, staring at me as if I were the prey he'd just ensnared.

Each time, I woke up in a cold sweat. Even though I knew it had only been a nightmare, my encounter with the mysterious man had been quite real, as had the way he'd commanded the Forest's pathways with ease, as if he were the life behind their enchanted movements. If they were really his servants, they could no longer be trusted, which meant I'd lost more than my sketchbook; I'd lost the trees themselves. I felt as if thousands of friends had died.

Yet still they beckoned, the wind pushing my body

towards the Forest in an earnest plea to return. I cautiously peered inside. In the sunlight that had finally penetrated the thick, stormy clouds, the Forest lost its ominous air, making a jaunt inside seem harmless. Even if it was no longer safe, I at least needed to try to retrieve my lost sketchbook.

After an earnest plea for its guidance and a deep, wavering breath, I took a hesitant step into the woods. Stepping within the trees again was like stepping into a dream, with everything fresh, bright, and green after the recent storm. With each step deeper inside, the anxiety that had tightened my heart eased. It was impossible to doubt the Forest now, when it was gently leading me along like an ever-constant friend. The beauty and peace of the woods almost distracted me from my quest.

The branches above me bent to form a canopy, dripping water onto my hair as I picked my way through the trees. The muddy path unfurled before me like a carpet, each twist and turn unfamiliar. Wherever the Forest was guiding me, it didn't seem to be towards my lost sketchbook. Where then was it leading me instead?

I pulled my cloak tighter around my shoulders as I looked around for any recognizable landmark, but everything looked different after the rain. I took the path much more slowly, frequently pausing to poke through the foliage for any traces of my lost sketchbook, which could have floated anywhere during the storm. An hour dragged by as I dug through mud and searched amongst the mossy vegetation, inching deeper and deeper into the Forest without success.

I sighed and leaned against a sycamore to stare up at the grey, dripping sky. The Forest was not only monstrous in size but was proving most unhelpful in where it was choosing to lead me. How would I ever find my sketchbook?

I squinted through the hovering mist as the path suddenly wriggled and shifted east. I took it without question, following the familiar beckoning lure of the Forest. Soon the surrounding trees thinned into a familiar clearing up ahead. Could it be…?

The moment I stepped into the clearing, I froze. The stranger who'd given me his cryptic riddle and had since haunted my dreams leaned against a birch tree. I stared in disbelief. Just as Rosie had hoped, the Forest had led me to him once more. What could its motive possibly be? Would I ever be able to trust it again?

The man smiled, not the same smirk he'd so generously given me several times upon our last meeting, but a real, slightly crooked smile that did strange things to my insides.

"I knew our paths would cross again. Even with the Forest's help it took longer than I thought, but I'm pleased to see you all the same."

I snapped my gaping mouth shut and turned and bolted. I'd barely gone a few feet when he seized my wrist and jerked me to a stop.

"Please don't leave. It's too soon to end our visit, considering it's only just begun."

I tried to wrestle from his grip, but though his hold was surprisingly gentle, it was like iron. "Let me go."

"I will if you promise not to run away."

"I'll make no such promise, not when it's my goal to be as far away from you as possible." How could the Forest do this to me *again*? It was most unfair.

His smile widened. "I'd forgotten how delightful you are."

"But I haven't forgotten what a rogue you are." I jerked my wrist but still couldn't break free. I growled in frustration and stomped on his foot. He swore, but aggravatingly, his hold didn't loosen.

"Feisty thing, aren't you?"

"I'll do whatever it takes, because whatever game you have in mind today, I do not want to participate."

"There's no need to worry," he said, his tone assuring. "As I've been trying to tell you from the moment we met, I'm not going to hurt you. Please don't be afraid."

I snorted. "Like I believe *that*, especially considering you've already harmed me."

His gaze flickered to the cut on my neck. "Your wound seems to be healing nicely."

"No thanks to you."

He lowered his eyes. "I didn't mean to hurt you. I only wanted a lock of your hair. I'm sorry." He brushed my scabbing cut with his fingertips. I slapped his hand away.

"Don't touch me."

"Just let me examine it."

"I said *don't touch me*."

He obediently dropped his touch from my neck but annoyingly still clutched my wrist.

I feebly tugged on his grip. "Please let me go. Are you waiting for me to beg?"

He laughed. "There's no need for that. Now, because you've said 'please,' I'll grant your request. Please don't run off." He released me. Despite his humoring me, I glared at him. He sighed. "This meeting isn't going as well as I'd hoped."

His meaning hit me. I narrowed my eyes. "Were you waiting for me?"

"I thought that was obvious."

"Why? Do you get some sort of sick pleasure in toying with innocent damsels?"

"I have something for you." With a boyish grin, he removed something rectangular and wrapped in maroon silk from his satchel.

I frowned suspiciously. "What's that?"

He held it out to me. "See for yourself."

I eyed it warily. "I don't accept gifts from strangers, particularly ones like you."

"I believe this will be an exception."

I hesitated but faltered at his earnest expression and my own curiosity. I took it and pulled off its covering. I gasped in disbelief. "My sketchbook!" Tears filled my eyes as I cradled it in my arms. It was in perfect condition, unsoiled by the recent rain. "I thought it had been destroyed. How did you—"

"I discovered it on the ground after you left. I admit I was tempted to keep it."

I protectively clutched it closely. "How did you know I'd return for it?"

"Because it's clearly something you treasure."

His tone, expression, and indeed this entire gesture were all so unexpectedly sweet that I felt unhinged. I caressed my sketchbook, unable to believe it hadn't been destroyed like I'd feared.

"Your talent is extraordinary," he said. "I've never seen such exquisite work."

Heat swarmed my cheeks. "You *looked* at them?"

"Of course," he said without the slightest remorse. "Isn't incredible artwork to be appreciated?"

"That's no reason to invade my privacy."

"Please don't be upset," he said in a cajoling tone that made me want to forgive him a bit too easily. "If not for me, all your drawings would have been destroyed. I didn't have to wait for you for three days in order to return it. My time is valuable."

I gaped at him. "You waited *three days* in the rain?" Why would he do that for a complete stranger? This man was proving to be quite the puzzle.

He shrugged. "I don't mind a bit of rain, especially with your smile as a reward for my efforts. Besides, I only came three times before deciding to wait for the Forest to summon me once you entered it. You certainly stubbornly resisted doing so."

The heat in my cheeks deepened. Clearly, I'd misjudged this stranger. I lowered my gaze. "Thank you. This means everything to me."

"You're welcome."

Silence settled over us. I shifted my weight back and forth, looking everywhere but at him.

"Eileen?"

I peeked at him through my long, dark hair. Whereas I'd previously thought his noble accent made my name sound filthy, now he made it sound almost like a caress.

"Because I sacrificed three days of my time for you, I believe you owe me something in return." He stated it in a business-like tone, as if he were about to draw up a contract.

Apprehension knotted my gut. "And what is that?"

"Perhaps I could get to know you better."

I snorted. "Because already possessing my name isn't enough?"

Despite my refusal, he grinned. "I take it you're not willing to go along with that plan? What would it require for me to become friends with you?"

I frowned as I studied him. Was this another game? "I'd like your own name, for starters. It seems unfair that you know mine but I have yet to learn yours."

He tilted his head, dark eyes teasing. "Perhaps you can guess."

I responded with a scowl.

He chuckled. "Clearly, you're in no mood for any more of my games. Because I desire to be in your good graces, I'll humor you: my name is Aiden."

"Aiden?"

He nodded. "And now we continue our proper introduction with the expected polite pleasantries. I bow"—he dipped into a deep bow, causing a single chestnut curl to dangle across his forehead—"and you curtsy."

"I'm not going to curtsy," I snapped. His lips twitched.

"I suppose we won't exchange a friendly greeting after all. Will your stubbornness extend to refusing polite small talk?"

I folded my arms. He cocked an eyebrow.

"Is that a yes or no to engaging in polite small talk?"

"Why do you want to get to know me better? After today, we're never going to see one another again."

"I wouldn't be so sure of that. Didn't you mistakenly assume that after our last meeting?"

I glared at him. He merely grinned cheekily in response. I wasn't sure what he was playing at, but his friendly smiles and the light filling his dark eyes were doing strange things to my heart, things I didn't like, making me almost desire to humor him.

He waited a moment, but when I still refused to play along by answering him, he sighed. "Are you always this untrusting?"

"Only towards mysterious strangers I encounter in the woods."

"How many such strangers have you met?"

"Just you."

"So you have no previous experiences to compare our interactions with, meaning you're basing everything on assumption rather than fact."

I raised my eyebrows. "Forgive me, but your behavior has done little to earn my good favor."

"You're correct; it appears another apology is in order." He bowed. "I'm sorry for my behavior at our last meeting. I was rather out of sorts, but it was still inexcusable. I'm now trying to make it up to you by returning your sketchbook and trying to get to know you better, but you're making it rather difficult. Can't we just start over?"

"Give me one reason why I should grant your request."

He grinned. "Because I'm charming."

I cocked my eyebrow skeptically. He sighed.

"I take it that's not a valid enough reason." A thoughtful pucker lined his brow. "I'm surprised you distrust me so easily. Considering we're both on good terms with the Forest, I would have assumed the opposite."

I frowned up at the trees swaying a bit too innocently, as if they found our exchange highly amusing. Mischievous creatures. Yet while their motives were questionable, they hadn't yet led me astray. Could I trust their judgment?

I glanced back at Aiden, who watched me a bit pleadingly. He wanted me to trust him. Didn't he realize that what he was asking was impossible to grant? I didn't trust, not when doing so was foolish. But his expression was so imploring that despite my best intentions, I felt the walls of my reservations crack. I sighed in defeat.

"Fine, I'll play your game...for now."

He beamed. "Excellent. Time for the small talk I fought so hard for. Do you come to the Forest often?"

"All the time."

Aiden looked up at the branches twisting together in an intricate canopy; the sunlight poked through the budding leaves to caress us in dappled gold. "I do, too. I love this place. It's my perfect escape: mysterious yet incredibly peaceful. I often feel as if the Forest is—"

"—alive," I finished. Heat tinged my cheeks as his gaze caught mine and his lips curved up.

"The Forest has led me to some wonderful places over the years, but the day we met, it was most insistent on leading me towards you. Perhaps we were destined to meet."

Goosebumps pinpricked my arms. Could that be possible? But what reason would the Forest have for me to meet a nobleman?

"Where are your favorite places to explore?" Aiden asked.

"Everywhere. Like you, the Forest leads me to whichever destination it has in mind, each more magical than the last. I feel it's always waiting to show me something new. It's taken me to lakes, meadows, orchards, groves of changing trees…"

Aiden gave me a cheeky grin. "…me?"

I scowled. He chuckled.

"I suppose it's too early for you to know whether our meeting was lucky coincidence or not." He glanced down at my sketchbook, which I still held like a shield in front of me. "Do you always bring your sketchbook wherever the Forest takes you?"

"Of course. It's my journal, preserving each of my experiences."

Aiden stepped closer, and I instinctively backed into a tree. "Warning: I'm about to be intrusive again." He tugged my sketchbook from my hands and opened it seemingly at random to a drawing of a lake reflecting the cloud-filled sky, lily pads dotting its surface. "In all my years exploring, I've never stumbled upon such a place within these trees. This is found in the Forest?"

I pressed my hands to my hips. "Nobleman or not, it's rude to grab someone's personal property without their permission."

He ignored me as he turned each page with reverence. "Your style is exquisite. I love your use of color; you use just enough to draw the viewer's attention to the focus of the piece."

"In case you're missing it, I'm hinting for you to return my sketchbook."

"This drawing is my favorite."

Aiden tipped my book to show me my panoramic view of

49

the Forest drawn from the attic window of my cottage, captured half in charcoal, half in colored wax. From left to right I'd created a timeline of the Forest passing through not only the day—from dawn, to dusk, to fading into night—but also experiencing all the seasons.

Aiden raised my picture eye level to more closely examine it. "You perfectly captured the majesty and mystery of the woods; the emotion practically crawls off the page. Stunning."

His generous praise pierced my annoyance. If he was trying to flatter me for whatever nefarious purpose he had in mind, it was working...but I couldn't let *him* know that.

"Aiden, please return my sketchbook."

Using his name finally got me a response. Aiden's gaze met mine. "Can't I admire your work a bit longer?"

"I need to return home before my mother returns from the market and realizes I snuck into the Forest."

He closed my book with a scoff. "How old are you?"

My cheeks prickled with another blush. "I'm nearly nineteen."

His eyes flickered over my small build and petite body. "I'll have to take your word for it."

Heat flashed through me. I scowled at him, but as usual, he ignored it.

"Why are you so concerned about your mother? Do they really cut the apron strings so late amongst the peasantry?"

Ugh, his nerve. "She's just worried about me," I said through my teeth. "And she has great reason to be."

"Worried about what? I assure you, there's nothing in the Forest to be frightened of."

"Except for *you*." And to reinforce my point, I motioned to the cut on my neck.

Remorse twisted his expression. "I told you that was an accident."

"And I'm telling you I don't care. Return my sketchbook. *Now.*" I yanked it from him. I expected to have to wrestle it from his grip, but surprisingly he didn't put up a fight. His crooked grin merely widened, as if I was the most entertaining spectacle.

"Spunky thing, aren't you?"

I took a deep breath. "I'm leaving."

He bowed with a flourish. "Be my guest."

"Goodbye and good riddance."

I turned towards the trees and sighed with relief that the path I'd used to arrive was still there. I'd barely stomped three steps towards it when Aiden called after me.

"We still haven't discussed my form of payment."

I froze before slowly turning back around. *"Payment?"*

He crossed his arms and leaned back against the same birch where I'd found him waiting when I'd first arrived. "Naturally. My time is valuable, so I expect compensation."

My heart hammered. "What kind of payment? I don't have any money."

"That does present a problem." Aiden rested his chin on his fist, considering, before mischief flashed in his eyes. "You don't happen to know how to spin straw into gold, do you?"

I gaped at him. Was he serious?

He chuckled. "No? Well, lucky for you, the payment I desire will be much more simple. What I want is"—he held up three fingers—"three days."

"Three days of what?"

"Your time. I spent three days coming to the Forest in order to meet you, so naturally I expect three days of your time in return. A fair exchange, wouldn't you say?"

I opened my mouth to give him my exact feelings on the matter, but he talked over me.

"And before you come up with any nefarious motive behind my request, allow me to reassure you that during our time together, I merely hope to get to know you better."

I swallowed the refusal I'd been prepared to give, for as much as I ached to deny it, I wanted to get to know him as well, for I admittedly found him rather intriguing. "What if the Forest never leads me to you again?"

He stroked the trunk of the tree he still leaned against. "I'm sure you've noticed how much the Forest likes me. Don't doubt it will do my bidding. The next time you step within its trees, you'll find there's only one path for you to take. I look forward to it."

With that, he bowed before walking down a path opposite my own. I watched it disappear behind him as the trees closed in and swallowed it up.

CHAPTER 5

Several days later, the trees were still beckoning me, their invisible hands reaching to pull me inside. I felt their urgency in each rustle of their branches. I slowly approached the Forest's border and peered into the dark foliage. Even without stepping inside, I sensed the Forest's desires to lead me to the mysterious Aiden, a man I didn't want to meet again. I tipped my head back so that even the Forest's tallest branches would see my determination.

"I don't understand your relationship with that Aiden, but I don't appreciate your leading me to him twice now."

The leaves merely swayed in response, feigning innocence despite my laying their betrayal at their roots.

"He might insist on your guiding me to him, but I refuse to allow it. If you want me to visit you at all, it has to be under my rules." My piece given, I pulled my shoulders back, lifted my head, and stepped within the trees.

The pathways immediately wriggled into a new position, undoubtedly ignoring my request. I tightened my jaw and determinedly stepped off the path into the dense foliage. The Forest would have none of that; a new path instantly appeared. I gritted my teeth and stepped off it once more, but only a few steps through the undergrowth, another trail appeared.

The Forest seemed intent on forcing my hand, but I was determined to ignore its guidance. How dare it dictate my actions after I'd specifically told it not to? So much for being my friend. I stomped my foot and glared up at the trees.

"I told you I don't want to meet Aiden again; I only want to explore."

A large gust of wind stirred the surrounding branches, signaling the Forest's disapproval. I took advantage of its distraction and scurried off the path—nearly tripping over a protruding root in my haste—before another immediately sprang into existence, twisting deeper into the trees, where Aiden undoubtedly awaited me. Even my attempts to go in the opposite direction only resulted in the path looping around to force me back onto the Forest's intended course.

I gritted my teeth. Mischievous Forest. Fine, it might not allow me to blaze my own trail, but it couldn't make me leave. I plopped down on the ground at the border, remaining in the Forest while still within view of the cottage. I glared up at the trees so they understood in no uncertain terms that I was miffed with them; they returned their annoyance with the resulting breeze that blew roughly through my dark hair.

I yanked open my sketchbook to a fresh page and began to draw in rapid, angry strokes a rather destructive scene of a forest fire, being sure to angle myself so the surrounding trees could see my picture and thus fully understand the extent of my ire. But as time passed, the tension tightening my chest slowly eased, especially as the Forest's harsh breeze gentled into a cooling caress, as if it were apologizing. I offered a repentant smile in return. I hated being out of sorts with such a good friend for long.

"Eileen?"

I glanced up to see Mother approaching, a basket of mending looped through her arm.

"I'm surprised to see you. I thought you might have gone exploring." She frowned at the Forest as she settled beside me. "I'm relieved you haven't, especially after I asked you not to."

Guilt knotted my gut. I'd only kept the promise—which I'd never intended to keep—for three days before going back to retrieve—

My grip tightened around my sketchbook in my lap, evidence of my disobedience. Mother's frown deepened as her eyes lowered to it.

"Is that…"

"A gift from Rosie."

I winced at my lie, one easy to give considering Mother assumed my old sketchbook had been ruined by the rain. She didn't deserve my dishonesty, but honesty would only cause her to worry, something she'd already done too much of these past several years as we'd struggled to survive without Father.

Desperate to distract her, I motioned to the basket resting beside her. "Do you need any help with the mending?"

She blinked down at it before shaking her head. "No, dear. Continue filling up your new sketchbook with drawings, and I'll tend to the mending. Do you mind if I sit with you?"

I shook my head and returned to my sketch of the Forest's demise. I frowned at the picture, additional guilt prickling my heart for drawing such a gruesome scene. It would be in my best interest to stay in the Forest's good graces, considering it had the power to get me hopelessly lost with a single shift in its pathways. I tore it out and crumpled it in order to start a new drawing; with the way the branches rustled above me, I knew the Forest approved.

We worked in cozy silence. I paused in my drawing depicting a much more pleasant portrayal of the Forest and watched Mother. She focused on the mending in her lap, a soft contentment filling her gentle, lovely features. I marveled at her quiet strength that had sustained us these last ten years since our lives had transformed so drastically.

My heart tightened to think of the times before Father's absence. I closed my eyes and touched the locket around my neck, transported to one such moment of our little family tucked inside our snug cottage around the fire as a storm raged outside. Mother and Father had snuggled together as they worked, while I'd lain on my stomach in front of the hearth, sketching. I looked up in time to witness Mother and Father exchange adoring smiles before Mother returned to her mending and Father to his whittling...until he'd paused and looked out the rain-splattered window. A small frown played across his mouth as the light in his eyes dimmed, a frown whose meaning still gnawed at me, even all these years later.

Father had eventually looked away from the window to notice my watching him. He grinned and stood. "Will you walk with me, sweetheart?"

I scampered over at his invitation, a common one considering Father never could sit still very long. Looking back, I now realized he possessed a restlessness that he could never quench. Was it this restlessness that had caused him to leave us?

He'd taken my hand with his rough one and we strolled the circumference of the room while Father recounted stories of adventure in far-off lands, ending with his usual, "Wouldn't it be marvelous to explore those lands for ourselves, sweetheart?"

At the time, the thought of going on a grand adventure with Father had seemed the most marvelous thing, but now my heart constricted at the thought. Father had loved us, but he'd clearly been unhappy with his simple lot. His thirst for adventure, his restless spirit...all had eclipsed his love. We weren't enough to satisfy him.

So he'd left us. If I'd only been a more exciting daughter, would he still have been so dissatisfied with his life and sought more?

I was tugged from my reminiscing as Mother stirred beside me. I peered over to see her frowning, eyes concerned. "What's wrong, Eileen?"

I hastily tore my gaze away before she could see my pain and know I'd been remembering Father, despite my fierce promises to myself over the years not to think of him. But her mother's instinct was stronger than my determination. She caressed my cheek to turn my head so our gazes met.

"I was thinking of him, too." She tipped her head back to stare up at the leafy branches. "Your father and I used to spend a lot of time here. It was our special place. I haven't been back since he left; it feels strange to be here without him." She smiled softly, wistfully. "He'd be pleased you love it so much. It makes me feel bad that my worries are keeping you from it."

I swallowed the lump quickly forming in my throat. "Why did Father leave us?"

She was silent a moment, her eyes glassy, before releasing a long, shuddering breath. "I don't know. But despite whatever might have happened to him, I know he loved us, still loves us."

"He couldn't have truly loved us if he left."

"I don't think he left of his own volition," she said slowly. "I just can't believe that."

"Why not?" I demanded.

She sighed again and returned to her mending. "He would never do anything to hurt me. Our hearts belonged to one another, so I trust that he would never intentionally break mine. That knowledge has allowed me to endure life without him. I've only maintained my strength by remembering his love and the joyful moments we shared together. Because I care for him so deeply, I need to believe the best of him. I wish you could, too."

While I wanted to, I just couldn't forgive him for leaving a hole in my heart, one that would likely never be healed. Father had broken both of us, and while Mother had managed to somehow rebuild her life, I still felt too weak to even pick up the shattered pieces. If Father's abandonment had left me in such a state, surely losing someone more dear in the future would destroy me completely. I couldn't survive being broken twice. Thus I had to protect what was left of my heart at all costs.

All the more reason never to meet Aiden again. The strange draw I felt towards him frightened me. But despite my urgency to avoid the man who was still very much a stranger, the Forest's lure continued chipping away at my defenses, urging me to step into the trees and allow them to guide me to him.

But I could no longer trust it. The thought I'd lost another relationship so dear to me sent a sharp pang through me. I pressed my hand against my heart in an effort to contain it. I eventually would. I was used to my heart hurting, for it had been broken when Father left, and nothing had ever been strong enough to repair it.

~

"Alright, I can't handle it anymore."

I paused in sweeping my bedroom and looked up at Rosie, hands propped on her hips and glaring.

"Can't handle what?"

"You." She gestured towards me with her dust rag. "You're keeping a secret from me, and I can't stand not knowing what it is a moment longer."

I bit my lip guiltily as Aiden's face unwillingly bombarded my mind before I could suppress it. I ached to deny I had a secret—especially one about a man—but Rosie had an uncanny ability to uncover such things no matter how much I tried to prevent her from doing so. She'd spent most of the afternoon casting me suspicious searching glances, her "Eileen is hiding something from me" senses obviously at work. Frankly, I was surprised her interrogation hadn't begun sooner.

For I did possess a secret. I'd managed to return home from my second encounter with the stranger in the woods (no, not a stranger—*Aiden*) with my sketchbook and had successfully kept it hidden in my room ever since. I couldn't risk Mother opening it and discovering it was my old sketchbook. Then I'd be bombarded with questions as she asked for further details about the mysterious Aiden, whom I was struggling—and utterly failing—to forget.

With that determined gleam filling her eyes, naturally Rosie would be the one to excavate my secret. At least I'd managed to keep it for a few days, a new record when it came to my best friend.

"What makes you think I'm keeping something from you?"

She rolled her eyes. "Did you really believe your ploy to dissuade me would actually work?"

"It was worth a try."

"Not when you have an impatient best friend who's dying

to learn what you're keeping from her. No, don't return to sweeping; you have a secret to share."

She snatched my broom. I attempted to grab it back, but she yanked it out of reach.

"Rosie, I need to finish my chores before Mother returns."

"You can finish *after* you tell me what you're keeping from me."

Knowing Rosie, there was no way to wriggle out of this without her getting what she wanted. I sighed in defeat.

"Fine, but we have to work while I share it with you." I managed to pry my broom from her and returned to sweeping around my bed.

Rosie muttered something indiscernible beneath her breath as she stomped over to my bed to change the sheets. Wait, she couldn't change them; that's where I'd hidden...

"Stop Rosie, don't—"

Too late. Before I could stop her, she yanked off my duvet and shrieked. She gaped down at my sketchbook, which I'd hidden beneath my pillow. I really should have chosen a better hiding place.

She slowly raised her wide eyes to mine. "Where did you get this?"

Rosie really had a knack for uncovering secrets. Annoying. "You're the one who encouraged me to return to the Forest and try to find it."

"Yes, but I expected that even if you succeeded in your quest, it'd be ruined." She examined my sketchbook, which possessed no signs of water damage. "Tell me at once how such a tragedy was averted."

I sighed as I settled on the bed. Rosie joined me with her usual expectant "tell me a juicy tale" look.

"Aiden returned it to me."

Up went her eyebrows. "*Aiden?* What an adorable name. What fine gentleman is the one who possesses it?" Before I could even answer she squealed again and scooted closer, eyes as bright as her smile. "Oh, please tell me it belongs to *him*."

"To whom?"

"Whom do you think? To your mysterious stranger you met in the woods."

I ached to deny it, but there was little point. If I didn't tell Rosie the story, she'd simply tell it herself, likely with her usual dramatics as she filled in exaggerated details to make it more like a fairy tale than what had actually happened, just to appease her romantic heart.

"Yes, he's the one who returned my sketchbook when I went looking for it," I said. "The Forest led me to him."

She seized my hands and beamed. "Oh Eileen, I just *knew* you two would meet again. I knew he was your true love."

"He most certainly is not my—"

"And what a heroic gesture to return your sketchbook," she continued as if I hadn't spoken. "You must tell me everything at once."

Seeing no way out of it, I reluctantly did, all while brushing over the confusing details I didn't want to share, such as how attractive I couldn't help but notice he was and the strange fluttery way he'd made me feel. Rosie listened to the recitation with ever-widening eyes, and when I finished she looked precariously close to floating in her delight.

"Oh Eileen, it's definitely true love."

"No, it's not," I snapped impatiently. "You keep saying that, but how could you know such a thing when we've only interacted twice?"

She gave me a knowing smirk. "For now. Don't you owe him three days? Over your next several meetings, I'm sure even you, who's stubbornly determined to be blind to love, will eventually see the obvious signs that he's your heart's match."

I gawked at her. "Are you really suggesting I give him the three days he's requested?"

"Of course you should," Rosie said. "He clearly feels something for you and wants to explore the relationship further. Besides, the Forest brought you two together."

"You mean it led me to a villain." But I regretted calling Aiden that the moment I did so. While he'd seemed foreboding during our initial meeting, he'd at least made an effort to be friendly during our last one.

Rosie rolled her eyes. "Villains don't return sketchbooks to beautiful maidens, Eileen."

"Unless the villain wants to ensnare her. What if it's a trap?"

"The Forest likes you too much to allow anything to harm you."

"It likes Aiden more. He has this uncanny ability to influence it." But despite that reservation, I still felt inclined to trust him—as much as I could trust anyone—simply because the Forest did. I also couldn't forget he'd made the effort to return my most prized possession, not to mention he'd never really intended to harm me at our first meeting.

But all those reasons were merely feeble attempts to justify the secret part of me buried deep within that *wanted* to see him again in order to get to know him. I didn't know where such a feeling came from, but I couldn't deny it was there, despite my not wanting it to be.

Rosie sensed my softening and smirked in triumph. "Not only is this relationship set up too perfectly for you to resist exploring it, but you're too honorable a heroine not to pay the three days of time Aiden requires of you. It won't hurt to at least create a friendship with him. You already have your love for the Forest in common."

By the mischievous way she smiled, I had no doubt she

harbored the ridiculous hope that any friendship we developed would deepen into something more.

"You know you want to," she continued. "Even someone as unromantic as you must be curious to see where such a serendipitous relationship will lead."

I opened my mouth to deny it, but my warm blush gave me away. I sighed in defeat. "You really think I should meet with him?"

"You *need* to," Rosie said. "There's undeniably a connection between you two. If it were me, I wouldn't be satisfied until I'd discovered what it was. Besides, you can't deny the Forest led you to him, not just once but *twice*. Don't you trust the Forest?"

And I did. Its opinion was what provided the excuse I secretly needed to take this unexpected path, one I knew I shouldn't want but did all the same. It wouldn't hurt to explore it for a *little* bit, just to see where it could potentially lead...

But wherever it did, I'd be sure to guard my heart. I wasn't certain why I was even worried about losing it to this man who was still a stranger, but I felt the fierce need to rebuild my fortresses around it all the same.

CHAPTER 6

I was insane to willingly meet with Aiden again. I told myself I didn't really have any choice. Not only had Rosie's unceasing pestering of the past several days compelled me to meet with him simply to appease her, but the Forest had been sending its own urges. Every day I felt its gentle tugs to enter it, a beckoning that came not only from it but also from inside me, as if my heart were being lured towards the woods.

I'd fought these strange enticements for nearly a week, knowing that the moment I gave in there'd only be one path to follow, before I couldn't stay away any longer. The trees were too alluring, especially with their dark, leafy limbs aglow in the rosy golden light of sunrise, the hovering morning mist casting them in an enchanted sheen. The moment I breached the Forest's border, the pathways quickly quivered and began to unfold in the direction it had determined for me to go.

The lure pulling my heart intensified as I picked my way through the thickening branches, venturing deeper into the woods. I knew exactly where the Forest was leading me. It was as if it spoke in a silent language only I could under-stand, one part of the gentle rustle of its overhanging branches.

Sure enough, the pathway widened then opened into the same clearing where I'd previously met Aiden. He waited, leaning against the same birch tree, and smiled in greeting. My stomach performed a strange flip-flop.

"You came," he said with undisguised enthusiasm. "After a week, I was beginning to be afraid you wouldn't."

I raised my eyebrows. "You've been waiting a whole week?" Would he require more payment for those days, too?

He shook his head. "Not to worry. Like before, the Forest only just summoned me, so I haven't been waiting around unnecessarily."

"The trees seem strangely determined we meet again."

His smile widened. "You knew they did, yet you chose to enter the Forest anyway."

"I can never stay away for long." I wanted to elaborate and explain the kinship I felt with the Forest, but before I could even find the words, his expression softened as he glanced up at the swaying branches, a canopy above us.

"I don't imagine you can. When one finds a haven, one yearns to visit it as often as possible. It's a similarity we share."

He reverently stroked the trunk of a nearby tree before he offered me his arm. I blinked at it and made no move to take it. He wriggled it encouragingly.

"You're supposed to accept a gentleman's arm when he offers it."

"Are you a gentleman, then?"

"Not always," he admitted. "I possess many undesirable traits, but you seem worth the extra effort to be on my best behavior."

He seemed sincere, so with a deep breath I tentatively

took his arm. Having spent a lifetime avoiding the local boys, I'd never been escorted before and wasn't entirely sure what to expect from the experience. A strange fluttering filled my stomach as my fingers curled at his elbow, a feeling I fought to ignore. It didn't work.

Aiden looked to the trees, and as if he'd issued a silent command, another path opened up, which he escorted me down. The moment we stepped onto this new path, the Forest swallowed it up behind us, preventing me from turning back. I bit my lip. Escape would now be nearly impossible.

"What did you have in mind for my first payment?" I asked, fighting to keep my voice steady. He couldn't know how nervous I was.

"You seem to know the Forest quite well, so I'm hoping to take you to places you have yet to discover, ones closer to my home where you likely haven't ventured before."

"And where is your home?"

"Hmm." He pursed his lips. "That seems to be too personal of a question for mere acquaintances."

"It hardly seems nosy when I'm placing so much trust in you, trust you have yet to prove warranted."

He chuckled. "You're here not because you trust me but because you trust the Forest. You couldn't stay away, and because the Forest listens to me more than it does to you, you were led here, just as I'd hoped."

I cast him a nervous glance and he gave my arm a reassuring squeeze. A jolt of heat rippled over me but I made no move to pull away.

"Don't worry, you have no need to fear me. With time I hope to earn your trust." He returned his attention to the path shifting before us. "The Forest is fascinating, isn't it? It can bridge any distance—no matter how vast—effortlessly by simply changing its paths. It can make any journey as short or as long as it wants and can lead one anywhere. It adds a bit of mystery to one's destination, doesn't it?"

While I'd never traveled beyond my own humble village, I'd seen enough maps of Sortileya to know the Forest touched nearly every village, town, and city. With the Forest's ability to shift, in theory a several-days journey by road could be accomplished in mere minutes within the trees if the Forest allowed it, making it a place of endless possibilities.

"So what you're essentially saying is that due to this skill of the Forest, you could live anywhere."

He nodded. "Exactly."

"Where is this particular path leading us?"

"Somewhere I hope you'll like."

I searched his expression, and the knots tightening my stomach slowly eased at the earnestness lining his hardened features. "So I'm not to be tortured?" I asked wryly.

He smiled. "The Forest may listen to me, but I doubt it would if I intended to harm you. I have much to learn about it, but I cannot deny it loves you. Its deep affection for you is one of my motives for getting to know you better so that I may discover why, considering it has few friends."

More of my unease melted away. I trusted the Forest, a trust I'd proven by returning to it despite knowing it'd guide me back to this mysterious Aiden. If the Forest trusted him enough to obey him, then perhaps I could continue this particular journey with confidence, despite not knowing the final destination. Hopefully, wherever it was, it would be somewhere wonderful.

With each step further down the path, the surrounding trees began to gradually change—from the blossoming buds of late spring to the leafy boughs of summer before the colors finally shifted to ruby, blazing orange, and gold, as if autumn had decided to arrive months early. I gaped up at the changing trees in awe.

Aiden smiled boyishly. "Is my quest a success?"

I slowly nodded in wonder. "It's beautiful."

"The seasons have their own time frame here. Right now it seems content with autumn, but if we wait a moment…"

As if attuned to his silent instructions, the air around us cooled as the leaves transformed into ice crystals, a taste of winter even in spring. After they had finished showing off, the trees donned their autumn-dappled leaves once more. Amazing. The Forest was full of surprises.

Our path led us through the vibrant trees to a creek before ending suddenly. "The place I want to take you is farther down the stream."

The creek twisted through the ruby and gold trees bordering the shore on both sides, leaving no bank for us to walk along. I frowned. "How will we get down there?"

"We have a bit of an adventure ahead of us."

He pointed to rocks zigzagging through the stream before releasing my arm and jumping lightly onto the first one, then the second. He paused on the third rock to glance over his shoulder, a wicked glint in his eyes.

"Don't you like adventure, Eileen?"

A challenge. With a stubborn lift of my chin, I leapt onto the first rock and nearly slipped into the creek. My breath caught. "Are you sure you don't mean to torture me?"

"Do you truly believe that an activity that's meant to be fun is really an elaborate plot for your discomfort?"

My laugh became trapped in my throat as I jumped onto the second rock. "It very well could be. I know little about you. We're still strangers."

"Hence I've requested three days to remedy that." He jumped to the next rock and paused to wait for me.

I hopped after him along the stepping stones through the

creek, heaving a relieved sigh whenever I didn't lose my balance and fall. "Then shouldn't you begin your interrogation?"

A mischievous glint filled his eyes. "Ladies first, considering I'm trying to prove myself a gentleman."

I paused on a large rock to catch my breath. I thought about what I wanted to learn about Aiden, only to realize I wanted to know everything. It was a strange sensation, one that made me wary. He waited patiently as I deliberated, his head tilted, curiosity filling his eyes.

I pointed to the healing scar on my neck. "Why did you do this?

"The moment the Forest led me to you, I felt an inexplicable draw towards you," he said. "I'd never experienced such a sensation like that before and I wanted something to remember you by, which was why I tried to take a lock of your hair. I know my behavior was unconventional and far too forward. I wish I had a better explanation for it." He nibbled his lip, his usual confident demeanor now rather vulnerable. "Do you ever feel that your worst self emerges?"

"What do you mean?"

He lowered his eyes to the flowing stream, as if he couldn't make himself meet my gaze. "When I first saw you… I can't explain what I felt, only that I was afraid of it. This explanation doesn't excuse my behavior, but it's the reason I was initially so rude. For that I'm sorry."

I wrinkled my nose, confused. Why would Aiden have any reason to be afraid of me? By the guarded look filling his eyes, I knew he had no intention of divulging that to me.

"That's what these payments are for," he continued. "I'm hoping to apologize for how I treated you as well as learn why the Forest led me to you."

His gaze penetrated mine, and I realized in that moment that I not only believed him but I was no longer afraid of him. It was why I'd allowed the Forest to lead me back to him. I also couldn't deny I felt *something* with him, too, something I didn't understand, and despite my reservations I wanted to explore these feelings and discover what they were, even when I was afraid of what I might find. How could I protect myself against these new emotions if I didn't know which ones I was fighting against?

Flustered, I leapt onto the next rock but underestimated the distance and slipped into the creek with an icy splash.

"Eileen?"

I shyly peeked up at Aiden's alarm-filled expression. He hopped along the rocks separating us until he reached me.

"Are you alright?"

Hopefully the water from the splash would mask the blush spreading heat across my cheeks. "This is mortifying."

His lips twitched as he extended his hand. "Even so, I'll help you up."

I seized his outstretched hand and yanked him down beside me with another splash. He scrambled to his knees, dripping wet and sputtering. I offered him my sweetest smile. "How kind of you to join me, Aiden."

He gaped at me. "I didn't think you were capable of something so devious."

I smirked. "Surprise."

He laughed as he clambered to his feet and proceeded to wring the water from his linen shirt. "I did want to get to know you better, but I didn't realize my quest would prove so dangerous." He offered his hand again with a suspicious look. "Are you one to repeat the same mischief twice?"

"You'll soon find out, won't you?"

I accepted his hand and couldn't help but notice that mine fit in his perfectly. His warm, firm grip enclosed it as he gently helped me to my feet. Even when I was steady he didn't release me. For a moment our gazes remained riveted to one another's, and despite being dripping wet, I no longer felt chilled. That didn't prevent a shiver from rippling over me, breaking our strange spell.

"Are you cold?" he asked.

I shook my head, but my chattering teeth betrayed me. Aiden wound his arm back through mine and helped me wade up the stream to clamber onto shore. There he pulled his velvet cloak off his shoulders and tucked it around me. It bathed me not only in warmth but in his alluring honey-musk scent. I burrowed my nose in the folds and breathed it in. It was intoxicating.

His concerned gaze penetrated mine. "Are you alright?"

I nodded as I tugged his cloak more tightly around me, but it did little to quell the shivers raking over me. To make matters worse, the surrounding autumn decided to fade into winter again; it began to snow, large flakes that caught the ends of my eyelashes.

Aiden scowled up at the trees as he rubbed his hands up and down my arms. "Believe it or not, I had a destination in mind at the end of our adventure up the stream, but perhaps we'll have to save it for next time."

I frantically shook my head, whatever trepidation I previously had for today's meeting with Aiden was now replaced with the strangest yearning for it to never end. "I'm too curious. Besides, I'm sure the snow will stop soon as the seasons change again."

He glanced up at the trees, and as if he'd given a silent command, the air began to warm, immediately stilling my shivers. He wiped stray droplets from my cheeks, leaving a trail of heat from his touch. Despite not knowing one another very well, the gesture felt strangely natural. "You sure you're up for it?"

I nodded as I met his seeping gaze. He searched my expression to gauge my sincerity before motioning for me to follow him through the still-fiery trees, now laden with icicles. The walk was beautiful. Even midst the gentle snow, autumn still filled the air and caressed the Forest with hues of gold and orange. Leaves fell gently around us, creating a carpet along the Forest floor that muffled our footsteps.

As we walked, Aiden and I took turns exchanging questions, each answer illuminating the smallest portion of one another's personalities and interests. In the course of my interrogation, I learned that Aiden was twenty-one, lived in the capital, and was a high-ranking nobleman—although he refused to share his exact title with me. From the basics, we moved on to more personal questions. No matter how many tidbits he revealed, I was eager to uncover more of his mysteries.

"What are my interests?" As with my previous questions, Aiden pondered the answer to this one with a lot of thought, as if it were a complex problem needing to be solved. "When I'm free from my duties, I spend my time either in the Forest, practicing swordsmanship, or reading."

"I like to read, too," I said, getting a strange thrill to have found yet another commonality between us. "Otherwise I'm always outside or drawing."

From there, Aiden inquired after my family. I swallowed the lump in my throat that always appeared when I thought of Father and instead told him of the adorable cottage I lived in with Mother and our adventures cooking, baking, weaving, and bottling jam. I also told him of Rosie—omitting, of course, her delusions that my relationship with him would develop into something more than friendship.

His lips twitched. "She believes everyone's life mirrors a storybook?"

I nodded. "She's even convinced everyone's story fits a specific genre."

Amusement danced in his eyes. "And which is yours? Romance?"

My face flushed with heat. "Definitely not." And before he could pry much further as to why I was so adamant about that—for the thought of discussing romance with him made me fiercely uncomfortable—I asked, "Which is yours?"

Aiden thought about it for a moment. "Mystery."

"And why is that?"

He wiggled his eyebrows. "It's a mystery."

I snorted and muffled it with my hand. He gave me an adorable lopsided smile, as if pleased he'd gotten me to laugh. His smile did strange things to my insides.

Just as the snow finally stopped, our path opened up into an orchard of apple trees, their fruit a garland of rubies dangling from the autumn-laden branches. I gasped in delight. "Apples in spring?"

Aiden plucked one and tossed it to me. I caught it easily. "Anything is possible in an enchanted forest."

The Forest truly was full of all manner of delights. I bit into my apple. Juice dribbled down my chin and my fingers as the taste danced across my taste buds.

"I stumbled upon this place some time ago," he said. "When I devised this scheme to take you to various places within the Forest, this was the first one I thought of."

I cocked an eyebrow. "You knew I loved apples? Can you read minds in addition to controlling the Forest, coming up with clever riddles, and frightening innocent maidens?"

He chuckled. "While I'm a man of many talents, the fact that you like apples is just a lucky bonus...or perhaps it's the workings of the Forest." He stared up at the apple tree whose boughs stretched over us. "The fruit that grows here changes upon each visit. The Forest knows your tastes well."

"As do you, apparently. This is the perfect place to have taken me."

He smiled, and after he'd picked his own apple, we settled on the ground beneath the tree knee-to-knee, where we continued talking. Time passed without my noticing, and all too soon Aiden paused. "Has it been too long?"

"Too long for what?"

Mischief filled his eyes. "Is your mother worrying because you've been gone from the nursery too long?"

I tossed my apple core at him but he easily dodged it. "How can you be friendly one moment and odious the next?"

"Impeccable skill."

I rolled my eyes. "And I have to serve as the victim you practice on?"

"Thank you for being so willing."

"I haven't much choice." But he'd unfortunately brought up a good point. I frowned up at the sky. The sun had traveled far across it, signifying the hours that had melted away without my noticing, meaning Mother would be expecting me shortly. "You're right, Mother will be worried. I really should go." I glanced at Aiden, needing him to understand. "I'm her only family."

His humor vanished and he nodded, eyes serious. "I can't begrudge you having someone care enough to miss you."

"What of your family?" I asked gently. He hadn't yet spoken of them, for when I'd initially brought up the topic he'd rapidly changed it. He sighed.

"We're not particularly close." He frowned. "Perhaps it's because I'm not a person people *want* to get close to."

It was the same fear I'd often entertained when I wondered why Father had left—that I wasn't worth caring about. And even though those insecurities still swirled through me—often untamed with no clear way for me to dispel them—I didn't want Aiden to experience the same painful emotions.

I leaned closer and lightly brushed against his arm. He

stiffened, and for a moment he stared at my hand touching him before he slowly raised his gaze to meet mine. He stared at me, unblinking, his eyes wide and glassy, before he rested his hand on top of mine.

"Perhaps it's not their fault but my own. I'm told I don't treat people well."

My lips twitched. "You were quite insistent on my catering to your way the first time we met."

He blushed. "I am rather accustomed to that arrangement, though I'm quite embarrassed by it now."

"You did get your way in the end," I said with a teasing smile. "You left our meeting with my name, just as you wanted."

"But at almost too high of a cost—that of pushing you away. I seem to push everyone away, yet for some reason I don't want to do that to you. But…" He took a steadying breath. "…if you don't want to meet with me anymore, you don't have to. Payment or not, I could never force you."

His voice was a whisper, as if he could barely force himself to say the words that would end this strange relationship of ours before it had even really begun. And it was only after he'd given me the option to end it that I realized I wanted this to continue, whatever it was.

"Why wouldn't I want to?" I asked. "I've had a lovely time with you." And it was true. Today had turned out entirely differently from how I'd expected. I searched his expression, as if the answer to this puzzle could be found from the man who seemed a riddle himself. "Why did you really bring me here today?"

His lips curved up and his dark eyes softened. "I'm intrigued by you. I've never met anyone quite like you. I hoped that perhaps…we could be friends."

I sucked in my breath and held it. In my mind I saw two paths unfold before me, one free from involvement with any man—the one that I'd determined to walk after Father left—and this new, unexpected path Aiden was offering, one that twisted and turned towards an unknown destination.

My initial response not to trust him compelled me to end this now, but there was something stronger than my fear that wanted me to explore it a bit longer. Uncertain, I glanced up at the trees, my friends and guides, seeking the permission I so desperately yearned for. The branches swayed. *It's up to you.*

Aiden waited earnestly for my response. My words became trapped in my throat so I nodded, an answer that I felt I'd always longed to give him, even before we'd met.

"I do have a debt to repay, after all," I managed. He beamed and my heart lifted at his elated expression. I wasn't sure where this new path would lead, but I couldn't wait to find out.

CHAPTER 7

"*E*ileen, what are you doing?"

I froze at Mother's taut voice and slowly turned to face her, praying I didn't look as guilty as I felt at having been caught breeching the Forest's border. By her narrowed eyes, my attempted innocent expression had failed dismally.

Mother stood with the basket of berries I'd collected for her that morning. Too late, I remembered my promise to help her make jam to sell in the village. I walked away from the Forest, ignoring the trees' annoyed rustling.

"Are you ready to make jam?" I asked nonchalantly.

My attempts at distraction didn't work. She frowned first at me and then at the Forest. "You were going into the Forest, weren't you?"

I bit my lip guiltily and she sighed. Her gaze lowered to my sketchbook that I hugged protectively, as if my special drawings would lend me strength for what was sure to be an unpleasant confrontation. Her frown deepened.

"That's not a new sketchbook at all; it's the one you lost in the Forest—a Forest you returned to even after you promised you wouldn't."

I crumpled. "I'm sorry. I can't stay away from it; it calls to me."

Hurt filled Mother's eyes. "Even though you know how much worry it causes me?"

I winced but said nothing. She sighed, sounding so...*weary*. After an agonizing moment of tense silence, she rested her hand on my shoulder.

"Let's make that jam."

I followed her into the house and pulled out a bowl. We worked silently side by side as we mashed the berries and cooked them over the hearth. Normally, the familiar chore was filled with cheerful chatter and laughter.

Not today. Each stolen peek revealed the weariness cloaking Mother, the worry furrowing her brow and filling her eyes. In the years following Father's abandonment, those worried lines had become a recurring feature. They'd gradually softened as we'd managed to forge a new life together and survive each hungry year and endless winter. Now, because of me, they'd returned.

"I'm sorry, Mother," I finally managed.

She didn't pause in her stirring. "I know you love the Forest. While I've always worried for you—convinced one day you'd get lost and never return—I've tried to suppress my fears, not wanting to take your special place away from you. But ever since you encountered that nobleman"—her gaze lowered to the cut from Aiden's dagger that scarred my throat—"I'm afraid for you, dear. You're all I have left."

"I know. I'm sorry I disobeyed you."

But despite my apology, I knew I'd return again. It wasn't just the trees that called me now, it was Aiden. I didn't understand my strong desire to see him again when we barely knew one another, only that I felt the pull. My need to ease Mother's heart fought with my longing to see Aiden. My chest tightened with guilt as I realized which side would win.

"Please promise me you'll never return to the Forest again."

Mother's desperate plea tore me from my thoughts of Aiden and what he'd planned for me today when I met with him, for I would. I couldn't lose that relationship just as it was beginning, while at the same time I couldn't hurt my relationship with Mother, which meant everything to me.

"Eileen?"

I slowly met Mother's gaze. I couldn't promise her, not when I'd only break it again. Instead of answering, I arranged the jars in preparation to pour the freshly made jam into them.

"Would you like to pour or should I?" I asked shakily. Behind me, I heard Mother remove the cooking jam from the hearth and come over to rest her hand over mine, stopping my nervous fiddling with the jars.

"Eileen, please promise me."

I shook my head. "I can't, Mother. I love the Forest. I can't lose it."

"And I can't lose you." Desperation filled her voice. She cupped my chin, forcing me to meet her eyes, which swirled with worry and pain. "You're all I have left. Every time you go into that Forest, I worry that, like your father, you'll never return."

"The Forest will never allow that to happen," I said. "It cares for me. You know how the trees work; they take a liking to certain people."

She blinked rapidly, as if staving off tears.

"I promise I'll always return."

"That's what he promised. He said the Forest would always protect him." Her usual careful composure cracked. "But something happened that took him away from me. What if something happens to you, too?"

"You can't keep me protected forever," I snapped. "I'm old

enough to make my own choices." I turned my back to her and seized the pot handle to pour the jam carefully into the jars. "I may have lost Father, but I can't lose the Forest." However, it wasn't the Forest I thought of midst my declaration but Aiden, the man I barely knew but desperately yearned to learn more about.

I finished bottling three jars of jam before I felt brave enough to risk stealing a glimpse at Mother's expression. The moment I did so I wished I hadn't. Raw pain filled her face and tears streaked her cheeks. My heart twisted.

"Mother?"

She shook her head, dismissing my attempts to apologize, and began placing the newly bottled jars into her basket. "I'll go to market to sell these. Wherever you wander off to, be back by dinner."

Guilt gnawed at my heart once more. "Mother, I don't have to—"

"You're right; you're not a child anymore, and I need to stop being afraid for you. An impossible task, no doubt, considering it's a mother's job to worry, especially about the only loved one she has left."

Tense silence settled over us as we finished our work. The moment the last jar of jam was ready, Mother left, slamming the door behind her. I stared after her before I glanced out the window at the Forest, its silent calls tugging me towards it.

Despite my guilt from my fight with Mother, I didn't want her to hold me back, not when I was so anxious to explore this new path I'd stumbled upon. I needed to see this strange new journey to its conclusion.

Yet despite my resolution, our fight lingered in my mind, and it took a while for the tension tightening my chest to ease.

~

"WHERE ARE you taking me this time?"

My words came out breathlessly, for my entire attention was focused on Aiden's hold as he led me deeper into the Forest. My heart pattered at the sensation of his fingers on my skin, the heat of his touch encircling my wrist.

Aiden grinned over his shoulder with one of his cute lopsided smiles. "You really expect me to ruin the surprise?"

My already rapid heartbeat escalated at the mischievous light glistening in his dark eyes. His eagerness for today's excursion had been palpable from the moment we'd met this afternoon, the thought of making me happy clearly pleasing him. It made the firm scolding I'd given myself after having once again allowed the Forest to guide me to a man I scarcely knew now seem unwarranted. Aiden was becoming a part of my Forest, a stable tree with deep roots.

He'd told me he had somewhere special in mind today. The moment he'd gently taken hold of my wrist, time had stilled. After several steps and a crimson blush, he paused to offer his arm instead, only just remembering to behave as a proper gentleman. His fluster made him all the more endearing, an endearment that made him more a threat to my heart.

The path we currently followed was extra twisty, as if it couldn't make up its mind about our destination. Aiden walked it with confidence, obviously having traveled this course many times already.

"Are we almost there?" For it felt we'd been walking for a long time.

"Almost. I know it's far, but I promise it'll be worth the journey. It's my favorite place in the Forest. I used to go there with my mother."

I wanted to inquire further about his mother but stopped at the guarded look suddenly filling his eyes.

The path eventually opened up to a rosy-violet-tinted lake, appearing as if its water had been dipped in sunset. Weeping cherry trees surrounded the lake like a halo, their pink blossoms falling like gentle snow onto the surface of the water, causing artistic ripples to dance across the surface of the lake. I stared in wonder as my gaze caressed the scene before me.

"I've never seen anything so enchanting," I finally managed to whisper, sure that speaking any louder would disrupt the tranquil reverence that filled this picturesque scene.

I sensed Aiden's pleased grin but couldn't tear my gaze away from the beauty before me, even for him.

"It's lovely, isn't it? This place has always been special to me. I once asked the Forest to keep others from stumbling across it, but you're welcome anytime."

My heart warmed at his invitation even though I knew I'd never accept it. I couldn't come here without Aiden. He was a part of this place. I could feel it in the swaying branches, each surrounding tree containing one of his memories, preserved forever within its limbs. Mesmerized, I watched their blossoms fall one by one onto the lake. Each ripple caused a tinkling sound like wind chimes. I cocked my head, listening.

"What's that?"

Aiden's grin widened. "I'll show you."

He released me—leaving me yearning for his touch—and walked to the base of one of the trees, all of which were surrounded by mauve stones. He crouched down and examined each before returning with a handful. "Have you ever skipped rocks?"

Father had always promised to teach me when I was a child. I swallowed the lump filling my throat and shook my head. Aiden searched my face with a small frown, eyes concerned, revealing he'd noticed the emotions I'd inadvertently allowed to slip through.

"I'll be happy to teach you." He handed me an oval-shaped stone that was perfectly smooth. Warmth rippled over me as our fingers grazed. "The best stone to use is one that isn't too big or heavy and is flat and uniform enough to skip across the water."

He stepped closer, closing the distance between us to stand directly behind me. My heart leapt to my throat as his warmth and honey-musk scent washed over me, making me lightheaded. I felt the strangest inclination to lean against his chest, but thankfully I resisted the ridiculous impulse.

"Hold it between your thumb and middle finger, with your thumb on top and your index finger hooked along the edge." He reached around me to arrange my fingers. I shuddered at his touch. "Now face the water at an angle and pull your arm slightly back." He adjusted my body to the correct position. "When you throw your stone, cock your wrist back in a quick flick to create the spin needed for it to skip across the water. Try it."

I took a few moments to catch my breath before I did. To my surprise and delight, the stone skipped across the lake's surface. With each of its patters and ripples, music resonated across the lake like the tune of a music box. I gasped.

"Oh!"

Aiden smiled and tossed his own stone across the water, creating more ripples and with them more music, this melody different than the first, one almost haunting in its beauty. I skipped a second rock for its tune to join his. The symphony of music waltzed around us, separate melodies that were still harmonious and beautiful.

We skipped several more rocks and listened to each of the lake's songs that filled the clearing with its sweet notes. When the last note had faded along with the dancing ripples breaking across the sunset-colored surface of the lake, a reverent silence settled over us until Aiden broke it.

"I haven't been here in so long," he murmured. "I'd forgotten not only how lovely it is, but how peaceful. I used to come nearly every day. Mother and I explored this instrument lake, trying to learn each of the notes found in the patterns of the water. She loved music. I like to think the Forest created this place just for her." He stared out across the lake, gaze unseeing.

"What made you stop coming?" I asked.

His soft expression immediately faded. He stooped down for another stone and tossed it jerkily into the water with such force it plunked out a harsh sound before sinking below the surface. Hardness twisted his expression as he turned towards me.

Whatever warm, fluttery feelings that had filled me vanished in an instant. Darkness filled his eyes, a brief flash of the man I'd met the day the Forest first led me to him.

The memory of that first meeting returned along with the feelings I'd experienced during it, ones which I'd fought and failed to entirely forget—the fear prickling my neck at the sensation of being watched, Aiden's dark eyes bearing down on me, the hardness filling his entire manner as he'd toyed with me, the suffocating sense of danger.

I flinched away, needing to put distance between us. How could I have wanted to be close to him mere minutes earlier?

The fierce lines of Aiden's expression vanished, replaced with sadness, leaving behind no traces of the darkness I'd caught a glimpse of, as if it hadn't been present at all. Only it had. I'd seen it. The walls I'd built around my heart—which had been crumbling brick by brick during each moment we spent together—were hastily built up once more.

The remaining stones in my hand slipped through my fingers to land at my feet. Aiden's brow furrowed as he glanced down at them. "You don't want to skip rocks anymore?"

I didn't answer. My heartbeat pattered wildly as if I'd run miles even though I stood frozen, the memory of his fierce expression still seared into my mind.

"Eileen?"

He stepped closer and I stumbled back, nearly into the lake, saved from an icy splash only by Aiden grabbing my waist to prevent me from falling. Once again his touch burned me, and my body betrayed me by shuddering before I yanked myself from his grip. His frown deepened.

"What's wrong?"

Everything was wrong. The tranquil moment was ruined. It was incredible how something so lovely could be so fragile and shatter so easily. I'd foolishly allowed my blind trust in a bunch of enchanted trees and their shifting pathways—along with Rosie's ridiculous fairy tale notions—to cause me to spend time with a man still a stranger to me. A kind gesture, a few conversations, and a handful of fun experiences together couldn't erase the fact that I didn't truly know Aiden, so trusting him was impossible.

I'd trusted Father, yet he'd betrayed my trust by leaving, teaching me I couldn't rely on any man, especially this dark stranger.

And yet…

"Eileen?" Worry filled Aiden's eyes as his fingers stroked down my arm, leaving behind a trail of heat before intertwining with mine. I jerked away from him and glared.

"Don't." My plea came out weak and strangled, a sign of my inner conflict. I hated the part of me that wished I hadn't pulled away, that wanted to hold his hand just to see what it was like, that wanted to believe in the Forest's judgment and ignore whatever I'd seen in Aiden's eyes.

"I'm sorry," he whispered. "Not just for touching you, but for…"

He trailed off, seeming not to have the words adequate enough to smooth over what had just transpired between us, but by the pain now filling in his eyes, he seemed aware of the darkness that had briefly overcome him and how it had affected me.

His gaze met mine, his eyes pleading yet uncertain. "Might we sit down? Please."

I wanted to say no and demand that he tell the Forest to take me home as quickly as possible, but I couldn't make myself say the words.

Against my better judgment, I plopped beside him on the damp shore. Silence settled over us, broken only by each musical ripple caused by the still-raining blossoms landing gently on the lake's surface. Despite the tension that had sprung up between us, it wasn't an uncomfortable silence.

"I didn't mean to allow my emotions to overcome me. I'm sorry if I upset you."

I said nothing. The fear he'd caused me to feel still pounded through my bloodstream. I needed to leave. Then why couldn't I make myself move?

"Ever since Mother died, I'm afraid the way I've treated people has been rather…rude, with complete disregard to others' feelings. I wasn't even aware of my behavior—nor would I have cared—until you made it clear how much it bothers you." His cheeks darkened and he avoided my eyes, tracing swirls in the damp shore with his finger. "I'm afraid I'm not a very nice person. I'm sorry."

I remained silent.

"This place is very special to me," he continued. "But it also brings a lot of pain. Although I love it here, years ago I vowed never to return. This is the first time I've been back."

"Why did you bring me?"

He didn't answer for a moment as he skipped his final stone across the water's surface, once more surrounding us with the lake's music.

"I'm not sure." His brow furrowed as he searched my eyes, as if the answer to that question could be found there. "I've wanted to return so many times, but I couldn't come alone. Yet because this place is so special, I couldn't bring just anyone..." His perplexed frown deepened. "I don't know."

Something flashed in his eyes, a secret. He was hiding something, another sign that I couldn't trust him.

My insecurities returned in a rush. I tightened my jaw and picked up one of my fallen stones to throw it into the lake, satisfied at the jarring note that reverberated through the clearing. "I don't understand why you not only brought me here but have been spending time with me at all. Who am I to you?"

He frowned. "I've upset you."

"You've done more than that. You've frightened me."

Vulnerability filled his eyes. "I'm not meaning to frighten you, but I suppose such an outcome is inevitable; I seem to frighten everyone." He sighed. "I've told you before that sometimes my worst self emerges and I don't know how to keep it buried where it belongs."

I understood that all too well. Sometimes when memories of Father's abandonment became too much, it felt as if my own pain and bitterness would consume me.

Aiden rested his forearms on his knees and stared unseeing out across the lake. "This place stirs so many memories, both happy and painful ones. Perhaps I hoped returning here would be healing. It's such a lovely place, isn't it?"

He gave me an imploring look, a silent plea not only to forgive him but to allow him to change the course of this unsettling conversation. I studied his expression, searching for any sign of insincerity, before releasing a long breath I hadn't realized I'd been holding.

I stared at the pink trees growing from the dusky-violet bank around the sunset-caressed water with its musical ripples, all seeming part of a dream. "I still can't believe such an enchanting place exists in the Forest."

"This was the first place the Forest ever led me to," Aiden said. "When I was young, the Forest frightened me. I felt as if the trees were guards surrounding my home, both constantly watching me and trapping me there. Even within the trees I was scared; I hated the thought there was no set path and thus I could easily become lost. One day Mother wanted me to overcome these fears. We entered the Forest together and it led us here. That moment changed everything. I learned to trust that the Forest's guidance would always lead me some-where spectacular."

His gaze slid to mine, intense and smoldering, causing my cheeks to burn. His smile lit up his eyes, completely dispelling the remaining darkness that had lingered there. "I hadn't come to the Forest for a long time until the day it encouraged me to step inside, when it led me to you." He tilted his head. "Perhaps that's why I brought you here today. It seemed fitting. I just hope that my childish insistence on demanding this payment of your time isn't hurting you—although considering I frightened you today, it's likely too late." Worry filled his eyes as he severed our gaze. "I don't want to frighten you. Please believe that."

Nor did I want to be frightened of him, but his volatile swings between the sweet Aiden and the hard one made me wary. The surrounding trees shifted, as if urging me to forgive Aiden and give him another chance. Why could I so easily place my trust in the Forest's guidance but not in my own heart? Their encouragement and the memory of the wonderful memories we'd forged so far gradually softened me.

Heart pattering, I hesitantly grazed his arm with my fingertips, a gesture which snapped his gaze back to mine. I still wasn't sure whether or not I could trust him, only that despite my moment of doubt, it felt natural to be here with him.

He stared at my hand resting on his arm, as if confused by its presence, before managing a smile, one that caused my heart to flutter. "Will you meet with me again?"

With the encouraging rustling of the surrounding trees, I nodded.

Only one more day of our strange bargain. A sense of sadness filled me at the thought. How could I allow our developing relationship to conclude when there were still so many unexplored emotions between us?

I found myself getting lost in Aiden's gaze once more and wishing that wherever my future would lead, Aiden would be waiting for me.

CHAPTER 8

"*E*ileen? *Eileen?*"

I reluctantly emerged from my daydreams to find Rosie no longer pacing the bakery's sitting room as she spun her latest tale but instead standing inches away from me, hands pressed on her hips, glaring.

I blinked rapidly as I struggled to reground myself. "Did I do it again?" For she'd been trying and failing to engage my attention the entire afternoon.

She sighed impatiently. "You certainly did. You scarcely said two words during our stroll and didn't even comment on my new tart. Now, I want all the juicy details. Spill."

My thoughts naturally drifted back to where they'd been torn from moments before. As much as I'd fought against thinking of Aiden since my last meeting with him, the wonderful memories filled my mind anyway, all eclipsing the brief moment of tension we'd experienced—the smooth and warm sound of his voice, the heat of his touch around my wrist, the fluttery feeling filling my heart whenever he looked at me, his crooked smile, the way the sunlight danced against the copper tints in his hair, and especially the look filling his black eyes that gave me the strangest sensation that my world was tipping upside down and nothing would ever be the same again.

I bit my lip to suppress the emerging smile that seemed to arrive whenever I thought about Aiden. "I'm not thinking of anything."

Rosie harrumphed. "You're the worst liar. I always know when someone has a fantastic story waiting to be told. You must do your best-friend duty and share it at once." She settled beside me on the settee and scooted closer with an eager gleam filling her eyes.

"It's nothing," I said again.

She delicately cocked an eyebrow. "Don't give me that. *Nothing* is merely code for *Aiden*."

The heat already filling my cheeks deepened. "Why would I be thinking of him?"

Rosie wrapped her arms around her legs and rocked back and forth, eyes bright. "I'm assuming you heeded my advice and have been engaging in clandestine meetings with him. And by your current blush and the way you've been floating around all afternoon, things must be going very well, as I knew they would. Now spill."

I groaned and buried my burning face in my hands. "I wish you couldn't read me so easily."

"I'm your dearest friend. Did you really expect anything less? Now stop stalling. I shall forgive your spaciness with every juicy detail you share about your Aiden."

"*My* Aiden?" I peeked through my fingers to see her mischievous smirk. "He's merely a...*friend*."

Admittedly, the word seemed too weak for the relationship we'd forged between us. I frowned, considering why, and couldn't come up with an adequate explanation that would sort out my jumbled feelings.

"Then why are you blushing?" Rosie asked, her annoyingly chipper tone far too knowing. "Why do you think about him so often with a dazed look? You two must have had many romantic interactions."

"Of course not," I said hastily. "We've only explored the Forest."

It seemed such an inadequate summary for how much I'd enjoyed the time we'd spent together, despite knowing it was unwise to feel this way, especially considering we hadn't been acquainted long and hardly knew one another.

Rosie predictably gave me an exasperated look. "Must you be so vague?"

I fiddled with the ends of my hair, avoiding her eyes. "I admit it's hard not to be when I'm rather confused myself."

She sighed, but I found her smiling when I stole a peek at her expression. "I suppose you're still trying to come to terms with your deepening feelings for Aiden."

My heart pounded rapidly. "My feelings? What feelings?"

Rosie rolled her eyes. "Isn't it obvious? You're developing a *tendre* for him."

My cooling cheeks ignited again. "Don't be ridiculous. I scarcely know him."

"Such a triviality was no obstacle for the Forest bringing you two together so that your hearts could recognize one another." She pressed her hand over her own heart with a wistful sigh. "It's terribly romantic, just like a fairy tale."

Father's tender goodbye embrace with Mother flashed through my mind, their last interaction before he left and never came back. Pain prickled my heart. "Life isn't a fairy tale."

"It would be if you'd stop being a villain by thwarting your own happily ever after," she snapped.

I sighed. "Stop reading too much into my relationship with Aiden. I told you we're just friends."

"Then why do you frequently daydream of him with a

starry look?" She smirked, daring me to deny it. I tightened my jaw, refusing to humor her, and her smirk widened. "I rest my case. Friendship is a wonderful start, but I have no doubt it'll soon lead to something *more*."

"It can't." Panic clawed at my heart at the thought. "It can't develop into anything. I won't allow it to."

Rosie pouted. "Why not?"

"Because love isn't in my future. It leads to nothing but heartbreak. After Father left, I vowed never to experience such pain again." My declaration built the weakening defenses surrounding my heart back up.

"Aiden isn't your father, Eileen," Rosie said softly.

I nibbled my lip. "I know that, but..." The image of the darkness filling Aiden's eyes returned, the memory of his cold expression eclipsing whatever warmth filled my other memories of him. "There are moments when something overcomes him, as if he's guarding a multitude of secrets. I don't know whether or not I can trust him."

Rosie pressed her thumb to her lips. "I admit distrust can be an obstacle difficult to overcome on the road to true love. What you must determine is whether he's honest with you, if you're comfortable enough to be yourself around him, and if you feel safe with him."

She made it sound so simple.

Rosie's frown deepened and her forehead wrinkled in concentration as she considered. Then she brightened with an idea. Judging by the mischievous gleam in her eyes, it was likely one I wouldn't like.

"We must create a situation that will guarantee you'll be able to determine whether or not he's worthy of your trust."

"And how do you propose we do that?"

She clasped her hands, her face lit with a radiant smile. "With a spelled dessert, of course—specifically, my famous truth cakes."

Before I could respond, Rosie scrambled to her feet and skipped into the kitchen. I reluctantly followed and found her tugging on a cupboard door that was quite firmly locked. She sighed and pressed her hands on her hips to look around the kitchen as if seeking inspiration.

"That cupboard has been locked ever since Mother caught me baking from it, but I was hoping luck would pay us a much needed visit and I'd find it unlocked for my plan. How inconvenient it's being so uncooperative. What a bother. I suppose I must find a way to break it open."

I eyed the cupboard warily. "What's in the cupboard?"

"*Enchanted Sweets and Delights.*"

I groaned. The last time she'd used her recipe book of magical desserts, it had ended in disaster. "Rosie…"

She waved my concern away as she strode the circumference of the room, searching for the appropriate tool for this particular scene in *Rosalina Bakes Up Trouble.*

"I don't have the recipe memorized, so it'd be best if I used the book so I can get it right," she said. "Wouldn't it be terrible if I inadvertently poisoned your true love?"

"*Rosie!*"

"Oh, stop fussing, Eileen; I've baked these cakes plenty of times. They're a Rosie specialty. Don't you trust me?" She gave me a wide-eyed, vulnerable look that tugged on my heart. Still, I refused to be so easily swayed.

"How do I know you're not going to create a love spell instead in order to get the ending you want in my story?"

"Why do that when you're well on your way to falling in love with Aiden already—if you haven't already done so?"

I opened my mouth to protest that particular point, but she merely talked over me.

"But if you're so worried, then watch me bake them so you can see for yourself I won't tamper with the recipe."

As I scrambled for another reason to dissuade her, she

returned to her pacing, scanning every inch of the kitchen. It was meticulously clean, everything in its proper order, leaving no spare tools lying about just waiting to pick a lock.

She suddenly froze and giggled. "How silly of me, I have the tool I need right here." She pulled out a hairpin. "This is how all heroines do it in mystery novels."

She returned to the cupboard and began working on the lock. Annoyingly, it actually clicked open. She flashed me a triumphant smirk.

"See how easy this is? We're definitely on the right path."

She pulled out a large and stained leather volume. Despite the heirloom having seen better days, it still had a glimmer about it, as if it not only taught how to brew magic, but that magic itself filled its yellowed pages.

She plopped the tome onto the counter and began to rapidly flip through the pages, muttering to herself. I sauntered over and stole a peek over her shoulder just as she reached the "Truth Cakes" recipe. She scanned it with her finger.

"It's an easy recipe, so nothing should go wrong.

Trepidation knotted my stomach. "And it won't, right?"

"Of course not. Stop worrying."

"But what if your parents return and catch us baking from this book?"

"They're in Draceria visiting my aunt and won't return until after dark. It's the rest day, so the bakery is closed, preventing any customers from interrupting our baking adventure. Any other protests?"

I gnawed my lip. "It's so...deceitful."

"But effective." Rosie began bustling around the kitchen, pulling out mixing bowls, spoons, and jars containing strange powders and colored liquids I'd never seen before, all with a determined gleam that made me realize I'd already lost the battle. But I refused to give up completely.

"We shouldn't bake Aiden truth cakes. It's wrong to tamper with magic when there's so much that can go wrong."

Naturally, she ignored such a sensible suggestion. She arranged the ingredients on the counter before opening the bag of flour. Humming to herself, she carefully measured it before pouring some into the bowl.

"Be a dear and fetch the unicorn tears?" She waved me towards an upper cupboard I couldn't hope to reach with my short height. I deliberated for a moment before sighing in defeat. There was no point arguing with a very determined Rosie. I dragged a chair over, telling myself that there wasn't any harm in humoring her since I didn't have to actually give the cakes to Aiden. This lie was so convincing I almost believed it myself.

The cupboard was stuffed to the brim with all sorts of strange ingredients: pixie dust, dragon's breath, petals from mystical flowers I'd never heard of, bottled starlight…. Even in all the fantasy stories I'd read and all the times I'd visited the magical Forest, I'd never encountered anything that would yield ingredients such as these. Where had they come from?

"Eileen? The unicorn tears, please."

I picked up the labeled jar containing a shimmering lilac liquid and scrambled down from my perch to hand it to her. She carefully measured out a spoonful before pouring it into her batter, which immediately turned a soft rose color. She smiled.

"Goodness, it's already so pretty, not to mention mine always turn out incredibly tasty. Aiden will gobble them right up when you give them to him. You should eat some, too, else he'll be suspicious."

"I suppose you fail to see the irony that I'm using deception in order to determine whether or not he's worthy of my trust?" I said wryly.

"One must use all the resources at her disposal," Rosie said, unabashed. "You're fortunate your best friend has an enchanted bakery." She sprinkled a glittery powder into the batter before handing me a spoon. "While it'd be preferable if you made these yourself so you're the type of heroine who takes charge of her own story, it's best if I do most of the baking so you don't mess up; we wouldn't want your story to end in tragedy. However, you can at least stir the mixture together."

I reluctantly accepted her spoon and proceeded to mix, alternating between clockwise and counter-clockwise stirring as directed by the recipe. "How do these truth cakes work exactly?"

Rosie dropped in three petals from a vibrant blue glowing flower. "They're really quite simple. With one bite the spell is cast, forcing Aiden to be truthful for several hours. It's a very subtle spell, so he shouldn't suspect anything is amiss, leaving you free to question him all you like. But don't be too heavy-handed; no man likes to feel interrogated. If you eat one, too, then you'll finally stop lying to yourself and admit you're falling in love with him."

"But I'm *not*," I insisted. She merely shrugged.

"We shall see, won't we?" And humming once more, she measured two spoonfuls of the crushed silver moon rock before snatching the mixing bowl from me and stirring with an excited fervor. The way she measured and mixed, she'd obviously created these quite often. I frowned suspiciously.

"Who have you baked these for?"

She paused, her cheeks pink. "A few crushes over the years, just to see whether or not they felt anything for me in return."

I groaned. "Oh, Rosie."

"There's no need to sound so disapproving. Except for my repeatedly breaking heart, there was no harm done. I needed these cakes to determine whether or not my crushes were *the one*, only for me to realize they weren't. But I'll find him one day. In the meantime, I can help you get together with yours."

"But Aiden isn't my—"

She gave me an exaggeratedly sweet smile. "Wait until you've eaten a truth cake before you try to deny it once more."

I knew I should continue arguing against Rosie's ridiculous idea, but it was difficult when I was already wrestling so much with myself, a battle made more difficult when I wasn't sure which side of me I wanted to win.

Once the batter was mixed, Rosie carefully arranged four cakes—each a different color—into round balls and placed them on the wooden peel. She carefully slid the peel into the hearth before rubbing her hands clean on her apron, eyes bright.

"Voilà! Four truth cakes, soon-to-be-baked to perfection. They'll keep for several days." Her eyes widened. "You are meeting him within the next several days, aren't you?"

"We're meeting tomorrow." My treacherous heart lifted at the thought, but I tried to mask my excitement. By the knowing look in her eyes, I hadn't fooled her in the least.

"Excellent. The spell works best when fresh. Oh, this is positively thrilling, Eileen. You must be sure to tell me the results afterwards."

As the cakes baked, we sat knee-to-knee on the floor as Rosie jabbered away about the latest rumors surrounding the Sortileyan royal family—particularly the Dark Prince and Dragon Princess—as well as all sorts of nobles I could care less about, considering none of the rumors were about Aiden. I fought to focus on the conversation rather than on my memories of Aiden that continuously fought for my attention. It didn't work, and thus I missed every bit of Rosie's juicy gossip.

Rosie checked on the cakes every ten minutes. Despite their small size, they took an hour to bake, which Rosie insisted was necessary in order to let the magic seep. When she deemed them finished, she removed the peel and sniffed the steam rising from the cakes.

"Aren't they perfect?"

They were quite lovely—small, colorful, and perfectly round, with a crispy outside and what promised to be a soft, fluffy inside. Their fruity scent tickled my nose and their appetizing appearance eased some of my anxiety. "They do look good."

"They're delicious, for truth is one of the sweetest things." She wrapped them in a napkin. "You must promise me you'll give them to Aiden the next time you see him."

I couldn't do anything less, not with the fierce look she gave me. "I promise."

With a satisfied nod, she reverently handed me the cakes. Their heat enveloped me as I cradled them close. The rest of my reservations melted away. Perhaps these were exactly what I needed.

Despite my continued denial against Rosie's suggestions that my relationship with Aiden was something deeper, I knew my heart was in danger—all the more reason why our next meeting should be our last. Even so, I couldn't deny I wanted to remove whatever barriers stood between us in order to know the true Aiden. Even if we never saw one another again, I needed to trust him—if for no other reason than to prove to my heart that it hadn't been nearly stolen by a man unworthy of it.

CHAPTER 9

*A*iden led us down the path deeper into the Forest, his hand laced through mine, having shyly taken it after kissing it in greeting. Ripples pulsed up my arm from our intertwined hands while nervous flutters tickled my stomach as I thought about the truth cakes tucked inside my satchel.

Due to these sensations, both his attempt at small talk and the beauty of the surrounding trees lit with golden sunlight were entirely lost on me. Each touch from his fingers sent a jolt straight to my hammering heart. Why was I allowing myself to hold his hand? We were only friends. I repeated this lie over and over while I still could, for once I ate a truth cake, I'd no longer be able to.

Around us, the trees were gradually thinning, hinting we were nearing the destination of my final payment. After today, I likely wouldn't see Aiden again...or rather, I *shouldn't* see him again. The thought sent a pang through my heart.

"We're almost there," Aiden murmured, and a few minutes later the path opened up into a clearing. My hand leapt to my throat.

"Oh, Aiden..."

Midst the clearing of colorful wildflowers permeating the air with their sweet perfume, a waterfall fell in a frothy cascade into a crystal clear pool. A glistening mist shrouded the air, casting a sheen of rainbows in the sunlight. A picnic blanket and basket were already arranged at the base of the falls beside the rocky outcroppings surrounding the pool.

Aiden beamed as he watched my reaction. I tentatively stepped closer, taking in the scene before us. The color of the waterfall gradually transformed from crystal blue to indigo to violet. My eyes widened. Like everything in the Forest, the waterfall was enchanted. Once again Aiden had chosen the most perfect place to take me.

"I'd always hoped there was a waterfall hidden within these trees," I murmured.

He wiped a spray of water off my cheeks with his sleeve. "I'm pleased I helped grant your wish. The Forest is full of many wonders, isn't it?"

He led me to the picnic basket and pulled me down to join him. There he unpacked all manner of delights—thick artisan bread, a variety of cheeses, slices of salami, an assortment of berries, and a pitcher of lemonade—and made me up a plate, which I accepted with a shy smile. He softly returned it, his gaze incredibly tender. I felt my heart constrict at his look. I needed to be careful; each moment spent with him weakened my defenses.

I placed some cheese on a slice of bread and took a bite. The crusty texture of the bread mingled with the sharp taste of the cheese danced on my taste buds. As we ate, silence hovered in the misty, floral-scented air around us. With each bite, the nerves filling me escalated.

"You're rather pensive today."

Aiden's voice tore my attention from the mesmerizing changing colors of the waterfall, which I'd watched transition through all the colors of the rainbow over the course of our picnic. He eyed my fidgeting warily.

"I'm just wondering how many more secret delights the Forest is hiding and how I can discover them all." I slipped my shoes off and slid my feet into the water. The smooth pebbles at the bottom caressed my toes.

He grinned. "Is this an invitation to explore more of the Forest with you?"

My cheeks warmed as I hastily tore my gaze away from his. "Isn't this the final payment?"

"It is...unless we change the terms of our bargain."

My heart lurched, both in hope and in terror at his suggestion. Each day I spent with him made it more and more difficult to imagine my explorations of the Forest without him. Desperate for a distraction, I lifted my foot from the pool and watched the water dribble down my ankle. A string of ripples extended from the splashes to dance across the water's surface.

"Eileen?" Aiden's imploring tone begged me to answer, but I couldn't—not when I didn't have an answer to give. "Please, Eileen, I very much want to meet with you again, if you're willing."

My heart pounded at his words but even more so at the smoldering look in his eyes when I finally looked at him, one that made me feel both lightheaded and warm to the core. Being with him now made me feel certain he was the path I was meant to take, despite it being one I couldn't walk—at least not until I was certain I could trust him.

I shakily removed the wrapped bundle of truth cakes from my satchel. "I brought dessert."

He unwrapped the truth cakes, whose vibrant colors and delicious aroma made them appear innocent, no hint of the spell one bite would trigger.

"Did you bake these yourself?"

"Rosie's family owns a bakery and we often bake together."

He handed me one. "In that case, perhaps you should test them for poison." He winked.

The nerves knotting my stomach tightened. I laughed breathlessly before nibbling at the end of a periwinkle cake.

Whether I imagined its effect or merely noticed it because I was aware of the enchantment, I immediately felt the spell seep through me, wriggling its way into the recesses of my heart, crumbling the barriers surrounding my closely-guarded secrets.

Aiden took a large bite of his own. I warily eyed his reaction to the spell; so far he didn't seem to notice the effects of the charmed dessert, just as Rosie had said he wouldn't.

"These are really good." He finished his cake and wiped his fingers on his handkerchief. I took another hesitant bite of my own and felt my need to tell the truth strengthen. Considering Aiden had eaten his entire cake, I had no doubt he'd tell me anything I wanted to know.

I took another cautious nibble, trying not to wince as my protective walls cracked further under the influence of the magic washing over me. There were so many questions I wanted to ask—about who he truly was, what had happened to his mother, how he really felt towards me—but I settled for the one that had nagged me the most.

"Do you remember the day we met?"

The first time I'd brought our meeting up, Aiden's guard had gone up, his black eyes stuffed to the brim with secrets. This time, however, everything about him became open as he answered without any hesitation.

"I remember wondering why the Forest had led me to you. When I first saw you, it was as if—I don't know, as if a light flickered inside of me for the first time in a long time. It both scared me and intrigued me. I knew I had to find out more about you, but you wouldn't even give me your name. It was all rather…disconcerting." His brow furrowed, as if something about his own answer puzzled him.

"Why?" I pressed. "What did I do to cause you to feel that way?"

He took a bite from another cake and stared at the cascading falls—now a fern green—as he chewed, as if he couldn't make himself look at me. "I was on a pre-determined path until meeting you pushed me off course. I've fought back, knowing any new path would never work."

My heart lurched. This admission and the magic working on my heart revealed a hidden truth that up until now I hadn't wanted to acknowledge—that despite my reservations, I *wanted* us to work.

"Why not?" I whispered breathlessly.

He offered me a wry smile as he lightly brushed my cheek with his thumb. "Because I'm already engaged."

Every other question I'd prepared vanished from my mind in an instant. The warmth filling my entire body at his heated touch immediately evaporated, as if doused by water. I choked on my last bite of cake. "You're *engaged?*"

He nodded. "We've been betrothed for many years now."

"*Years?*"

A strange prickling emotion burned through my veins, intense and festering, begging for release in either anger or a wave of tears. "Who are you engaged to? When are you to be married?" My questions tumbled out, ones which I needed the answers to but whose responses I dreaded receiving.

He shoved the last piece of truth cake in his mouth. "She's actually my friend's younger sister. We're to be married next year."

My lip quivered. I blinked rapidly to stave off the tears burning my eyes. I took a deep, steadying breath to calm myself. It didn't work. "If you already have a girl, then what are you doing here with *me*?" The words were poison on my tongue and the jealousy raged further, like a monster begging for release.

"She's not my girl." His entire expression twisted, as if tasting something unpleasant.

"She is if you're engaged."

"The engagement was arranged by our families a long time ago." His attention returned to the waterfall, his expression pensive. "I was indifferent about it before, considering I never believed I'd find love myself, but now…"

His gaze shifted to mine, soft and piercing, making me feel at once both turned inside out and caressed. I leaned closer, eager to be near him and to hear the rest of his thought. "But what? Please tell me."

His eyes filled with pain and unmistakable yearning. "Everything is different now. What used to be an arrangement I felt indifferent towards now fills me with"—his mouth twisted as he struggled to find the correct word —"*hopelessness*. I don't want to be part of my arranged engagement any longer. I didn't realize just how much I didn't want it until I realized what I *do* want…or rather, *whom*."

He glanced at me shyly. I found myself lost in his dark eyes while the intense emotions I never expected to feel raged within me—emotions the enchantment of the cakes now forced me to acknowledge—and I suddenly wished I'd never baked them.

Aiden shook his head. "No, I can't want you. We can't work. It's impossible." Even as he spoke, he touched my hand with the tip of his finger. I jolted at the contact even as I welcomed it. "From the moment we met, I knew we couldn't be together. That's why I wanted a lock of your hair, so I'd never forget what I might have had. Besides our differing stations being an insurmountable obstacle, you deserve better than me."

At his rejection, heartache washed over me, drowning me in sharp, searing pain. This was what I'd worked so hard to avoid—before the spell had shattered the barriers protecting my heart, leaving me raw and vulnerable.

Aiden began tracing swirls on my hand, nearly unraveling me completely. It took every ounce of willpower not to look at him, certain I'd drown in my yearning with a single glimpse into his dark eyes.

"Perhaps these obstacles can be overcome," he murmured. "Perhaps we can still work."

His words caused my heart to pound frantically. "Aiden…"

The intense longing I felt for him, unlocked by the power of the enchanted cakes, overcame me. I cradled my legs against my body, as if the act could protect me from my own terrifying emotions as well as the warmth seeping over me from Aiden's tender expression.

Aiden plucked a violet and scooted closer, bridging the distance between us to gently tuck it into my hair. I shuddered as his hand grazed my cheek. I didn't move. I didn't even breath. His stroking touch felt amazing.

"You're so beautiful," Aiden whispered.

My breath became trapped in my throat. Aiden's fingers moved to caress my face before he wrapped his arms snugly around me to pull me close. I instinctively curled against him, my arms looping around him as I nestled closer. Aiden ran his nose up and down my neck before burrowing his face in my hair. I shuddered.

What was happening? I shouldn't be cuddling with Aiden. He was engaged! I needed to end this. But despite my firm instructions, I found myself leaning deeper into his soft hold to rest my cheek against his beating heart, unable to resist the lure I felt towards him. The enchanted cakes had broken down all my defenses and I could no longer lie and pretend I didn't want this; I'd never wanted anything more in my entire life.

I tilted my head towards his. There were no words to describe the intense emotion filling his eyes, but it was one that enveloped my heart all the same. His breath caressed my mouth as he leaned closer. His fingers lightly traced my cheek, my nose, and finally my lips, his expression incredibly soft, his eyes never leaving mine, not even for a moment.

Slowly, he began closing the distance separating us, and in that moment I realized what was happening: Aiden was going to *kiss* me. I melted into him—until the sharp reminder that he wasn't mine, no matter how much I wanted him to be, shattered the spell. I jerked away. He blinked at me, confused.

"What's wrong, Eileen?"

My thoughts swirled. We'd almost *kissed*. I was angry both at him for attempting it and at myself for stopping it. I glared at him, needing to unleash the bitter disappointment burning through me. "Were you trying to *kiss me?*"

He blushed crimson as he opened his mouth, closed it, and opened it again, at a loss for words. "I'm so sorry, Eileen." His voice broke. "I don't know what's come over me. All I can think about is you. I didn't realize how much you'd come to mean to me until today. Nothing will ever be the same now."

Our gazes locked, and the emotions I felt towards Aiden that I'd been fighting to suppress washed over me—a sweet, beautiful, and powerful feeling that blossomed inside of me and made my heart want to burst.

"What are you saying?" I whispered. He stared intensely at me, his eyes filled with such sweet tenderness. I flinched. "Stop. Don't look at me like that."

He obediently lowered his gaze. "I can't help it."

"You can't look at me like that," I said.

"But you can't deny there's something between us. There was the moment we met."

I ached to deny it, but the truth spell prevented me. "I know. I feel it too, but you're engaged," I stuttered. "It'd be dishonorable for you to kiss me when you're firmly attached to another."

He was silent a long moment before his serious expression became hopeful. "Perhaps that unfortunate circumstance can be remedied. I admit it'll be difficult, but not impossible. How can I marry another now that I've found you?"

My breath hooked. I stared into his gorgeous ebony eyes, and once more the beautiful foreign feelings burst, as if my heart had broken open, causing them to tumble out.

Why had I allowed Rosie to bake these truth cakes? My heart wasn't strong enough for the truth—the truth that despite not knowing one another long, I could no longer deny that *something* existed between Aiden and me, something that drew us closer as effortlessly as when the Forest's pathways had brought us together.

But circumstances being what they were—he was *engaged*, for goodness sake—it'd be morally wrong for us to continue pursuing a relationship. The fact that I now knew it was forbidden made me fully realize how much I wanted him.

I forced myself to stand and turn my back to him. "I have to go."

He scrambled to his feet and seized my wrist. "Please, Eileen." His tone was pleading and compelled me to look back at him. Pain filled his eyes.

"This is wrong," I said. "We can't be together."

"Perhaps not immediately, but I won't rest until we can." He stepped closer. I closed my eyes and allowed all that was Aiden to wash over me for the last time. "I have an idea," he continued. "I just need some time to work out the details, but I won't act unless I know: do you feel anything at all for me?"

I ached to lie with every fiber of my being. But I couldn't. I opened my eyes and met his gaze once more. "Yes."

He beamed as his hand trailed down my arm to lightly squeeze my fingers. "I do, too." He leaned down and pressed a soft kiss on my cheek, causing my heart to jolt. His warm breath caressed my ear as he pulled away. "We'll see one another again. Trust me."

I knew he could easily manipulate the Forest into allowing us to meet again, but how could he do that now with the obstacles keeping us apart? "We can't, Aiden. It won't work." The thought was agonizing.

"I'll find a way."

I forced a smile. "After all, you always get what you want."

"Exactly." His dark eyes seeped into mine as he raised my hand and lightly kissed it. "Thank you for the time you've spent with me. I look forward to our next meeting. Things will be different then, I promise; I have a plan."

Despite my reservations, his assurances enveloped me. I wasn't exactly sure what he was promising, only that he couldn't lie, not when I'd enchanted him. Even without the magic of the cakes, I knew I'd never be able to doubt the intensity filling his eyes as he looked at me like that.

$\mathcal{I}$ couldn't see the Forest through the curls of fog that hung over Arador, completely masking the trees. A shiver rippled up my spine. I didn't like not being able to see my Forest.

Beside me, Rosie stuck her hand out of the open window and beamed as it was swallowed up in the thick, hazy fog. "What a perfect night for a sleepover," she said.

I shuddered. "I feel as if the fog is smothering us."

"It adds atmosphere." She spun away from the window to take in my bedroom, tucked cozily up in the cottage attic, but by the way her eyes glistened, I suspected she was imagining a far different scene for whichever story she was currently experiencing. "We're princesses trapped in a castle surrounded by a cursed fog that casts whomever ventures into it under a spell."

"What sort of spell?"

She tapped her lips thoughtfully. "A spell of eternal sleep that can only be woken by true love's kiss. Now all we need to do is await our princes."

"Wouldn't they also fall under the spell if they attempted to rescue us?"

Rosie ignored this argument. "Aiden would brave even the most sinister curse in order to win your heart. You know it's true, Eileen, so don't even try to deny it."

The denial was pointless. I'd found Rosie waiting for me the moment I'd left the Forest following my waterfall picnic with Aiden, a picnic that had been both beautiful and heartbreaking.

She'd immediately begun her interrogation before the spell from the truth cakes wore off, finally forcibly excavating my true feelings for Aiden. Thankfully, her learning about my tendre for Aiden had spared me enduring further questioning about the picnic, allowing me to keep the hopelessness of our situation to myself...for now.

With time, the enchantment had faded and allowed me to once more see sense: a future with Aiden seemed impossible. He was engaged and thus off-limits, no matter how much I wished otherwise. Clinging to what I couldn't have would only invite heartache, and I'd had enough of that already.

Rosie snatched a biscuit from the plate left by Mother. "You can't continue denying it; I've heard your confession and won't let you forget it."

She finished off her biscuit in three bites and wiped her crumb-coated fingers on my quilt before settling on the bed and arranging her skirts daintily. She patted the spot beside her and I joined her, bracing myself for another Rosie interrogation.

"I've been fulfilling my best-friend duty and trying to extract juicy tidbits about your Aiden from Gavin," she began.

"You've been doing *what*?"

She rolled her eyes. "What's the point of having a cousin who's a member of the court if I don't use him? Despite having spelled Aiden, you wriggled precious little information from him, so I must do my part to remedy that blunder."

All the questions I'd meant to ask Aiden had seemed irrelevant after learning about the insurmountable barrier of his engagement. My heart tightened at the memory. It would have been easier to let him go if I hadn't realized how much I felt for him.

"You can't ask Gavin about Aiden anymore." It would be disastrous if Aiden's fiancée learned he'd nearly pursued a relationship with another girl.

"Stop your worrying. He wasn't suspicious about my inquires, considering my fishing for rumors is nothing new. It's my duty to stay up to date on all the latest gossip, and grilling a member of the court is the best way to do it." She furrowed her brow. "Although for some reason he seemed eager to cut our conversation short, which he's done a lot lately. Unfortunately, this resulted in my learning little about your Aiden; Gavin didn't even know who he is, but he wagers he's probably some stuffy duke."

Her failure to retrieve any information about Aiden was both a relief and a disappointment.

She wrapped her arms around her pulled-up knees and gave me an expectant look. "Speaking of Aiden, when are you going to see him again?"

I nibbled on the end of my own biscuit and avoided her eyes. "I'm not."

Rosie's mouth fell open. "But *why*? You love him."

My cheeks warmed as I once again remembered the feelings that had filled my heart after I'd eaten a truth cake, feelings that were both beautiful and frightening at once. "I don't *love* him."

She sighed. "Fine, you're in the process of falling in love with him, but how can you continue if you never see him again?"

"I don't want to see him again."

She rolled her eyes. "Why wouldn't you want—"

"He's betrothed to another woman."

Her hands flew to her mouth. She stared at me in disbelief, eyes wide and glassy, before a strangled sob escaped through her fingers. "Oh Eileen...really?"

I swallowed the lump in my throat. "Yes. The fact that he was involved with me at the same time shows what kind of man he is: one I could never be with, even if I was determined to get in a relationship, which as you well know I'm not."

Rosie bit her lip as she rested her hand over mine, her expression soft with sympathy. "I'm so sorry, Eileen."

For a moment we sat in silence, Rosie with her forehead furrowed and me trying and failing to ignore the pain tightening my heart.

Rosie's expression set in determination. "Engagements are easily broken, especially if he feels more for you than he does for her. You need to fight for him and your happily ever after."

My heart fluttered in hope before I forced myself to once again quench it. "I can't."

"*Eileen.*" Rosie scooted closer, expression fierce. "True love comes once in a lifetime. How can you allow him to slip away now that you've found him?"

I sighed. "Oh Rosie, please just let it go."

"I won't. From what you've told me, you two seem far too perfect for one another for you to give up now. We need to come up with a plan for you to thwart—"

"I won't interfere with his engagement," I said firmly. "Even if I managed it and he became engaged to me"—I tried and failed to ignore the way my treacherous heart lifted at the thought—"it would be foolish to enter an agreement with a man who doesn't take his romantic commitments seriously."

Rosie snapped her mouth shut, for once at a loss for anything to say. But naturally, she couldn't remain silenced for long. "Then why did the Forest lead you to one another?"

I didn't care to decipher the hidden motives of an enchanted bunch of trees and their mischievous pathways. "It doesn't matter. All that matters is that I've paid my last day of payment to the man it led me to and am now determined to never see him again."

"Even though you want to?"

I tightened my jaw and didn't answer. The horrified look that filled Rosie's face was as if I'd just announced I'd decided to carve out my heart and live my life without it. I tried to ignore the feelings sneaking past my careful barriers telling me that I may well be doing exactly that.

Rosie sighed and rolled her eyes towards the ceiling, as if appealing for divine assistance on how to deal with stubborn me. Then, as if she'd received an answer, her attention focused on my sketchbook. My heart jolted as I predicted her plan. I made to grab it, but she snatched it before I could and rapidly turned the pages, smirking in triumph when she found what she was seeking.

"Ah-ha: proof you're not willing to completely let him go yet." She tipped the book to showcase Aiden's portrait, which I'd drawn as I'd lingered near the Forest and fought its lure to step within the trees, unable to handle meeting Aiden again should that be where the Forest's paths took me. Yet my determination to forget him hadn't prevented me from drawing him.

It was my finest work. His face was expressionless yet possessed a hidden gentleness, found in the slight curve of his mouth and the dimple in his firm chin. My favorite part of the drawing was his eyes. I'd worked hard to capture the darkness and depth in them, particularly the way they guarded his emotions like sentries protecting a fortress.

Rosie's own eyes widened appreciatively as she hungrily took in Aiden's portrait. "Oh my, he's utterly adorable." She raised her gaze to mine with a knowing smile. "You need to fight for him."

Her words made another attack on my heart. Even if Aiden cared for me, I wasn't remarkable enough for him to throw away a prestigious arrangement for. I crossed my arms, as if the gesture would better protect me from the emotions washing over me at seeing Aiden's portrait again. But they didn't. Instead, my throat closed up and my eyes burned. I bit my lip so hard it bled.

"Please let it go," I pleaded. "Even if he weren't engaged and Father's abandonment wasn't holding me back, we're of differing stations. His family would never allow such a match. It could never work." The disappointment of my own admission clawed at my heart.

"True love has no such silly obstacles," Rosie said. "It's splendid how you've captured the heart of a noble, just like a real life fairy tale."

All desire to cry evaporated as my anger flared. "Life isn't a fairy tale, Rosie. You need to stop living in your fantasy worlds and finally realize that. Imagining otherwise is too painful."

Her expression crumpled and she lowered her eyes. Remorse for hurting her filled me, while the truth of the emotions I'd fought so hard to ignore once again threatened to drown me.

ROSIE CAST me frequent disapproving looks throughout the remainder of our sleepover, scrutiny I tried and failed to ignore. It was a relief to finally hug her goodbye following breakfast the next morning. The moment I closed the door behind her, Mother approached.

"May I talk with you, dear?"

I rested my forehead against the door to brace myself for her unwanted interrogation before turning to face her. Worry lined her brow and concern filled her eyes. Whatever her reason for initiating a heart-to-heart chat, it likely wouldn't be pleasant. I forced myself to smile anyway, hoping it would mask the nerves already tightening my stomach.

"What is it?"

She tipped her head towards the settee and I obediently sat, perching myself on the very edge. I tried to keep my hands still but found myself anxiously bunching the fabric of my dress. Mother rested her hand on top of mine, her blue-grey eyes piercing.

"Are you in a relationship?"

The denial I ached to give lodged in my throat. I swallowed several times before slowly shaking my head. It wasn't even a lie; Aiden and I weren't in a relationship—not the way Mother meant, anyway.

Mother frowned, disappointment filling her eyes. "There are many wonderful young men in Arador. None have caught your fancy?"

"None." That at least I could be completely honest about. "You know I avoid the boys in the village."

She sighed wearily. "I've noticed. It saddens me that you're not even looking for love."

"I don't want it."

She raised her eyebrows. "Why not?"

I bit my lip. I couldn't bring up Father to her, not after I'd watched her painstakingly attempt over the years to heal the wounds his leaving had caused, wounds impossible to be made whole unless Father returned. But he wouldn't. I'd long since given up hoping he would, given up on both him and any man in my future. It was easier and far less painful this way...although this previously firm resolve was becoming increasingly more difficult to cling to the longer I missed Aiden.

Mother was still waiting for an answer I didn't want to give, one I couldn't without hurting her. I shrugged instead, hoping to appear nonchalant. "I'm simply uninterested in romance."

"Really? *All* romance?" She gave me a look that was a bit too knowing, revealing she'd detected my lie in the uncanny way only a mother could, as if she alone had the keys to access the locked-away secrets of my soul.

I gnawed at my lip. "Of course."

"Then who's Aiden?"

My heart fluttered at the sound of his name. His face and all the wonderful memories we'd forged together immediately bombarded my mind, despite my determination not to think of him. Forcing myself to stay away was difficult enough already.

"He's no one. Just...a friend."

"A *friend*?"

"Well..." I twirled a loose strand of my dark hair around my finger and avoided her eyes. "A *good* friend." But I wouldn't admit more than that. I couldn't.

"I see."

Mother fell silent, during which I felt her silent pleadings for me to confide in her. I kept my gaze resolutely in my lap, afraid of the emotion I'd discover filling her eyes if I looked up, one I was certain would unravel me completely.

"Eileen?" Mother's gentle voice finally forced my gaze to meet hers, one full of sad understanding, just as I'd feared it'd be. "I heard your conversation with Rosie last night."

I released the pent-up breath I hadn't realized I'd been holding. "You did?"

"Yes. I know you've been meeting a man named Aiden that you've grown to care for, yet you're choosing to turn away from him."

"He's no one. He's just…" *Absolutely wonderful.*

Mother squeezed my hand. "He's not just anyone. Such light wouldn't be in your eyes if he were." She furrowed her brow in thought. "I'm not sure I know any boys named Aiden. Is he someone from the village?"

"Not exactly. I met him in the Forest—"

Mother gasped sharply, her gaze lowering to the now-healed cut scarring my throat. "Is he the same man who gave you that cut?"

I ached to deny it, but it was impossible to keep anything from Mother. "Yes, but it was an accident; he never meant to harm me. The problem is he's a nobleman, a man far above my station. It could never work between us."

There were so many other things I wanted to share about Aiden that I didn't dare. My thoughts drifted to each moment he'd made me smile, and the barriers around my heart faltered. My exposed feelings must have shown on my face, for Mother's entire expression softened.

"Oh, Eileen." She gently cradled my cheek. "He's become special to you, hasn't he?"

I shook my head but I knew the gesture was pointless, as I was certain Mother could read the truth in my eyes.

"If you care for him, why are you turning away?"

"Because he's engaged." I blinked back the tears burning my eyes. "But even if he weren't, I couldn't be with him. Love is too painful. Finding out Aiden is engaged has only proven it."

She sighed. "Even if your Aiden is unavailable, please don't give up on all love. I know your father hurt you deeply when he left, but you can't allow his choices to affect your future."

"I need to. How can I know that any man I choose won't be just like Father? He shattered my trust in men when he left, and it's impossible to reclaim."

Mother stroked my cheek. "I loved your father. I still do. I cherish every moment we had together, not to mention our union brought you, the light of my life." She squeezed my hand again. "Even knowing what I know now, I would still choose him, over and over again."

"But he left."

She winced, and instantly remorse for my biting words filled me.

"I'm sorry," I said hastily.

Mother squeezed her eyes shut and took a deep breath. "I don't understand why he never returned, but I know your father. Something must have happened. There could have been an accident—"

"It doesn't matter what happened," I said. "Loving him has caused us nothing but pain."

"I can't deny how difficult it's been, but loving him has caused far more joy. Giving your heart isn't without risk, but it's the most beautiful experience you could ever imagine. I'd hate for you to miss such an incredible experience. I can tell how special your Aiden is to you by the way you talked of him last night, and I can see how much pain choosing to stay away is causing you now."

I ached to deny it, but I was tired of lying, of fighting these emotions. It was exhausting. I crumpled in defeat. "Isn't the pain I'm feeling now less than if I choose him and he breaks my heart?"

"I'm not sure where your own romance will lead, but you won't know unless you take the risk. I promise it'll be worth it. Please don't allow your past pain or your father's choices deprive you of any future joy. Take a leap of faith."

She kissed my brow, and after one final squeeze of my hand she stood to begin cleaning up from breakfast. Rather than join her, I sat frozen, awash in her words—words that caused doubts about my previously firm decision, making me feel lost and confused.

Which path did one take when they had no idea where they wanted to go?

CHAPTER 11

*T*he trees were whispering to me, their beckoning becoming more and more insistent with each passing day. And it wasn't just them; I felt my heart constantly tugging me towards the Forest, pleading for me to step inside and to allow the paths to lead me where it yearned to be.

Weeks had passed since I'd last seen Aiden, but it felt like several lifetimes. I didn't understand the Forest's motives for continuing to guide us to one another when Aiden was betrothed to another woman, but I knew if given the opportunity it would do so once more. Aiden had seemed so certain our paths would cross again in the future; with his influence over the Forest, I knew he had the power to make it happen, but only if I stepped into the Forest.

No matter how many twists and turns the Forest used to try to dissuade me from my predetermined path, nothing would sway me, yet it was becoming increasingly difficult to continue to resist doing so. The longer I was away from Aiden, the more agonizing our separation became, until it had become nearly as painful as when Father had abandoned me.

I embraced an oak at the Forest's border as I peered into the shadowy greenery of the trees. No paths appeared; that only happened if I stepped into the woods, and I was still deliberating whether or not I should.

But the lure gently pulling on my heart finally won out. I readjusted my bag that contained my sketchbook and drawing supplies, took a deep breath, and stepped within the cool, pine-scented woods.

A path immediately unfolded before me. Whatever lay at the end of this particular path, I hoped Aiden would be there waiting for me. I picked my way along as it twisted and turned, weaving around trunks and through thick undergrowth. After several minutes, I ducked beneath a low-hanging branch and frowned as the path stopped abruptly. I slowly looked around. The Forest had led me nowhere in particular, and Aiden wasn't anywhere in sight.

I sighed, fighting against the disappointment prickling my heart, and settled on a log to sketch. I quickly grew restless. Normally, an afternoon of drawing while enfolded by the tranquil stillness of the woods would have satisfied me, but I now yearned for more; I ached for Aiden more than the trees.

I couldn't concentrate on my drawing. My once faithful muse had become too slippery and fleeting. I abandoned the log to lie on my stomach and propped my sketchbook against a tree, hoping a different vantage point would encourage my creativity. When this new position failed to make drawing any easier, I began mindlessly turning the pages of my sketchbook until I reached Aiden's portrait. My heart leapt as I stared at him, my fingers tracing his face over and over while my mind swirled with the memory of his dark, soulful gaze seeping into mine and his endearing, lopsided grin.

Around me, the air gradually grew cooler and what had started out as a pleasant breeze became a biting wind. My tracing hand froze as thunder rumbled. I gnawed at my lip and looked up at the sky peeking through the Forest's branches. Thick grey clouds were gathering and the air smelled of approaching rain.

I quickly gathered my art supplies and shoved them into my satchel, my stomach twisting into knots. Would I make it home before the storm hit? I'd no sooner scrambled to my feet when it started to rain. I ran for the cover of the trees, but the budding branches above did little to provide shelter.

I waited, shivering, for the Forest to show me the path I should take. One slowly quivered into view, as if reluctant to be of assistance. I took it without question. Although I trusted the Forest to lead me home, its familiar pull was now absent, as if whatever enchantment had breathed life into the trees had vanished.

After several minutes of brisk walking, lightning flashed across the sky, briefly illuminating the path before me. I stumbled to a stop, my breath catching. The pathway that I'd been walking had disappeared. I frantically looked around, struggling to see through the thick rain. Nothing. Panic clawed at my heart. Darkness and shadows made it impossible for me to determine the correct direction. If there wasn't a path, how would I ever find my way out?

The rain picked up, pelting me in heavy sheets and soaking me to the bone. I shivered and forced myself to press on, trudging through the mud. Through the tumult of rain blurring my vision, I continued to search for a path. Still nothing. I glanced up at the trees, seeking aid, but they were uncannily still, as if the entire Forest had fallen asleep, leaving me to my own devices.

The storm raged on. I wasn't sure how long I'd been wandering—-with the thick clouds blocking the sun I had no measure of time—but with the increasingly suffocating darkness, I knew it was nearing night.

Suddenly, the pathways stirred from whatever slumber had kept them so still and unhelpful. A path finally appeared, wriggling and shifting. I slogged down the muddy path snaking through the trees, branches scratching my flesh. Whenever I considered venturing off course, the trees closed in around me, narrowing the path and leaving me no choice but to take the one it desired.

The road widened. I squinted through the thick rain and caught a glimpse of the Forest's border, where I knew home lay just beyond. I managed a cold grin and quickened my pace. Soon I'd be within the comforting walls of my cottage, sheltered from the biting wind and in front of the warm hearth.

I burst from the Forest and froze. Rather than the village of Arador greeting me, tall, ominous gates stood like sentries guarding the grand royal Sortileyan Palace, its gilded marble glistening in the sliver of moonlight penetrating the thick clouds.

I stared, my foggy mind unable to comprehend what my eyes were seeing. How had I ended up dozens of miles north, in the capital of Sortileya, and at the residence of the royal family? But now was not the time to decipher the complicated workings of the Forest's pathways. With a wavering breath, I approached the gate, and was immediately blocked by two guards standing rigidly in front, their swords drawn. I froze.

"State your business," one stated fiercely.

"Please," I said. "I need—"

"Wait, it's the one we've been waiting for." The other guard lowered his sword. "We've been expecting you."

They opened the gate. I cast them a puzzled look before gratefully staggering up the cobblestone path that led to the towering front doors.

A knocker in the shape of a dragon head protruded from the massive door. I grasped its metal ring and knocked frantically. My knock was swallowed up in the wind. I pulled my wet shawl closer and leaned against the door as I waited, hoping that the storm wouldn't prevent my desperate knock from being heard.

The door swung open and I stumbled into a frowning footman wearing a smart violet uniform with the royal crest embroidered in silver, a uniform I'd now just gotten all wet. Not the best first impression.

I managed to right myself as his disapproving gaze slowly raked over my drenched form. "How may I help you?" His tone was cold, as if helping me was the last thing he wanted to do.

"Please, I got lost in the woods and was hoping I could—" The rest of my plea was swallowed by a sneeze. The footman flinched away.

"You're disturbing His Majesty and Their Highnesses because you lost your way?" He glared at someone behind me. I turned to see two guards flanking either side of the doors, nearly masked by the shadows. "You allowed a commoner into the palace at such an hour?"

"She seems to be in need of assistance."

The footman sniffed in disapproval. "The royal family are already entertaining many distinguished guests and are preparing for the arrival of many more. Now please escort her out of—what is it, Guard Alastar?"

A tall, broad-shouldered guard had appeared. After a long look at me with a stoic expression that betrayed no emotion, he leaned down to whisper in the footman's ear. The footman's eyes widened and he hastily turned to me with a crisp bow.

"Forgive me for my rudeness. I didn't know who you were, Your Highness."

Your Highness? "Oh, no, I'm—I mean, there must be some mistake, for I'm not—"

"Please, come in out of the rain."

He summoned me inside, and I was too cold and too tired to argue any further. The door closed behind me with a resonating *thud*, cutting off the howl and biting chill of the wind, leaving only the whispers and titters of the servants as they surveyed me with wide-eyed curiosity. The footman snapped his fingers and a maid bustled over to take my wet shawl. Even when freed from my soaking garment, a violent shiver raked over me.

"She's chilled to the bone," the maid tittered. "How long were you out in the rain, Your Highness?"

"Hours. I got caught in the—" My answer was swallowed by the chattering of my teeth. I rubbed my hands up and down my arms to get warm.

"And what happened to your things? Your escort?"

Another maid's arrival cut off my second attempt to explain myself. She gasped when she saw me, taking in my hair hanging in wet clumps and my hem dripping water all over the marble floors.

"Oh my goodness, what happened to the princess?"

"She lost her escort and has been wandering the woods," the other maid said. "Alaina, will you show her to her room and prepare a bath for her?"

"Right away. Come, Your Highness, let's get you out of those wet things."

This time I made no protest as Alaina wrapped a motherly arm around me and led me away from the apologies of the now-flustered footman and up the grand staircase.

"I'm so sorry for all the trouble, Your Highness," Alaina said as we ascended the stairs. "We didn't expect you to arrive so late and in such a state." She frowned at my soaked dress, obviously quite plain and not befitting a princess. "Good thing you were wearing your traveling clothes. Why, there's mud all along the hem."

I wanted to protest her ridiculous assumption that I was royal, but the storm lashing the windowpanes was a persuasive incentive to remain silent. Yet with each step further down the elegant corridor, I wondered whether shelter from the storm was worth becoming entangled in what was sure to be a mess.

"What a pity you've lost your things. Not to worry, Your Highness, I don't doubt His Majesty will allow a wardrobe to be made for you. In the meantime, I'm sure Princess Seren will allow you to borrow some of her dresses."

The infamous Princess of Sortileya, more commonly known as the Dragon Princess? There were many rumors about her cold and sullen demeanor. While gossip revolving around her wasn't as prevalent as that surrounding her brother, the Dark Prince Deidric, I'd heard enough not to doubt that being caught wearing her clothes would surely earn me a dungeon sentence, even before my true identity was discovered. Terror clenched my heart at the thought.

"Oh, I couldn't."

Alaina frowned at me before nodding curtly. "You're right, Your Highness, for you're much shorter than she is. That wouldn't do at all."

"No, I meant—"

"The royal family is currently entertaining numerous guests, both royalty and nobility. I'm sure one of them has something you could borrow. Perhaps Her Highness, Princess Elodie of Draceria, will have something suitable. From the glimpses I've managed to get of her, I'd wager she's about your height. I'd hate to impose such a request on a prestigious guest, but considering I'm doing it in the service of another…" She chewed her lip in thought. "What to do, what to do…ah, here we are."

She bustled into a room. I started to follow but froze in the doorway with a gasp of awe. The room—a vision of marble, satin, and opulence—was bigger than the entire ground floor of my cottage.

Alaina scurried to the hearth to stoke the fire as I walked in a daze to the bed. The mattress was higher than my waist and looked unbelievably comfortable. I stroked the coverlet with a hesitant hand and nearly moaned at how soft it was; it was like touching silk. Alaina bustled around heating water for my bath, only pausing when she noticed I wasn't in front of the fire.

"Come, Your Highness, you need to warm up."

She gently led me to the hearth. My objections that I wasn't a princess and that my being here was a mistake died in my throat as the fire's blissful warmth washed over me. Now that I was no longer numb, I was quite reluctant to be thrown back out into the rainy night, let alone the dank dungeon. I could always wait to confess in the morning, after the storm had passed…

"Your bath is ready, Your Highness. Let's get you out of these wet clothes." To my horror, Alaina yanked my dress over my head. I jerked away.

"Are you *undressing* me?"

"Well, you haven't your own lady's maid to do it, so I'll happily do it for you."

She worked quickly and efficiently, and before I could fully register the embarrassing process, my undergarments lay in a sopping pile on the floor and I'd been pushed into the heavenly bath. My protests died immediately as I melted deeper into the tub with a contented sigh. Alaina nodded with approval.

"There, nothing like a hot bath to set you right. Now if you'll excuse me, Your Highness, I shall fetch a nightgown for you and something to eat." She curtsied and headed for the door. She paused in the doorway to glance back, brow furrowed. "Did you need me to aid in your washing?"

"No, no, no, that won't be necessary, thank you." To my utter relief, she accepted this answer before leaving.

I stared at the closed door, the gravity of my circumstances slowly settling over me. I'd somehow ended up in the royal palace miles away from home, having been led here quite forcibly by whatever mischievous motives the Forest had in mind. Just great.

Alaina soon returned with a tray of soup and sandwiches. The mouthwatering scent emanating from the soup's steam was the only thing strong enough to pull me from my bath. The food was far richer than any I'd eaten before, but I was too hungry to savor it. I shoveled it down in a most un-royal manner as Alaina fluttered around me, dressing me in a toasty velvet nightgown before running a brush through my hair. When she'd finished, she gently guided me towards the grand bed.

"You should get some sleep now. Is there anything else you'll be requiring, Princess Gemma?"

Princess Gemma? Who was that? "I'm sorry, I'm afraid you have me confused with someone else." I yawned as I hoisted myself onto the softest mattress I'd ever laid upon. "There's no need for *princess,* because I'm not—"

"But Your Highness, it wouldn't do for me not to address you by your proper title." Her eyes widened at the thought. "I'd lose my place. I may be currently under your charge, but please don't ask me to go against a direct order from His Highness."

I wrinkled my nose in confusion. "What do you mean?"

"His Highness has informed me I'm to tend to you for the duration of your stay."

"My stay?" My exhaustion was making everything so confusing. I snuggled deeper beneath the covers, for this was truly the most comfortable of all beds. "My stay for what?"

She slid a warming pad beneath the blankets at my feet. "Why, for the Princess Competition, of course, for His Highness's bride."

My drooping eyes widened and I bolted upright. "The *what?*"

"Goodness, Your Highness, you must be tired. Aren't you here by royal invitation from the crown prince?"

I cringed at her formal address. "What are you talking about? What competition?"

Alaina's forehead furrowed at my ignorance. "His Highness has decided that his former betrothed, Princess Rheanna of Draceria, is no longer suitable. Thus he's invited all royalty and the most eligible noblewomen throughout the surrounding five kingdoms to participate in a series of tests to determine who's worthy to be his bride."

I gaped at her. "You think I'm here to try and win the prince?" Of course she would, as if my situation wasn't ridiculous enough.

"It's not my place to say, of course, but the rumors about him aren't…well…" Her cheeks darkened as she avoided my eyes, becoming extra preoccupied with smoothing out nonexistent wrinkles in my duvet. Her response was oh so reassuring.

"Regardless, your arrival signifies you've accepted his invitation to potentially become his bride, which means you'll be required to stay here to see whether or not he'll choose you. I can't imagine why he doesn't want Princess Rheanna; she's such a sweet thing. I don't understand the mind of royals…meaning no offense." She shrugged rather helplessly.

I continued to gape at her. Was I really expected to stay for His Highness's ridiculous scheme? I might have inadvertently fooled the servants into thinking I was royal, but to think I could fool the other princesses or the Dark Prince himself…my stomach knotted.

"I have to leave." I scooted to the edge of the bed to do just that, but Alaina pushed me firmly back down.

"You're exhausted, Your Highness. Get some sleep. You'll need it for tomorrow."

Panic clawed at my throat, threatening to swallow me whole. "You don't understand; I can't stay."

"Surely you can't leave," she protested. "I've just told you that His Highness has ordered all the princesses and noblewomen to stay as his royal guests."

"But if he doesn't know I'm here—"

"Oh, but he does," she said. "I encountered him on my way to fetch your food, and he asked how you were faring. It was uncharacteristically thoughtful of him, come to think of it." She frowned.

My heart hammered at this news. Prince Deidric already knew I was here? That would make escaping far more difficult, but I was still determined. The moment Alaina left, I'd sneak out. I eyed the window, where rain lashed against the panes as the storm continued to rage.

Perhaps not tonight, not when I'd only just warmed up and my smothering exhaustion was luring me towards much-needed sleep. But tomorrow for certain. I'd wake up extra early and slip away before I found myself tangled further in this mess.

Alaina finished fluffing my pillows before picking up my dinner tray. "Anything else, Your Highness?"

I wearily shook my head. "No, thank you."

She blinked in surprise at my gratitude before smiling warmly in return. "It's a pleasure, Your Highness. Have a good night. I'll see you in the morning."

No, she wouldn't, for by the morning I'd be long gone. I watched her leave the room before snuggling deeper into the mattress, prepared to allow what promised to be my most restful sleep claim me...only it didn't.

Despite being on one of the softest mattresses in the kingdom, I couldn't get comfortable; each position I attempted was more uncomfortable than the last. I tossed and turned, all while the wind and rain swirled angrily outside.

Not only did the heavenly bed feel far too fancy for mere common me—a reminder I was nothing more than an imposter—but thoughts of Mother's worry when I hadn't returned home tonight gnawed at my heart. I needed to escape as soon as possible, not only for her, but because each moment I remained at the palace put me in greater danger. If I couldn't even sleep on a royal bed, I'd never be able to fool anyone into thinking I was a princess, nor did I want to. The truth would be exposed even before the Dark Prince's competition for his bride had begun.

CHAPTER 12

*M*y exhaustion from my wanderings through the Forest followed by several hours of tossing and turning before sleep finally claimed me foiled my intentions of rising early. I woke to a tentative tap on my shoulder, as if the one administering did so with the utmost hesitation.

I groggily stirred from sleep, noticing I was far more warm and comfortable than normal when waking in my attic bedroom. I struggled to open my eyes. Golden sunshine tumbled through large gleaming windows, framed by silky curtains and still spotted from last night's rain. I blinked at them, confused, and rolled over.

The maid Alaina hovered over me. "I'm so sorry to disturb you, Your Highness," she said in an uncertain whisper. "I hesitate to wake you, especially due to how tired you must be after last night's ordeal, but breakfast is soon and I need to help you dress."

Her words washed over me, failing to penetrate the thick drowsiness hovering over my senses. Then in a rush everything came back to me: getting lost in the Forest, stumbling upon the palace, and the delusion the palace occupants were under that I was a princess—and not just any princess, but a *Princess Gemma*, whoever she was. How I'd become entangled in such a ridiculous notion was beyond me, but one thing was certain: no true royal would fall for the façade. And I'd just slept through my prime moment to escape.

I groaned and covered my face with my hands. "This is a nightmare. Please tell me I'm still asleep and dreaming."

"You're quite awake, Your Highness," Alaina said hesitantly, as if afraid to contradict me. "And now that you are, I shall assist you in getting ready."

I struggled to formulate a plan, a difficult feat with my foggy head and every inch of my body aching from my wanderings the night before. I managed to grasp at the end of one. I forced myself to sit up.

"I shall dress myself." That would get Alaina out of the room and allow me to more easily slip away. But Alaina was already shaking her head.

"That won't do at all, Your Highness. You certainly can't dress yourself, and since you're without your own lady-in-waiting, I will assist you."

I opened my mouth to retort that I'd been dressing myself just fine since I was a child, but with the stubborn gleam in Alaina's eyes, I knew that this was a battle I'd lose regardless of my arguments. I snapped my mouth shut with a sigh of defeat. So much for that plan. Time for another: go along with the charade until I was finally away from this maid who was proving to be more guard dog than servant and, with luck, not get hopelessly lost in the palace hallways before finding my way outside.

That decided, I managed to drag my aching body to the edge of the bed. As I did so, Alaina surveyed my face and her eyes widened.

"Goodness, Princess, there are bags beneath your eyes. Did you sleep at all?"

I yawned and stretched. "Not much."

Alaina tittered as she shook her head. "I'll fetch some cosmetics to hide the evidence of your restless night. You need to make a good impression if you hope to win the prince."

I sighed. I didn't want to win the prince; I wanted to leave the palace as soon as possible so I could return home and ease my frantic mother's heart. I hopped off the bed and stumbled in a most ungraceful manner. Alaina steadied me, her brow lined with concern.

"Are you alright, Your Highness?"

"I'm merely tired. Perhaps you can allow me to rest awhile longer." Anything to get her out of this room. Unsurprisingly, she shook her head at that suggestion.

"Begging your pardon, Your Highness, but I have my orders to prepare you to go down for breakfast."

I bit my lip to stifle my growl of frustration. I doubted royals vented their emotions in such an unsophisticated way. I untangled myself from Alaina's arms and staggered to the fireplace. I picked up my muddy dress drying in front of the fire cracking merrily in the hearth.

Alaina immediately fluttered over like an overexcited bird. "Goodness no, Your Highness, you can't be seen wearing *that*. Just look at it! It's dirty and torn beyond repair. Why you wore such rags in the first place is beyond me."

"Because I'm not a princess," I snapped, finally managing to get the words out.

Alaina seemed not to hear me in her agitated state as she snatched my dress and, to my horror, tossed it into the fire.

I leapt forward. "No!"

But it was too late. I gritted my teeth as I watched one of

135

my only dresses go up in smoke. Fine, I supposed wandering the Forest in my underclothes would have to do.

Unfortunately, my jailer still had me on a tight leash as she took my arm and led me to the wardrobe, where she held up the most beautiful gown I'd ever seen—soft blue-grey silk with floral patterns embroidered in silver thread and pearls lacing the bodice. I gaped at it.

"It's *beautiful*." I tentatively reached out to touch the dress. The silk felt smooth between my fingers.

"Princess Elodie was kind enough to lend it to you. Isn't that sweet of her?"

If this belonged to a real princess, I couldn't wear it, no matter how much I longed to. Alaina stepped forward to begin dressing me. I flinched away. "I can't wear that."

"You must. You haven't anything else."

And whose fault was that? I glowered at the ashes in the hearth. But I had no excuse adequate enough to resist wearing the dress, especially as my protests died in my throat the moment it slid over my head. It not only fit like a glove, but the silk gown was so soft I felt as if I were wearing water.

I stared wide-eyed at my reflection as Alaina arranged my dark hair in the most elegant style I'd ever worn. By the time she'd finished I truly felt transformed, for me and the woman in my reflection couldn't possibly be the same person.

I raised my hand and pressed my fingers to the glass, causing my fingers and the mirror Eileen's fingers to touch. "Is that really me?"

"Of course it is, Your Highness."

I continued to stare. I'd never considered myself beyond merely pretty, but the woman in the mirror was stunning, simply from wearing an elegant gown and hairstyle.

I felt like the biggest fraud.

Alaina surveyed me with approval before motioning for me to follow her. "I'll escort you to the dining room so there's no chance of your getting lost." She opened the door to reveal the guard from the night before waiting for us. "Guard Alastar." She curtsied.

He bowed crisply in return. "I'm to escort Her Highness to the dining room."

I took in his strong guard build and the sword strapped to his waist and sighed. He would be impossible to slip away from. That didn't mean I wasn't going to try, though.

"Thank you, Alastar. That would be most helpful; I have other duties I need to attend to." Alaina curtsied to me before bustling away, leaving me at the mercy of this guard. For a moment, he studied me with the same serious expression he'd worn last night, as if trying to discern whether or not I was an imposter. Did he suspect?

"If you'll follow me, Your Highness." After another bow he strode into the hallway. I reluctantly followed him.

The splendor of the palace corridors had been lost on me the night before, due to the dark shadows and my escalating panic at the strange situation I'd found myself in. I rubbed the material of my gown between my fingers as I took in everything with wide eyes while also searching for my opportunity to slip away. I seized it when we reached a fork in the gilded marble corridor—Guard Alastar took the right, and while keeping a wary eye on his towering form, I took the left, but I'd no sooner stepped into the other hallway—

Guard Alastar gently took my arm and guided me down the opposite corridor. He didn't smile, didn't betray any emotion whatsoever, but for a brief moment I was certain his eyes twinkled. "He told me you'd try to escape."

"Who did?"

Guard Alastar said nothing. Annoying.

He continued to lead me in stony silence, not releasing my arm. I tried to wriggle away, but his grip was firm. "Are you going to let me go?"

"I'm not of the mind to do so after your attempt to slip away, Your Highness. It wouldn't do for you to become lost while under my charge."

"Isn't it against some royal law to manhandle a princess?"

His lips twitched. "It's not my intention to do anything of the sort. I'm doing my best to treat you with the utmost respect while still keeping you within sight. I notice you seem keen on escaping, and I'm afraid I can't allow that."

"Observant and efficient." A bit too much so.

"I'm a guard, Your Highness."

I wished he'd stop calling me that, but not nearly as much as I wished he would falter in his escorting duties to give me the escape opportunity I was desperate for. But the guard's attention didn't waver even for a moment, making escape impossible. All the same, I kept my eyes peeled for an opportunity.

After descending the grand staircase and walking down another corridor, Guard Alastar stopped in front of two wide doors that opened to an opulent dining room. He bowed.

"Your destination, Your Highness."

I hovered in the doorway and peered inside. My stomach tightened. There were dozens of nobles all wearing the fancy clothes and jewels showcasing their rank, all of which were far above my own. I moaned quietly. Guard Alastar's stoic expression faltered slightly and a glimpse of concern filled his eyes.

"You must be nervous."

"There are a lot of nobility."

"Hopefully your own kind will help put you at ease." He gave me a look that almost dared me to defy his statement. My breath hitched, but I bravely lifted my chin and with a deep breath entered the room.

My feigned bravery crumbled the moment I stepped into

the dining room. I stood frozen and stared at the sea of strangers, my heart pounding. While most ignored my entrance, the curious looks from the several who'd noticed me was enough to cause me to spin towards the exit—only to have Guard Alastar block my way. While his expression didn't falter, encouragement filled his eyes. I tightened my jaw and took a tentative step further into the room.

A golden-haired princess sat at the end of one of the long dining tables laden with fancy china and mouthwatering dishes. Her entire manner lit up when she spotted me. She gracefully motioned for me to take the empty seat beside her. I eyed the windows as I inched closer but dismissed that potential escape route due to the unfortunate presence of so many witnesses.

The princess stood in greeting, her entire form short and willowy. "You must be Princess Gemma. I'm Princess Elodie of Draceria." Her smile brightened as she looked me over. "I knew this was the perfect gown to lend you, but it's even more lovely on you than I imagined. The blue-grey even matches your eyes. You mustn't borrow it at all. Consider it yours. And you must raid my closet for more gowns, considering your luggage was lost and I have plenty." She looped her arm through mine as if we were already the best of friends.

We took our seats—Princess Elodie with fluid movements, me plopping down with enough inelegant force to jiggle the table—and the princess turned to her seating companions, all of whom possessed matching golden hair and bright blue eyes.

"May I present my siblings: Crown Prince Liam, Princess Rheanna, and Princess Aveline. Everyone, this is Princess Gemma."

All three gave me polite smiles, all of which were different—Princess Rheanna's was tinged with shyness,

Princess Aveline's was stiff and formal, while Prince Liam's was a cheeky grin accompanied by a wink. I smiled timidly in return. Despite their kind reception, my heartbeat escalated in trepidation.

Princess Aveline looked down her nose at me, her elegant expression suspicious. "My apologies, Princess Gemma, but it was my understanding a missive arrived from Malvagaria stating that you and your sister weren't expected to attend."

So Princess Gemma was a Malvagarian princess. That complicated things. If I should be caught claiming to be this Princess Gemma, it would end in disaster, but how else could I ward off Princess Aveline's suspicion? Before I could scramble for an answer, Princess Elodie leaned close, as if to share a secret.

"Is your family really cursed?"

I blinked at her. "Cursed?"

"The rumors are that all the children of the Malvagarian royal family are cursed in different ways. Whatever curses surround your two older brothers remain a mystery, but it's been said that the eldest princess of Malvagaria has been locked away in an enchanted tower, while the younger has some sort of sleeping curse. An official invitation was sent and rejected, but I'm happy you've decided to come after all." She gave me an impressed look. "If you escaped, it's no wonder you haven't an escort or any luggage."

Princess Aveline wrinkled her nose at her sister's claims. "Really, Elodie, princesses shouldn't listen to rumors."

She rolled her eyes delicately. "I have two working ears, haven't I? What am I supposed to do when I hear a rumor?"

"Choose not to listen, especially to one as ridiculous as a princess getting locked in a tower."

As they squabbled, I nibbled the inside of my lip, deliberating. The number of royalty to impersonate were few. If there was any truth about this particular rumor and the

Malvagarian Princess—whether trapped in a tower or simply desiring not to attend—hadn't arrived and was unknown to those in attendance, she was my best option of whom to impersonate—my *only* option.

"You're correct, I do hail from Malvagaria, but being trapped in a tower is merely a rumor."

Princess Elodie's bright eyes dimmed in disappointment. "Such a shame. And are your brothers and sister cursed?"

"Last I saw, they were in perfect health."

While Princess Elodie managed to slump in a way that still maintained her perfect posture, Prince Liam leaned back in his seat with a goofy grin.

"It's a shame your tale is so dull, Princess Gemma. I'm an excellent weaver of interesting stories. Allow me to make yours more exciting."

"Oh, please, Liam, not another one of your silly theories." Princess Aveline buttered her toast with a disapproving sniff. "Whatever comes out of your mouth is always ridiculous."

Naturally, Prince Liam protested, and the two siblings began bickering quietly. I seized the opportunity to look around the elegant room. It was overwhelming how many people there were, people who could potentially discover my deception.

Princess Elodie leaned closer. "Locked in a tower or not, I do know your family has been elusive and thus you're likely not very familiar with the other kingdoms' nobility. Shall I point out those I know?"

I nodded gratefully and Princess Elodie proceeded in a discreet manner. "You've met my own dear family. We come from Draceria, a lovely kingdom of rolling hills and country-side. Our hosts come from Sortileya, which, as you can see from your stay so far, consists primarily of woods. Bytamia is a tropical kingdom across the ocean, and they haven't any daughters. Three of the four princes—Prince Daman, Prince

Jaron, and Prince Owen—have come as official representatives of Bytamia, but I believe that's only a cover for their true purpose: to look for a potential wife amongst all of these eligible maidens. Their eldest brother, the crown prince, is currently at sea. Then there's the mountainous kingdom of Lyceria, with Crown Prince Nolan and Princess Lavena."

She motioned towards a beautiful princess with dark hair and dark eyes. At her mention, Prince Liam snorted, his nose wrinkled in disgust. Two of his sisters ignored him while Princess Rheanna gave him a sympathetic look.

Princess Elodie continued her introductions. "Now for the nobility whose names I know, starting from the far end of the table…" She bombarded me with a multitude of names and faces that I couldn't even hope to remember. My hand tightened around my fork with each one.

"Are the Dark Prince and Dragon Princess in attendance?" I asked when Princess Elodie paused to take a breath.

"Prince Deidric isn't, but that's the Dragon Princess over there, Princess Seren." Princess Elodie motioned with her chin to a dark-haired, pale-eyed princess who, while beautiful, looked as sour as her name implied, and she so happened to be glaring directly at me.

I flinched and hastily looked away, but I could still feel the heat of her gaze watching me, as if she sensed an imposter in her presence and meant to expose me.

"Are you quite alright, Princess Gemma?" Princess Rheanna whispered, her voice as quiet as she'd been throughout the conversation.

I lowered my own voice. "Princess Seren is staring at me."

Princess Elodie subtly glanced over and narrowed her eyes while Prince Liam snorted. "Oh, she's a real gem and is an expert at making friends. You'll get along swimmingly with her."

Princess Aveline whacked his arm. "Be nice, Liam. Seren is a lovely girl."

Prince Liam gaped at her as if she'd lost her mind.

Princess Aveline daintily bit her lip. "Although I admit she does tend to have interesting moods…"

Prince Liam muttered something indiscernible beneath his breath before turning a charming smile towards me. "Ignore her; it's what everyone does. And if you are forced to interact with her and discover she doesn't like you, don't take it personally; she doesn't like anyone. She's really quite—"

He broke off as Princess Lavena rose gracefully from her seat. He gasped and ducked beneath the table. Princess Elodie giggled while Princess Aveline looked aghast.

"Liam, get off the floor at once. You're a prince."

He didn't emerge, but his voice drifted from beneath the tablecloth. "No, thank you. I'm having an enjoyable morning so far and don't fancy it ruined, which it will be if *she* spots me. Tell me when she's gone."

We all watched Princess Lavena motion to one of the attending servants lining the wall—a woman who looked uncannily similar to her—and walk towards the door. She paused in the doorway to smirk towards Prince Liam's empty seat, as if she knew she'd riled him and was pleased by her achievement. After she left, Princess Elodie peeked beneath the table.

"She's gone."

Prince Liam released a pent-up breath as he settled back in his seat and leaned his head back. "Disaster averted."

"So is this the new approach to dealing with Lavena?" Princess Rheanna asked. "Rather than ignore her, you feel it prudent to hide from her instead?"

"Ignoring her doesn't always prevent our interacting. Why take a chance?"

I swirled my eggs around my plate with my fork. "Why do you dislike her?"

"She's my *intended*." Prince Liam spat the word out like a curse. "I almost didn't escort my sisters to Sortileya when I heard *she'd* be here."

"Why is your fiancée competing for Prince Deidric's hand if she's already engaged to you?"

"In case he miraculously wants her," Prince Liam grumbled. "As far as I'm concerned, he can have her."

Princess Rheanna frowned sympathetically at her brother. "Poor Liam is having difficulties with his arranged engagement, but Father won't let him wriggle out of it, no matter how many schemes he tries to come up with in order to do so."

Prince Liam groaned. "I'm not giving up. Until we're stuck together, there's still hope of escape. After all, you managed to break your own arrangement."

Princess Rheanna gave a small smile that didn't quite reach her eyes. Ah yes, she was *that* Princess Rheanna, the Dark Prince's ex-fiancée. I surveyed her objectively. She not only seemed charming—why hadn't Prince Deidric wanted her?—but she seemed in perfect health, with no signs of having been slowly poisoned by her fiancé. Naturally, that particular rumor of Rosie's was unfounded.

A sharp pang filled my heart with thoughts of dear Rosie and poor, worried Mother. By now, Rosie had likely come up with a myriad of tragic stories to explain my absence. I only hoped she didn't share any with Mother, who was undoubtedly frantic enough without any help from my overdramatic, story-loving best friend. They likely believed I'd fallen victim to some horrible fate.

"I have a brilliant idea, Liam." Princess Elodie's cheerful voice yanked me from my worries. She swiveled in her seat towards me, expression hopeful. "Make a match with another princess while you're here and perhaps Father will allow the engagement to be broken. Gemma seems the perfect choice."

My cheeks burned as Prince Liam straightened to study me. He smiled approvingly. "You're truly lovely, Gemma, but unfortunately my execution warrant has already been signed, sealing my fate." He made a show of pretending to stab himself with an invisible knife, throwing his head back, and slumping.

Princess Elodie's face crumpled at seeing that her matchmaking had failed. "I suppose it wouldn't have worked if Deidric had picked her."

My heart lurched. Oh no, he couldn't pick me. He wouldn't even have the opportunity to. As soon as breakfast was over, I'd make my escape, somehow.

"What do you know of the prince?" I asked.

"Surprisingly little, considering our engagement," Princess Rheanna said.

"That isn't surprising at all." Prince Liam concentrated on stacking his empty dishes into a pyramid while Princess Aveline looked on with disapproval. "I don't know anything about Lavena except that I don't like her. I couldn't even tell you what color her eyes are, not that I care."

"You've never attempted to get to know her," Princess Aveline said. "And stop stacking your dishes like a child."

He flashed her an unrepentant smile as he carefully balanced cutlery at the very top. "Before you go on about my embarrassing myself, may I remind you that I'm not here to woo the prince, and I doubt our friendship will change over stacking a few plates."

I startled. "You're friends with the Dark Prince?"

Liam chuckled. "I am indeed friends with the *Dark Prince*." He shuddered theatrically. "He hates it when I call him that, hence I do it at every opportunity, even when he's not present. Despite his reputation and my antics, I've managed to survive our friendship thus far, despite some close calls." He winked and I managed a smile.

"How did you become friends?"

"During the many frequent diplomatic visits between him and dear Rhea. He often escaped their outings to spend time with me instead. You never seemed to mind, did you, Rhea?"

He ruffled Princess Rheanna's hair. She blushed and lowered her eyes to her lap. "Considering he's already rejected me, my presence here is nothing more than a formality."

"Is he as fierce as everyone says?" I asked.

"We shouldn't gossip about His Highness," Princess Aveline said cooly as Princess Elodie eagerly leaned closer.

"He is. Darkness fills his soul. No one dares cross him. Rhea is fortunate he broke off the engagement. He'd not be fun to be married to." She giggled and Prince Liam rolled his eyes.

"We've met several times over the years," Princess Rheanna said. "He's admittedly very handsome but quite fierce and..." She trailed off, seeming to have run out of descriptions.

Princess Elodie continued the explanation. "He's rather intense and is always cold and distant towards poor Rhea."

Princess Rheanna once more lowered her eyes. "To be honest, I'm rather frightened of him."

"It was nothing personal, Rhea," Prince Liam said. "Elusiveness is just his way, especially around women. Over the years, I've done my best to teach him how to treat ladies, but has it done any good?" He shrugged.

Princess Aveline raised her eyebrows. "*You* tried to teach him how to treat ladies?"

"Certainly," Prince Liam said. "After all, do you know anyone more charming than me?"

Princess Aveline pursed her lips and made no comment.

With this less-than-reassuring assessment of the prince's character confirming the rumors I myself had heard about him over the years, I could only imagine what he'd do to me if he discovered that I, a mere commoner, had lied in order to enter a competition to become his bride. The already strong urge to escape this scenario intensified.

I spent the remainder of breakfast formulating escape plans. I'd rather be lost within the Forest than forced to participate for the hand of the Dark Prince, for I'd inevitably be found out and subsequently thrown in the dungeon...or worse. My blood chilled at the thought.

No, it wouldn't come to that. I refused to allow myself to become tangled in this scheme. I would escape. Tonight.

CHAPTER 13

*W*hile everyone else was mingling, I spent the entire day pacing the circumference of my room as I plotted, pausing only to look out the window in order to measure the sun's progression across the sky, too tense and worried even to draw.

I only left for lunch, where Prince Deidric was once again absent. The royalty of Draceria informed me they'd learned he wouldn't make an appearance until the end of the competition, which would be a series of tests that would begin the following night after everyone else had arrived, a fact which only increased my desire to leave as soon as possible.

As I paced, I fiddled with my necklace and went over my plan yet again, desperate for something to do to fill the endless day. While being led by Guard Alastar through the labyrinth of elegant hallways that held me prisoner, I'd noticed that guards flanked both the entrance to the palace and, from the view of my window, the outer gate. They'd be difficult to slip past, but I hoped they wouldn't question me when I tried, considering they were under the delusion I was royalty.

I stared out the window at the surrounding Forest, longing for the safety found within the trees. Once away from this gilded cage, I'd have to rely on the Forest to lead me home. If it proved as mischievous as yesterday when it'd gotten me into this mess in the first place, I'd be forced to travel home on the roads. The capital was several hours north of Arador by cart, meaning walking would take ages, not to mention I'd be out alone after dark. And what if I succeeded in escaping but the Dark Prince came after me? But as frightening as that possibility was, the alternative of remaining was far worse.

I went over every possible detail for as long as possible, for if I stopped planning, my fear would eclipse my thoughts. But one could only plot for so long. I eventually collapsed backwards onto my bed and frowned at the ceiling, the worry I'd fought to suppress washing over me in waves, gnawing at my heart until I feared it'd swallow me whole.

Mother.

My heart twisted to think of her, frantic with concern. I'd slipped into the Forest yesterday afternoon and had now been missing for an entire day. Mother was likely in hysterics wondering what had become of me. She'd never approved of my Forest wanderings, and now I'd vanished without a trace, just like Father had. The thought that I'd broken her heart was torturous.

I stilled. I'd done the same thing as Father had when he'd left and never returned. But my situation was different. I hadn't abandoned Mother; I just currently found myself unable to return home. Yet the reason didn't matter; Mother's pain was the same. For the first time since Father's disappearance, I wondered whether something really had happened to him after all, that rather than abandoning us, he'd instead been prevented from returning.

I shook my head to clear it. Wondering did me no good.

The fact was he was gone. But unlike him, I'd find a way to return to Mother. Somehow. If I could sneak away tonight and make it home, all would be made right and this strange experience could become nothing more than a memory.

By the time the dinner hour arrived, my anxiety had made me physically ill. My stomach churned as Alaina bustled around midst her excited chatter as she helped me prepare, tugging on another gown borrowed from Princess Elodie—this one a soft fern green like the leaves of the Forest —before plopping me in front of my mirror to fuss with my hair.

Her tittering paused as she surveyed my reflection. "Are you feeling alright, Your Highness? You're looking a bit pale."

The nerves twisting my stomach and making my head throb made my plans to feign an illness unnecessary. "I have a horrible headache. I don't feel up to attending dinner."

"But Your Highness, tonight is the welcome feast. You can't possibly miss it."

My forehead pulsed at the thought. The longer I lingered amongst real royals, the higher the likelihood this façade would crack, landing me either a lifelong dungeon sentence or a trip to the gallows. I groaned, causing Alaina to flutter around in a panic.

"Oh dear, you don't seem well at all. How shall I serve you, Your Highness?" She rested a cool hand along my brow. "You're quite warm. Shall I open a window? Are you near a faint? Shall I fetch the smelling salts?"

My surroundings swayed and darkness lapped at my senses. I buried my head in my hands. "I need to lie down. I'm in no state to go down tonight. What a horrible impression I'd make if I fainted during dinner."

That seemed to be enough for Alaina. She wrapped her arm around me and guided me towards the bed, where she helped me settle. I sank into the mattress. Unlike last night, its feathery softness immediately began luring me to sleep. No, I couldn't sleep. I needed to use the time everyone else was at dinner in order to finally escape. I forced myself to keep my eyes open.

Alaina stroked my hair back, a gesture that caused me to miss my own mother fiercely. "What can I do for you, Your Highness?"

I waved her towards the door. "I'm sure I'll be fine after a bit of a rest." Especially if come morning I was far away from the palace. I'd much rather take my chances wandering the Forest than posing as a princess.

Despite my insistence, it still took Alaina far too long to finally leave, precious minutes of lingering daylight I didn't want to waste being cooped up in this room. She promised to check on me in a few hours and bring a dinner tray, which was bad news as that gave me limited time before she discovered me missing and informed the guards. But I had no other choice.

I waited several minutes after she'd tiptoed from the room to see if she'd return. When she didn't, I slipped from bed and frowned down at Princess Elodie's gown. Such finery would be nothing but a hinderance while traipsing through the Forest, but the buttons lining the back were impossible to undo myself. It was while I was mumbling several choice curses about my predicament that a knock sounded on the door.

I bit back a sigh, both of impatience and relief. So Alaina had returned to assist me after all. "Come in."

I gasped as the door swung open, for it wasn't Alaina who stood there but—"*Aiden?*"

He beamed, his eyes lighting up as they settled on my face. Warmth seeped over me to see him again after all these weeks, and my heart performed several cartwheels as he stared at me, his expression tender.

"Aiden!" I fell into his arms, burrowing myself against him.

He nestled against my hair. "It's wonderful to see you. I admit I thought it'd be much longer before our paths crossed again, and I'm pleased that's not the case."

I tipped my head back to gape up at him. "Wait, what are you doing here?"

"An excellent question, one I was about to ask you. May I come in?"

I slowly nodded. He shut the door behind him, his eyes never once leaving my face. The shock of seeing him at the palace of all places slowly subsided and I tentatively smiled. "I can't believe you're here. I never thought I'd see you again."

He returned my smile with a lopsided one of his own and my insides fluttered. "I promised we would. How are you?"

I sighed. "Your timing is rather bad. I'm in a bit of a predicament."

He raised an eyebrow. "Indeed. So you're a secret princess keen on trying to persuade the prince to marry you?"

I pulled a face. "No, this is all some horrible misunderstanding."

"Is it?" He folded his arms and leaned against my bedpost. "And how did a common girl end up in such a plight?"

I narrowed my eyes at him. A secret danced within his dark eyes, taunting me. "You don't happen to know the answer, do you?"

He chuckled, and the warm sound I'd fiercely missed washed over me. "I do, actually." But instead of explaining, he looked me over, his gaze as soft as a caress. The heat in my cheeks deepened. "Your finery suits you. You look beautiful."

I glanced down at my gown and wrinkled my nose, never mind it truly was lovely. "A pretty dress can't transform a common girl."

"I disagree. Now your apparel finally reflects the woman inside the dress." He gave me a look that ignited my insides.

I shook my head to clear it. I couldn't afford distractions, not when I had an escape plot to execute. "Are you going to tell me how I ended up in this mess and help me escape?"

His smile widened. "I've really missed you, Eileen. I'm so glad you're here."

"Why *am* I here?" I pressed my hands on my hips and glared at him, demanding he answer me.

He straightened and came over until he stood directly in front of me, enveloping me in his warmth and causing the strange sensations that only came from him to fill my heart. "It so happens I witnessed your unexpected arrival last night."

"What are you even doing here?"

"Isn't it obvious? I'm a member of the court."

My brow furrowed. "I don't understand. How does your witnessing my arrival explain why I now find myself trapped here?"

"Because thanks to my position, it wasn't difficult to convince the guards that you're one of the princesses come here to woo the prince." He winked.

I gaped at him, my heart pounding furiously. With each beat my insides burned, my anger searing and poisonous. "You told them *what?*"

He frowned. "I told the guards that you're a princess."

"You mean to tell me," I hissed through gritted teeth, "that it's your fault I'm tangled in this dangerous mess?"

Perplexity twisted his expression. "Mess? It's an opportunity."

"An opportunity for what, exactly? To be executed?"

He rolled his eyes. "Why so dramatic?"

My fists tightened. "If I'm caught posing as a royal, what do you think will happen? You think the royal family will merely have a good laugh before releasing me? No, they'll send me to the gallows." My blood chilled. I needed to escape. I stomped to the door, but Aiden blocked my exit.

"You're not going to get caught." But worry now marred his expression, which wasn't at all reassuring.

"Your empty promises make me feel loads better." I tried to walk around him, but he blocked me once again. I darted to the other side and he matched my movements. Angry tears burned my eyes. "Get out of my way."

"Please, Eileen." He seized my shoulders, his grip both firm and gentle. "Don't be upset. I just wanted to see you again and spend time with you."

"How do you expect to do that after I'm thrown into the dungeon?"

He flinched. "I'm so sorry, Eileen. I'm so selfish. I never once considered the potential consequences for you."

I yanked myself from his grip, his touch burning. "Well, now that you're aware of them, if you have any decency, you'll help me leave while I still have the chance." I made for the door, but he blocked me once more. I stomped my foot. "Aiden!"

"Didn't the Forest lead you here?"

"Yes, and like you, it's proven to be nothing but a betrayer."

"I didn't betray you." He stepped forward, reaching out to touch my cheek, but I flinched away with a glare. "I was just trying to help you. Would you rather have been thrown back into the storm?"

"Better risk catching a chill from the rain than risk execution for participating in this charade you thrust me into."

"It's not a charade." Aiden's voice was all gentleness, cajoling me to forgive him even though he didn't deserve it. "I just want us to be together. I told you I have a plan—"

I snorted. "*This* is your plan? How will having me impersonate a princess allow us to be together? It's the last thing that will change our circumstances or make me happy. The only thing worse would be to actually *be* a princess."

Aiden seemed on the verge of saying something, but at my words, his mouth snapped shut and his forehead furrowed. "I...I thought you'd welcome this opportunity. Don't all girls want to become princesses? That's what fairy tales always seem to be about, anyway."

"Well, not me. I'm perfectly happy with my simple country life, thank you very much."

He merely stared at me, seeming both stunned and at a loss as to what to say next.

"Besides," I continued. "It sounds like a fate worse than death to be forced to marry the Dark Prince."

He finally found his voice. He cocked an eyebrow. "The Dark Prince?"

"I'm sure you've heard the rumors about him. You are a member of the court, after all."

He didn't answer. I ignored his silence. Since the door was obviously not going to be my form of escape thanks to *him*, I tried the windows. Locked.

"What is this, a prison?" I fiddled with the latch but couldn't figure out how to make it work. I growled in frustration. "A little help here?"

He sighed and came over to unlock the window and push it open. A rush of cool evening air caressed my flushed cheeks. Together we peered down to the manicured gardens below. My stomach lurched. From the third floor, the ground was quite a ways down.

"You'd fall to your death trying to escape this way."

He was likely right. I gnawed at my lip as I scanned the room. "The bedsheets." I stomped towards the bed, but Aiden seized my wrist to stop me. Despite my anger, my stomach still jolted at his touch.

"Please don't climb out the window. You could get hurt."

"How can you possibly care about that after already putting my life at risk?" My voice stuttered, on the brink of tears. I swallowed. I would not cry in front of him.

He pressed my hand against his chest, his eyes wide with remorse. The feel of his hands enfolding mine and his heart pulsing beneath my palm did strange things to my insides and made it difficult to think.

"I'm genuinely sorry for entangling you in this, but I promise not to abandon you. I'll help you not fail."

I gaped at him. "You want me to try to win the Dark Prince?"

Sharp betrayal pierced my heart. After our near kiss, I thought he felt more for me. My jaw tightened. He obviously didn't. He was just like all men: fickle and unreliable. I refused to allow him to hurt me any longer. I yanked my hand out of his. "I don't want your help."

"Please allow me to give it to you." He reached for my hand again but I jerked away.

He winced at my rejection and I inwardly smirked. *Good, let him be hurt.* He deserved it.

"I don't want to marry a prince, so your help isn't at all welcome."

"But you don't want to be caught as an imposter either," he said. "If the prince doesn't pick you, then you can go home."

"But what if he does?" Not that I thought such a situation likely; no matter how much Aiden tried to help me, I would never be princess material.

"There are plenty of other eligible brides for him to pick instead," Aiden said. "Now, will you accept my help?"

I eyed him warily as I folded my arms like a shield over my frantically pounding heart. "How could you possibly help me?"

He had the audacity to grin, causing my treacherous heart to flip-flop. I silently cursed my body's reaction. "As a member of the court, I've been forced to be part of the shallow world of the nobility my entire life. I know exactly how to play the game. And in the meantime, we can spend time with one another again." He reached for my fingers and curled his own around my fingertips, giving me an earnest, hopeful look.

In that foolish moment I almost told him yes, for I secretly wanted that very same wish. But I locked those ridiculous desires away. This couldn't happen, especially with a man who was very much engaged. I yanked my hand away as if he'd burned me.

"We can't do this."

He flinched, eyes wounded. "But you told me you were developing feelings for me."

"That was *before* you betrayed me by making the court believe I'm a princess. Besides, you're still engaged."

"But Eileen, you don't understand." He reached out as if he meant to embrace me, but I stepped away until my back pressed against the bedpost. He gaped at me. "Have your feelings changed?"

They hadn't, but caring for him didn't mean our relationship was right. "You're engaged to another. It's wrong for you to betray her in order to be involved with me." Men were far too fickle. Thank goodness I'd learned Aiden's true character before I'd involved myself further.

Aiden's expression crumpled. "Please, Eileen."

"Perhaps I didn't make my meaning clear," I said slowly, forcing myself to say the words that burned on my tongue. "I never want to see you again." I pointed to the door, my entire body shaking. "Get out. Now."

"But Eileen—"

"Go away!" My tears finally escaped. He reached a thumb

out as if to wipe them away but froze at my glare. He slowly backed away.

"Very well, I'll leave. But please don't try to escape, Eileen; guards are posted everywhere, and it'll look more suspicious should you inevitably get caught. The best course of action is to stay."

I gritted my teeth. He was right and I hated it. His words were bars, trapping me in this prison. There was no escape. Defeated, I crumpled to the ground and pressed my tear-streaked face against the side of the mattress.

"Please leave," I whispered.

To my surprise, he obediently heeded my wishes.

Despite the anger raging war against my breaking heart, a sense of loss washed over me the moment he left the room. The earlier joy I'd felt at seeing him again was now swallowed up by his betrayal. Despite everything we'd experienced together, Aiden was like all men, always hurting you in the end. I made myself a determined promise never to trust my heart to him again.

CHAPTER 14

*D*espite Aiden's warning, I wasn't inclined to entirely give up trying to escape. Rather than spending the following day cooped up in my room, I explored the palace corridors, searching for potential escape routes, trying every door I passed—most of which were unfortunately locked—and exploring every unlocked room that didn't appear off-limits.

After several unproductive hours of this, I ventured outside to the towering gilded gates, which were flanked by two rigid guards. I pressed my face against the bars and stared longingly at the Forest and the freedom it represented, so near yet still beyond my reach. My neck prickled. I glanced over to see both guards watching me with suspicious frowns.

I straightened. "Open the gates so I might go exploring." I tried to sound authoritative, but the command sounded weak even to my ears.

The guards exchanged long looks. "Forgive us, noble lady, but the Forest is off-limits. It's an enchanted Forest prone to getting wanderers hopelessly lost."

I jutted my chin out. "Be that as it may, I'm ordering you to let me wander it anyway."

"Forgive us, but His Highness has given strict orders that no one is to leave the palace grounds."

What good was it being forced to pose as a royal if my orders weren't obeyed? I wanted to argue but knew doing so would only draw more unwanted attention. Once again I'd failed.

As I turned away from my now-forbidden Forest to trudge gloomily back into my palace prison, a figure hastily ducked behind a hedge, a man who looked suspiciously like that guard, Alastar. I frowned. Was he following me?

I kept a sharp lookout for him as I ascended the palace steps, but I didn't see him, just as I hadn't seen him during my earlier explorations, but I couldn't shake the feeling that I was being not only watched but followed.

When I went down to lunch, I took my usual place at the Dracerian Royalty's end of the dining table.

"I've been looking for you all morning," Princess Elodie said the moment I sat down. "Where have you been?"

Princess Aveline sniffed disapprovingly. "Princesses shouldn't go looking for anything; that's what servants are for."

"Where's the fun in sending them to do something I'm perfectly capable of doing myself?" Princess Elodie said. "Do tell me where you've been, Gemma."

My cheeks burned. I didn't want to admit having spent the entire morning traipsing around the palace and its grounds. Prince Liam grinned cheekily as he leaned back in his seat.

"I know where you've been, Princess. I'll keep it a secret in exchange for your crumpet."

I lowered my eyes to the crumpet on my plate before

tossing it at him. He caught it easily, eyebrows raised in surprise, before an easy grin lit his face.

"You tossed a crumpet at the table?" Princess Aveline gaped at me. My stomach sank at my mistake and I wanted to groan at my stupidity. Rosie always tossed baked goods at her brother whenever I dined with her family, and Prince Liam seemed the epitome of an annoying older brother, making the impulse to throw my crumpet impossible to resist.

"I often throw crumpets at my brothers, so I don't see why I shouldn't bestow the same courtesy to Prince Liam." The princess I was imitating was said to have two brothers, right?

Prince Liam threw his head back and laughed. "I like you, Gemma." He took a huge bite from the crumpet I'd given him, completely ignoring his own waiting patiently on his plate. "Very well, I'll keep your secret."

"No fair," Princess Elodie said. "I want to know what Gemma has been up to. It must have been something exciting considering it's a secret."

"She's been exploring the palace, quite thoroughly, too."

I glared at him and he held up his hands defensively.

"Don't look at me as if I just betrayed your trust. I never said how long I'd keep your secret for." He winked, a gesture which effectively disarmed me. Why were princes so charming?

"That was a cruel trick, Liam," Princess Rheanna said.

"But an effective one; it got me an extra crumpet, didn't it?" He shoved the rest of it into his mouth, dripping crumbs onto his velvet tunic, which he brushed off onto the floor.

Princess Aveline rolled her eyes before eating her own crumpet with exaggerated formality. "You must work on improving your manners for when you're king and attend state dinners with important diplomats."

"But we're not at a state dinner with a bunch of stuffy diplomats, are we, sister dear? Thank heavens for that." He tugged her earlobe playfully before jabbing at his rosemary chicken. "Did you find anything interesting in your explorations, Gemma? I expect you were searching for the many secret passageways to be found within the Sortileyan palace's walls."

My heart gave an excited leap. "Passageways?" A secret passageway could either get me hopelessly lost or lead me to much-desired freedom. Either scenario presented a better fate than the predicament I currently found myself in.

Prince Liam twirled his knife between his fingers. "Come now, don't tell me you haven't heard the rumors. The Sortileyan palace is famous for its labyrinth of secret passageways, ones I'm keen to discover each visit."

"Have you found any?" For while I hadn't exactly doubted Rosie's imaginative claims that such things existed, I hadn't made searching for them a priority compared with other possible exits.

He sighed. "Unfortunately not, but that doesn't keep me from looking. I've pleaded with the prince to show them to me, but his only hint is that all of them share a feature that's the trick to finding and opening them."

"Do you know whether any of the passageways lead *outside* the palace?"

"I'm told there's one that leads directly to the Forest."

At last, there was hope of escaping after all. My mood brightened considerably and I beamed at Prince Liam; he flashed me an excited grin that lit up his bright blue eyes.

"Ah, I recognize that determined gleam. I wish you much luck on your quest. Perhaps I'll do some searching of my own this afternoon. If we split up, we'll cover much more ground."

The passageways became that afternoon's quest. I combed every wall I passed for potential knobs and switches but found nothing in the smooth, ordinary marble, not even when I tentatively peeked around lavish tapestries, suits of armor, or other decorations lining the hallways.

I huffed a frustrated sigh. This was getting me nowhere, but I couldn't give up, not when the alternative would be the impossible task of continuing to pretend I was a princess. Getting caught was inevitable. I gritted my teeth. This was all Aiden's fault.

No, I wouldn't think of him, not when his betrayal was still so fresh. But despite the anger attacking my heart, I unconsciously looked for him during my palace explorations —especially amongst the attending nobles during meals—for despite how much I pretended otherwise, I wanted to see him again.

But I never encountered him; it was as if he'd disap-peared...or perhaps he was avoiding me. I tried to tell myself it was for the best, for with his engagement he was very much unavailable to me. Still, his absence hurt all the same.

As I continued to search, I couldn't shake the feeling I was being watched. It began as merely a suspicion—sensing someone behind me only to turn around and see no one there, or catching the occasional movement from the shadows—but after spotting Guard Alastar in the gardens, I became certain he was the one following me. I tried to ignore him, but soon his trailing presence became too unnerving to do so any longer.

I waited until we'd reached an abandoned corridor before spinning around to stare at the apparently empty hallway. "I know you're following me."

He stepped into view and bowed. "Good afternoon, Princess Gemma." He emphasized my name, as if he doubted it. My heart flared in paranoia. Was he following me because he found me suspicious?

"I saw you in the gardens." I glared at him, challenging him to deny it. His stoic expression didn't even falter.

"I was careless. I wasn't sure whether you would attempt to force yourself past the guards flanking the gate, so I stepped into the open in preparation to come after you."

I tightened my jaw. "So you are following me. Why?"

"I have my orders, Your Highness."

Undoubtedly, Aiden had put him up to this. The question that remained was whether he'd done it in order to protect me or to prevent me from escaping. I pressed my hands to my hips. "I see I'm not the only one Aiden is ordering about."

"He doesn't order me," Alastar said. "He merely makes requests, but considering our friendship, I take them as seriously as if they were direct orders from the crown prince himself."

I frowned. He hadn't denied it was Aiden's bidding he was doing, the man I was still quite annoyed with, although my anger lessened the longer my true identity remained undiscovered. Admittedly, I longed to see him again more than I wanted to remain upset with him.

"I knew it was Aiden's doing."

"You make it sound like an accusation."

"Because it is."

Alastar's lips twitched but not into a full smile, as if he considered smiling below his position as guard. "I can see why he's taken a liking to you. He needs someone to put him in his place."

"I'll do more than that," I grumbled. "Next I see him I'm going to murder him."

Alastar frowned. "What's the reason for your ire?"

I tightened my jaw but remained silent, no excuse adequate enough that wouldn't give me away. I couldn't very well admit the façade I was being forced to participate in, but by the knowing look in this guard's eyes, I had the sinking feeling he already knew the full extent of my situation.

"Why is Aiden having you creepily follow me?"

Alastar cocked an eyebrow. "*Creepily*? I was going for *discreetly* and *protectively*."

"So you claim Aiden wants to protect me?"

"Can you doubt that?"

That flared my temper. "If he's so concerned, he shouldn't have been the one to lie about me being a—" I snapped my mouth shut before any more condemning words escaped. Alastar made no indication he found my outburst incriminating.

"Whatever his choices that you may or may not approve of, he's still clearly concerned for your welfare, Your Highness. Shouldn't that be taken into consideration?"

For once his use of my false title caused me to relax. Surely he wouldn't address me so formally if he suspected I wasn't who I claimed. "Why would he be concerned with my welfare?"

"He thinks very highly of you—something quite impressive considering he rarely thinks highly of anyone."

Despite my annoyance with Aiden, I couldn't quite mask my pleasure at Alastar's words. "And my grumpy mood and snappy retorts don't make you believe he's delusional, I take it?"

"Not at all." Alastar's stoic expression didn't even waver as he met my gaze. "Please don't be angry with him."

Against my better judgment, his request softened me. It wasn't that difficult, considering I didn't *want* to be angry with Aiden. The longer I was the more wrong it felt, as if any negative emotion wasn't meant to exist between us. "It would be easier to forgive him if I knew why he did it."

"I'm not at liberty to say, Your Highness, but what's

important is that his motive is significant to him. He carefully considers all his decisions before he makes them." He frowned thoughtfully. "Although admittedly, this one was more impulsive. Regardless, he didn't mean to hurt you; of that I can be certain."

"Despite that, he still hasn't fully repented for his offense. Until he does, I have the right to remain upset with him."

"Hopefully with time, your anger will fade."

I tilted my head and studied him with a thoughtful frown. "You truly think highly of him, don't you?"

"As I've said before, Your Highness, he's a good friend."

"Then you must know a lot about him." My anger momentarily faded, replaced by the unsatisfied curiosity that constantly filled me concerning Aiden's many mysteries. "What's Aiden's title?"

"One far above my own," Alastar said. I frowned at his ridiculously vague answer.

"What of Aiden's background? His relations?"

Hesitation pierced Alastar's stoic expression. "Forgive me, but I'm not at liberty to divulge such information without his permission."

Of course he wasn't. This was getting me nowhere, and I was growing tired of this game. I turned and stomped towards my room. It came as no surprise when Alastar followed me. I sighed. "This is going to get quite annoying."

"I apologize if I'm inconveniencing you. If it bothers you so much, take it up with Aiden."

"Next time I see him, I have other more pressing words to spout to him."

Alastar's lips twitched in response.

We walked back to my room in silence, the only sound our footsteps echoing through the marble corridors and the occasional direction from Alastar when I was about to take a wrong turn. Curiosity compelled me to pause outside one of the locked doors I'd encountered during my earlier explorations.

"What's beyond that door?" I asked.

"A portrait gallery, Your Highness, filled with several generations of Sortileya's royalty."

I made another tug on the handle but it didn't open. "Why is it locked?"

"I couldn't say, Princess Eil—*Gemma*."

My heart flared to life as I slowly turned to face him. His stoic expression hadn't faltered, but regret filled his eyes. He knew my real name. Aiden must have told him, which meant Alastar was in on the secret that I wasn't who I claimed to be.

"Is something the matter, Princess Gemma?"

I ached to confront him, but his clear determination to address me by the part I played deterred me. I shook my head and we resumed walking.

When I reached my bedroom, I eyed Alastar warily. "You're not ordered to follow me into my room, are you?"

"No worries, Your Highness. I'll wait for you out here."

I frowned. "All evening?"

"I'll have the opportunity to stretch my legs when I escort you to dinner."

Another awkward formal dinner, and with it, the revelation of the first test—a test I'd been distracted from dwelling on in my search for a way to avoid it. I groaned. "If only I could find a way to wriggle out of it."

He tilted his head. "Why Princess, you're beginning to look a bit ill, if you'll forgive the observation."

I sighed. "Unfortunately, I already used that excuse yesterday."

"Quite unfortunate indeed. I shall entertain myself with coming up with other possible excuses for you. It'll help pass the time."

I managed a smile. I liked this stoic guard.

Alastar turned away from the doorway but paused to glance over his shoulder. "If you'll forgive my asking, Your Highness, how is your quest to uncover the palace's secret passageways going?"

My face heated. "How did you know?"

He raised his eyebrow. "I've followed you most of the day and witnessed your poking around."

That was true. "Do you happen to know where they are?"

"I do, but unfortunately I can't divulge their whereabouts; they're secret for a reason."

I sighed. How disappointing. That meant I had no choice but to face the first challenge, one I wanted both to pass and to fail. I didn't want to do well, considering I had no interest in marrying the prince, but I couldn't do so poorly that I'd be found out as a commoner posing as a royal. My head throbbed at the fine line I had to balance. So overwhelming.

As if sensing my discomfort, Alastar offered a sympathetic smile. "Don't worry, Your Highness. All will be well."

I studied him with a frown. He definitely knew my secret. Was it his relationship with Aiden that prevented him from turning me in?

"Do you trust Aiden?" Despite the pain of his betrayal, I still cared for him. I needed a reason to forgive him in order to begin rebuilding the fragile trust he'd broken.

Alastar's already serious expression intensified as he met my gaze. "With my life. He's a noble man and a wonderful friend, incredibly loyal and caring, even when he chooses to hide those traits. Whether or not you approve of him wanting me to watch over you, I have to do it; our friendship runs too deep for me to risk hurting him, which would happen should any harm befall you."

I allowed his words to wash over me before I nodded and slipped inside my room, where I collapsed onto my bed and stared at the ceiling. Even though my head told me it was foolish to hope, my heart ached to give Aiden another chance. The more I analyzed this desire, the more my searing anger began to fade away.

CHAPTER 15

The first task arrived immediately following dinner. I shakily broke the royal seal and unfolded the gilded stationery:

A princess is a symbol not only of the royal family, but of the kingdom and the people whom she serves. Thus a true princess should be one who showcases the proper etiquette and decorum in all situations with which she is presented.

My panic escalated, tightening my heart. It was only the first task and I already found myself overwhelmed, for not only was there nothing proper about me, but I had a single night to transform myself from a common girl to the elegant royal they expected.

After many wrong turns to arrive at my destination before Alastar took pity on me, I spent the evening combing the library shelves for a miracle. A wasted hour crawled by, then two, with little to show for my efforts. An etiquette manual was likely a useless volume to keep in the royal library since princesses were bred from birth for their role, but I refused to give up.

As the sun sank below the horizon and darkness tumbled

through the library windows to smother the shelves in shadows, my failure to bring a candle forced me to abandon my search. It appeared I was now back to the plan of tying my bedsheets together and escaping through my bedroom window.

"Princess Gemma?"

I gasped and spun around to see the Princesses of Draceria, their eyes wide with remorse.

"I beg your pardon, Gemma," Princess Elodie said. "We didn't mean to startle you."

I pressed my hand to my frantically pounding heart and didn't answer.

Princess Elodie stepped forward with a friendly smile. "Are you here to prepare for the first task?"

I nodded mutely.

Princess Rheanna's brow furrowed. "What do you think of it? Personally, I was expecting something a bit more challenging."

Of course she'd find it easy. This fact only escalated my panic.

"I, for one, am not surprised at the task," Princess Aveline said. "Proper decorum is the foundation for being a queen fit to rule. I hope the tests increase in challenge; I mean to prove myself."

This one was challenging enough for me. How could I cram a lifetime of social graces into a single night when I couldn't even find a guide to aid me? I glanced outside at the disappearing dusk. I was wasting too much time. I began inching towards the door.

"Where are you going, Gemma?" Princess Elodie asked. "We were hoping to spend the evening with you."

I forced myself to smile when, inside, I wanted to cry that they were so confident in their own royal graces that they had time to spend so frivolously. "I want to make sure I'm properly rested for tomorrow."

"You're looking a bit pale. Are you well?"

Not in the least, not when I was on the brink of fainting. "It's been a long day. If you'll excuse me…" And before they could call me back, I scampered from the room.

The marble hallways seemed entirely transformed by the shadows cast by the glowing lanterns guiding my way. After wasting more precious time taking several wrong turns before Alastar—lips twitching, as if my being lost had been highly amusing—again took pity on me, I finally located my door and with a fierce sigh of relief slipped inside my room.

For a moment I stood with my back pressed against the door, eyes closed, taking several deep, steadying breaths. I needed a plan, something far better than trying to fake my way through social graces. Yes, the bedsheets would have to do. That decided, I pushed myself away from the door and opened my eyes.

I screamed, and Aiden slapped his hand over my mouth. "Shh, I don't want to be found out."

From outside my door Alastar called, "Is everything alright, Your Highness?"

"Yes, I'm fine. Thank you." I pushed Aiden away, my hands lingering far longer than they should on his firm chest. "What are you doing here? Do you mean to frighten me half to death?"

"I'm sorry, I didn't mean to startle you."

"Then why were you lurking in my dark room?"

"I was waiting for you. I did initially knock."

"And since I wasn't here to invite you in, you took my silence as an invitation to hide in the shadows and wait for me?"

He crunched the end of his hem and bit his lip. "That was a bad idea, wasn't it?"

His obvious remorse softened me, but only slightly. I folded my arms across my chest, fighting to ignore the excited patter of my heart at seeing him again. So much for my grudge. "Aiden, you shouldn't be alone with me in my room."

His brow furrowed. "Why? I'm here to help you. Don't worry, Alastar will ensure no one disturbs us."

I narrowed my eyes. "I seem to recall telling you I *didn't* want your help."

"I know you said that, but what else are you to do?"

"The current plan is to use the bedsheets to climb out the window."

Aiden gave me an exasperated look. "Like I told you before, even if that worked, there are guards posted at the gates."

Oh yes, them. They definitely presented a problem.

"Besides, need I remind you that your room is on the third floor?"

I frowned at my bed. As large as it was…"The bedclothes wouldn't be long enough, would they?"

"Likely not, which means…" He gave me a rather sweet, hopeful look. "Will you please accept my help now?"

My frantic breathing slowly subsided, leaving in its wake a swirl of confusing thoughts. Even though I'd pushed him away, Aiden had still returned. He hadn't abandoned me. "You really want to help me?"

"I do." He stepped forward and took my hand. I reluctantly let him. His earnest gaze met mine. "I got you into this, so I won't leave you to face it alone."

In spite of his mistake, he'd returned to atone for it. I desperately wanted to trust him, but one gesture wasn't enough for me to determine whether or not I could. Despite my reservations, I didn't pull my hand away.

"What's the first task?" he asked.

I went to my desk to retrieve it. He read it rapidly and rolled his eyes.

"*This* is the task chosen by the king?"

I cocked an eyebrow. "Not by the prince?"

"From what I understand, the prince asked for the opportunity of choosing his own wife, but the terms were that the king would determine how the choice was to be made."

I wrinkled my forehead. "The Dracerian royalty mentioned the prince isn't even going to witness the competition until the very end. How can he choose a bride when he has no opportunity to even see his choices? Doesn't that seem rather strange?"

Aiden raised an eyebrow. "It does. He likely has his own criteria for choosing his bride. Perhaps he's already chosen who he wants, and this competition is merely a formality to appease the king and his ridiculous dictates on whom he believes to be suitable." He waved the paper. "Apparently, all one needs in marital happiness is a *proper wife*."

"He must believe a proper wife is graceful on both the inside and the outside."

Aiden snorted. "Not in the least. Etiquette is both a mask and a part one plays. Anyone can learn to do it, and thus it cannot measure one's true character."

I sighed. "It doesn't matter, for I'm doomed to fail. I searched the entire library for a book on etiquette and found nothing."

"Then I'll teach you myself. I just so happen to know all the rules."

I raised a skeptical brow. "In one night?"

"It won't take long, for propriety is common sense once one knows how the game is played. Now, will you allow me to help you?"

He gave me such an earnest look. I nibbled my lip, deliberating. I seemed to have no other option. "If I say yes, then let me be clear that this changes nothing. I'm still upset that your lies entangled me in all this." Although admittedly forgiveness was forthcoming.

His expression crumpled. "I truly am sorry. I just wanted to"—he hesitated for just a moment—"see you again."

I nodded, not trusting myself to speak. He smiled and stepped closer, enveloping me in his comforting warmth.

"First is posture."

He gently rested his hands on my shoulders. I shuddered at his touch as he pressed his fingers against my back until I straightened.

"That's too straight; relax your shoulders and keep them back. Good. Now lift your chin to keep your head in a natural, upright position."

He hooked his fingers beneath my chin to raise it, his touch lingering to stroke my jaw.

"There." He stepped back with a nod of approval. "See? This isn't so hard, is it?"

"Until I start to move."

His lips twitched. "Come now, Eileen, don't be so harsh on yourself. Part of posture is confidence."

"How can I be confident when I'm terrified every moment of being caught as an impostor? I'm on the brink of an anxiety attack."

He cupped my chin. "I won't let anything happen to you. I promise. Don't you trust me?"

I narrowed my eyes. "I trust no one."

He frowned as he dropped his hand. "I hope one day you'll learn to trust me."

"I want to trust you," I said. "Really I do. But how can I when your lies hurt me so much? You only thought of yourself when you got me involved in this."

He flinched, expression tortured, and despite my prickling anger, I felt remorse at his pain. In spite of everything, I still cared about him, more deeply than I wanted to admit.

"I'm sorry," I whispered. "I shouldn't have said that."

He was silent for a moment before he raised his gaze to mine with a wry smile. "You only spoke the truth. I'm a selfish person. I always have been, and I need to change. I want to be a man you can always rely on. You deserve nothing less."

My heart constricted. How could he say things like that when he was engaged? I searched his eyes. Sincerity filled his gaze, and once again I felt my fierce resolve slacken. I smiled, and when he tentatively offered me his own smile in return, I felt the tension that had festered between us begin to melt away.

The lesson in decorum continued. From proper posture, we moved to learning to walk with grace and poise, something Aiden seemed perplexed on how to teach. After several minutes of pondering, he gave a helpless shrug.

"They just seem to glide. I don't know how they do it."

"Small steps?" I attempted my hypothesis. Aiden watched, head tilted.

"That's not quite it. Goodness, this is ridiculous. You walk just fine now. Changing it won't change *you,* so how would walking gracefully determine your worth?"

"I doubt the Dark Prince cares about my worth either way," I said as I experimented walking the circumference of the room with different-sized steps.

"I don't see why he wouldn't," Aiden said. "Does his title mean he doesn't desire marital happiness like everyone else?"

I shrugged. "Is that important to any man?" I knew the assessment was rather unfair, but I couldn't bring myself to retract my words.

"It's important to me."

My gaze snapped to his, and for a beautiful moment we

stared at one another. I broke our connection first, my cheeks warm. "It's getting late. Shall we continue?"

Since Aiden seemed at a loss on how to explain the process of strolling gracefully, he experimented with different walks. I bit my lip to stifle my laughter as Aiden strolled in exaggerated dainty ways around the room, his walk becoming more and more aggressive as his frustration escalated. Soon I couldn't contain my giggles any longer and they wriggled free, causing him to pause with a chuckle of his own.

"Do I look as ridiculous as I feel?"

"You certainly do. I wish you could see yourself." I laughed again and his smile widened.

"I love hearing your laugh."

"Then keep walking like that. And here I thought you an expert on social graces. You disappoint me, Aiden."

"If I were teaching you to walk like a nobleman, I'd have succeeded by now. But I refuse to give up until I've fulfilled my promise to you, even if it takes all night." His eyes flashed with determination and once more warmth seeped over me, causing me to little by little begin to believe him.

After much more amusing experimenting, Aiden determined that the key to walking gracefully was dainty steps, a straight spine, drawing in the abdomen, and keeping one's hands naturally at one's sides while looking directly ahead. He beamed as I practiced.

"Exactly. I knew I'd figure it out. I'm ready for my accolades."

"Why humor you when you've already given them to yourself?" I smiled, one of many this evening. With each passing moment with Aiden, not only was I reminded of how much I loved spending time with him, but my terror about tomorrow gradually began to abate. Perhaps I wouldn't be as much of a disaster as I'd initially feared.

Aiden picked up a book and rested it on top of my head. "Now to practice. My sister trained by walking with books on her head. The goal is not to let it fall off."

"You have a sister? Why isn't she here offering her expert advice?"

He smiled wryly. "Unfortunately, she's not one who likes to extend her assistance."

We practiced with a book perched upon my head until I managed to walk around the room without it tumbling off, and then we sat at my vanity with it still in place as I practiced the motions of eating with the correct posture. From there we went over basic table manners and table place settings, the proper volume to keep one's voice while conversing, and how a proper lady extended her hand to be kissed. Before Aiden could demonstrate on me I yanked my hand away, afraid of what his lips touching my skin would cause me to feel. I immediately regretted doing so when my rejection caused Aiden to wince.

We ended the evening practicing how to properly curtsy. Every time he curtsied low, I fell backwards onto the settee, clutching my sides as I laughed. Finally, Aiden gave up that particular lesson and joined in.

When we managed to catch our breath, I rolled onto my side and propped onto my elbow. "Is that the end of the lesson?"

"It is. You'll be perfect tomorrow."

The anxiety that had previously twisted my insides slowly eased. Perhaps I wouldn't fail after all.

"Thank you for your help, Aiden."

His gaze seeped into mine. "It was my pleasure." A strange energy passed between us as we stared at one another. Aiden's crooked grin broke the spell. "We still have the matter of payment."

I groaned. I should have known. "What is it with you and

payments? Very well, what would you like? I warn you I haven't much to offer."

"That's where you're wrong." He thoughtfully pressed his thumb against his pursed lips before his gaze settled on my sketchbook, the corner of which poked out from beneath my mattress where I kept it hidden. "A portrait."

"A portrait?"

He nodded. "Yes. In exchange for your decorum lessons, I'd like a portrait of you."

"Of *me*?"

He offered a boyish grin. "Please?"

I nibbled my lip. "I don't know…"

His smile faltered. "Does that make you uncomfortable? You don't have to."

I searched his expression, so open and sweet, and I realized in that moment that I'd not only forgiven him but that I trusted him more than I'd been allowing myself to admit. I retrieved my sketchbook and settled cross-legged on the floor in front of the full length mirror. I started to open the book, but he crouched down and rested his hand on top of mine, stopping me.

"Really Eileen, you don't have to do this if you don't want to."

I met his gaze and once again felt turned inside out by the tender way he looked at me. "I want to."

"Then might I watch?"

I nodded breathlessly as I turned to a blank page and selected my pencils, sliding them into my bun for easy access. Aiden sat directly behind me—so close I could feel the heat of his body seeping into my back—and it took all my willpower to resist leaning against his chest.

I tried to study my reflection but my eyes were repeatedly drawn to Aiden's, who hovered just above my shoulder. He met my gaze in the mirror and smiled. I swallowed and looked away to study my face with as artistic an eye as I was capable of while so attuned to his closeness.

I rested my pencil on the page. I'd attempted several self-portraits before, but I could never get them exactly right. "It may not be very good."

"Doubting your talent?"

"No. It's just that the more I know a person, the more difficult it is to capture their portrait through mere lines on paper. I know myself best of all. How then can I portray all that I am in a drawing?"

He tucked my hair behind my ear. I shuddered at his touch while the instinct to lean against him intensified, as did my efforts to resist the impulse. "I can fill in the missing lines, especially the more I come to know you myself."

I rather liked that idea. With this promise, I took a wavering breath and began. I adored this process: beginning with a blank page and then line by line creating shapes that I sculpted to resemble a person. Drawing was similar to the process of coming to know someone; over time, more and more about an individual was revealed, until one had a complete picture.

I felt as if my relationship with Aiden was a sketch I was creating. Each interaction together drew lines on my heart, and although I still couldn't see the entire picture, I knew that with time I would...if I kept drawing. And I found that the longer I worked on this picture, the more excited I was to see the finished product.

As my pencil caressed the paper in long, fluid strokes, I tried to forget Aiden's presence behind me, but it was impossible. I had to pause several times to still my shaking hand and school my pattering heartbeat. I tried to resist looking at him in the mirror but I couldn't escape the feeling of his soft gaze upon me, caressing, nor his warmth enveloping me, as if I were curled in front of a hearth.

Aiden broke the tranquil stillness first. "I know you claimed not to be able to adequately capture yourself in a drawing, but so far it's remarkable. You're incredibly talented. Perhaps I should request my portrait next."

"No need, I've already drawn one." The words escaped before I could register them. I froze and my cheeks flamed. "That is...*oh*." I closed my eyes and groaned. "I can't believe I just admitted that."

"You've drawn my portrait?" His fingertips lightly traced my warm blush, his tone delighted. "Please don't worry; I'm flattered. Might I see it?"

"Perhaps that can be your next payment."

He chuckled but didn't remove his stroking fingers. I was secretly glad. I felt so alive when he touched me. "Can you give me a hint on how it turned out?"

"It looked like you, but I couldn't quite portray the layers protecting your secrets."

"Now I'm even more eager to see it. I'm dying to know how you see me."

Our eyes met in the mirror. "I'm not even sure I know the answer to that. How do you want me to see you?"

His gaze intensified as his fingers curled around my still-burning cheek. "As a man you can trust."

If only he knew that's how I desperately wanted to see him. After tonight, I saw him as that man even more.

The clock on the mantle chimed, signifying the late hour. I tugged one of my pencils from my hair as I returned to my portrait, pulling out my bun. My dark hair cascaded down my back. Aiden's attention shifted from the careful strokes of my drawing to my hair. After a moment's hesitation, he ran his fingers through it. I froze.

"Am I distracting you?"

"Yes," I murmured breathlessly. "If you keep doing so I won't be able to finish."

His hand wound around my hair, caressing the strands between his fingers. "Perhaps this is a better payment. I love your hair." He paused. "I'm sorry. I should have asked your permission before touching you."

He met my gaze in the mirror, seeking the desired permission with his eyes. I could barely nod in order to give it. I tried to calm my breathing in order to continue drawing, but the task proved impossible. My heart raced at the sensations caused by each of Aiden's touches as he stroked my long hair down my back, sending ripples all over my body.

Aiden eventually pulled away, leaving me aching for his touch. I had to bite my tongue to keep myself from asking him to touch me again.

"I could play with your hair all night, but I really want your portrait." He leaned over my shoulder, enveloping me in his honey-musk scent and making me lightheaded. "It's really coming along."

Even midst my tumult of emotions, I managed to stare at it with a critical air. "It doesn't seem…me."

"I should say not. What is a piece of paper to the remarkable woman I have the pleasure of sitting beside?"

He rested his chin on my shoulder and after several shuddering breaths, I managed to unthaw and finish the portrait. It was almost done. I used my thumb for the final shading and held it beside my face.

"Finished. What do you think?"

Aiden glanced back and forth between it and me and nodded in approval. "Flawless. Well, almost." He lightly traced around my eyes, his own full of an intensity that ignited my insides. "You couldn't capture the light dancing in your eyes nor the brightness of your smile." He pressed his fingertip against the corner of my lips before withdrawing. "I suppose a portrait can't fully capture a person."

"I did warn you."

"But it's still wonderful and I'm happy to have it." He took it reverently after I removed it from my sketchbook and admired it with an appreciating smile. "Thank you, Eileen; I'll treasure it forever."

He glanced at the clock on the mantle. I sighed. "You have to leave?" It was impossible to keep the disappointment from my voice. What a contrast: this evening I'd gone from not wanting his presence to aching for him to stay.

"I do, but I'll see you tomorrow after the task."

"If I survive the experience."

"You will, I have no doubt." He stood and extended his hand to help me to my feet, holding mine long after I'd risen. "Until tomorrow."

He lifted my hand and pressed a kiss on my fingers. This time I let him, and just as I'd feared, it caused my heart to patter so rapidly I was certain it'd explode. It didn't settle even after Aiden bowed and left the room, and it took even longer for me to tear my gaze away from the closed door, especially considering I was now more frightened by the despair I felt at his absence than by tomorrow's test.

CHAPTER 16

I blew the ink dry on the note I'd spent the morning writing to Mother. It was such an inadequate explanation for the fierce worry she'd undoubtedly been experiencing since my disappearance, but at least she'd be assured I was alive; it was better than nothing.

I gnawed my lip as I reread it. It was far too vague, but telling Mother the extent of my situation would likely cause her to fret even more. For now she'd at least know I was well and that I would hopefully be home soon.

I folded it and tucked it away before my gaze settled on the tiny package that Alaina had delivered with my breakfast tray. Without even needing to check the card, I knew who it was from.

I closed my eyes as memories from last night washed over me—the sweet look filling Aiden's eyes as he looked at me, the ripply sensations his touch had caused me to feel, and the way my heart yearned for his presence when we weren't together. Certainly whatever was in this package from him would only intensify these already confusing emotions.

With a deep breath, I shakily untied the ribbon and lifted

the lid. I gasped. For a moment, I stared at Aiden's gift before I lightly traced each shimmering pearl of the necklace with my fingertip. It was both elegant and simple. Aiden knew my tastes well.

I picked up the accompanying note that had fluttered to the desk when I'd opened the box: *Wear with confidence, for no amount of etiquette can match the true poise you already possess.*

My emotions swelled and I had to blink back tears. I gently removed the necklace and draped it around my neck, my fingers tracing it as I stared at it, dazed. I'd never possessed something so beautiful. Even the locket from Father couldn't compare to this. His locket...

A lump formed in my throat as I tugged the locket from beneath my collar, the locket I hadn't taken off since Father left. While wearing two necklaces didn't seem dignified for the princess I supposedly was, I didn't care. I needed to wear both to give me strength for what was to come. My stomach knotted further as I glanced at the time. I was due downstairs soon.

Half an hour later, I waited with the rest of the court in the rose parlor, fidgeting. Despite the large size of the elegant room, it was crowded with nobility, pressing around me in their finery, making me moments away from a faint.

I wove through the smothering crowd as best I could, searching for Aiden. Considering he was a member of the court, surely he'd be here. Hearing his sweet assurances and seeing his endearing smile would help ease my nerves so I could face the first challenge. But no matter how many times I scanned the room, carefully examining every face, I didn't see him. My disappointment was more pressing than the crowd.

"Looking for someone in particular?" Prince Liam appeared at my elbow, a knowing smile on his face. "A good-looking bloke, perhaps? Because if so, here I am."

I smiled indulgently before resuming my search. "Are all members of the court present?"

"A good number of them are."

It only made Aiden's absence more acute. His obvious disdain for court—which he'd repeatedly expressed with fierce grumbles the night before—made it unsurprising he'd chosen not to come. But shouldn't his desire to see me and wish me luck have compelled him to come anyway? My heart prickled at his neglect.

"Are you alright, Princess Gemma?"

I reluctantly tore my scanning gaze away from the crowds, which Aiden clearly wasn't amongst, and forced a smile for Prince Liam. "Just admiring the room. It's lovely."

He smirked, and mischievousness filled his piercing stare. "I see. Looking for someone in particular in this lovely room?"

I sighed in defeat. "I was hoping to see my friend before the luncheon."

"A female friend or a male friend?"

My cheeks warmed. "Merely a good friend."

"And you feel *he's* abandoned you?"

I tightened my jaw, clenching it to stave off the embarrassing tears already gathering, my exhaustion from my late night making me overemotional. Certainly princesses didn't blubber in public. "He didn't exactly promise to meet me. I'm sure he has a good reason…" But my words did little to abate the tightening of my heart. Why weren't men ever there when you needed them?

I didn't hear Prince Liam's next several comments or even notice when he finally excused himself. When he left, I seized the opportunity to escape into a corner and take several steadying breaths. There I spotted another familiar face. I gaped at Rosie's cousin, the noble relation who always caused her to bristle with family pride; from what I remembered, he now worked in Sortileya's trade negotiations.

"Sir Gavin?"

He turned at the sound of his name and blinked at me before faint recognition filled his expression. He came over. "I remember you. Rosie's friend, right?"

"Yes, Eileen." I gave my real name in a whisper. "But due to circumstances beyond my control, everyone believes me to be Princess Gemma. Don't ask. And you're Rosie's cousin?"

"Princess Gemma, huh?" Gavin smirked. "And Rosie and I aren't exactly cousins. Is that what she's told you?"

Only countless times. With the way she went on about 'dear cousin Gavin,' I'd assumed the relationship was close, both by blood and friendship. "She has. Are you two even related?"

"In a sense. We're fourth cousins..." He scrunched his forehead, considering. "...twice removed, I think, although with the way she clings to me and milks me for information whenever I visit other relatives in Arador, I think she'd like the relationship to be closer."

Unsurprising. Leave it to Rosie to lay more kinship to a distantly related nobleman than actually existed. Such a classic Rosie gesture made me miss her more than ever. Would I ever survive this experience in order to see her and Mother again? The thought made the first task feel more daunting than ever. In my escalating anxiety, the crowds and walls seemed to close in on me, suffocating.

My increasing discomfort was lost on Gavin, who was looking at me with renewed interest. "What are you doing here?" His eyes widened as if the answer to his own question had just occurred to him, and his grin widened. "Oh, you're *Aiden's* Eileen."

My astonishment grew, as did my pleasure to be referred to as *Aiden's Eileen*. "You know Aiden?"

"Quite well. We've met on and off over the years and have become good friends." His stare became suspicious. "And how do *you* know him?"

"Certainly you know the answer to that, considering it sounds as if he's talked about me." A tiny flutter of pleasure filled my heart at the thought.

Gavin gave a rather strange smile. "He has. Quite often, in fact. When Aiden told me of the woman who's besotted him, I never would have expected he was referring to you. I should have realized when Rosie started milking me for information about Aiden that she was doing it on someone's behalf. My apologies I lied to her and pretended I didn't know him; I wasn't comfortable sharing anything about my friend to someone who's a huge gossip." He looked around at the surrounding nobles. "You've become entangled in quite the mess."

So Gavin knew of that, too. It was somewhat reassuring that should anything happen to me today before I could post my note to Mother, someone would at least be able to share my fate with her.

I scanned the room once more, still hoping for Aiden to emerge from the crowd. "Considering you two seem to be good friends, care to enlighten me on where he is? Why isn't he at court? Doesn't he want to witness what is sure to be a spectacle?"

"Of course not. He loathes court and avoids it whenever possible."

"And he's allowing this dislike to prevent him from attending when I need to see him?" I sighed. "Some friend he is."

Gavin frowned sympathetically. His pity only made me

feel worse. "He knew you'd be upset with him. He almost came just for you."

"But he didn't." And none of Gavin's prepared excuses would be enough to change that fact.

"No, he didn't, but he has a very good reason as to why."

I folded my arms across my chest in an attempt to smother my disappointment. "And this reason is more important than anything else, including me?"

"No," Gavin said. "He's told me enough about your relationship for me to know that nothing is more important to him than you."

Strange how Gavin didn't seem scandalized at the thought that Aiden cared more for me than his fiancée. Despite knowing it was wrong, my heart lifted at the idea and I silently cursed it for being so easily swayed. "He has a funny way of showing it."

Gavin offered a wry smile. "True, but perhaps he's showing it in the best way he can. He's never been much of a gentleman."

As he spoke, he swiveled around to seize two glasses of champagne from a passing footman. He offered me one. I shook my head. With a shrug he kept both, sipping from the first.

"Since I've found you, may I offer Aiden's most sincere apologies for not being able to wish you good luck in person and for any additional distress his actions have caused you. He feels sorry having to beg forgiveness from you yet again, especially so recently after his apology for involving you in this in the first place."

Something flashed in his eyes, a secret, as if he had the answers I so desperately sought. "Do you know the reason he did it?" For I sensed there was more to Aiden's motive than he'd shared.

"I do, but…"

I scowled. "But you're not going to tell me."

He shook his head. "No, I'm not. What kind of friend would I be if I so easily betrayed Aiden's trust?"

I harrumphed, frustrated, but did my best to reign in my emotions. I was still trapped amongst a crowd of nobility and thus had a part to play, as unwilling as I was to perform. "I'm sure he expects me to grant my forgiveness, but you'll have to disappoint him, especially since he sent you to do his dirty work."

"My apology is merely a precursor to his own, for he also wanted me to assure you that a proper apology is coming. Best of luck, Eileen...I mean, *Princess Gemma*."

Gavin winked before departing with a bow just as the parlor doors swung open and lunch was announced. All thoughts of Aiden immediately fled as I forced myself to concentrate on the overwhelming task before me: fooling the entire court and the visiting royalty that I was one of them.

I followed the excited crowd into the dining room. Although I'd already dined here many times, the opulent room now seemed more foreboding. The light spilling through the windows did little to abate the terror smothering me or the nerves knotting my stomach. Would this be where I finally exposed myself for who I truly was?

I shakily took my seat at my usual place beside the Dracerian royalty. Princess Elodie immediately leaned towards my ear. "It seems strange that our first test is dining, something we've already done many times before."

But I'd already noticed several notable differences. The place setting had far more dishes and cutlery than our previous meals, meaning we'd be engaging in one with multiple courses. My gaze settled on each piece of silverware in turn. Aiden's late-night tutoring had extended to the proper use of each, but that had been long after midnight when exhaustion had begun to press against my senses, making the memory of that particular lesson a blur.

"Are you *glaring* at the silverware, Gemma?" Princess Rheanna whispered.

I rapidly raised my gaze in time to see Prince Liam pick up his knife and examine it with a frown. "Can you blame her? It does seem rather offensive."

He offered me a reassuring grin and cheerful wink. I gave him a grateful smile before glancing towards the other side of the room, where several stuffy, elderly noblemen sat along the wall, portable writing desks perched in their laps for notes, which many were already scribbling. My stomach clenched.

Princess Aveline watched them thoughtfully. "Already taking notes. They must have observed our entrance to see if we walked with the necessary poise befitting a true queen."

My mind scrambled back to how I'd walked to my seat. Had I done so with the proper posture and graceful manner Aiden had taught me? I couldn't remember. My hand fluttered to the necklace Aiden had given me this morning as I took several steadying breaths. No matter what happened during this luncheon, Aiden believed I had poise. Some of my unease abated at the thought.

Before the meal began, the doors suddenly swung open and everyone rose as an elderly, regal man with hard black eyes strode in with all the pomp and circumstance befitting a royal. He sat at the head of the table, and with a wave of his ring-laden hand, we all took our seats.

I tried to ignore the piercing stare from His Majesty as the first course began and a waiting footman placed a light salad at my place. I nibbled my lip as I looked at the many forks before copying Princess Elodie by selecting the farthest one on the left. I stabbed a big forkful before remembering Aiden's instructions to eat with small bites. Several bites later, I realized I'd forgotten to put my napkin on my lap, and a few bites after that I noticed I'd been slouching slightly. I immediately corrected my posture and cast a worried glance towards the stern-looking noblemen watching me with sharp attention. It appeared my slip-up hadn't gone unnoticed. At least I'd managed to avoid spills.

"We should converse with charming smiles and witty comments," Princess Rheanna leaned over to whisper. "Surely a proper queen isn't expected to be so solemn at state functions."

Princess Aveline cocked an elegant brow. "Are you still trying?"

"Of course not; I just want to prove I wasn't discarded simply by being unsuitable." But despite her words she blushed.

Princess Elodie promptly launched into this new plan with enthusiasm and started up a dull conversation about foreign relations, keeping her voice at the proper volume and inflections. Despite the tedious topic, the others' smiles never faltered. Goodness, they were so proper. Was royalty all about appearances? Surely the Dark Prince wanted more than a wife who was the portrait-perfect image of a queen.

I pretended to listen to the conversation swirling around me but didn't feel brave enough to contribute myself, especially when I was thoroughly enjoying the delicious salad, seasoned with herbs, berries, seeds, and a light coating of dressing. I hadn't realized just how hungry I was. I was nearly halfway through when Princess Elodie leaned towards my ear.

"Remember not to eat it all."

I frowned. "Why not? I'm hungry."

"You'll appear gluttonous."

"That's ridiculous."

Prince Liam snorted while Princess Elodie's eyes widened

at my loud-whispered outburst. I sighed and obediently set down my fork in the proper way Aiden had shown me to signify I was finished. I watched sadly as the salad was whisked away by an attentive footman and I was presented with a bowl of strawberry soup. I took as dainty a sip as I could and managed not to draw attention to myself. Never had so many bowls of soup been eaten so quietly; no one made a slurp.

Several courses followed, and I was soon quite stuffed and exhausted from eating with so much focus. I seemed to do well enough until I picked up my bread during the fifth course to scoop up some gravy. Another mistake followed in the next course when a spoonful of my sorbet plopped right into my lap. Thank goodness my napkin caught it so I didn't ruin my dress—another one borrowed from Princess Elodie, this one a rose silk.

She unfortunately noticed, as did the king. After my gravy-scooping error—which she'd sweetly pointed out to me—Princess Elodie scarcely tore her attention away from me, seeming genuinely concerned for my performance. As I tried to subtly clean up my fallen sorbet, she leaned over.

"Do relax, Gemma; you're far too nervous. Remember the essential trait of all royalty: *confidence*."

I took a steadying breath and nodded. The meal was almost over. I could do this.

After the bowls of sorbet were removed, I resisted the impulse to lean back in my seat with a sigh of relief that I'd survived. Surely that had been the final course. My hopes were dashed as a tall goblet of water to wash down our meal was placed in front of me. I picked it up and drank several gulps. It was cool and refreshing, with a slight lemon taste.

The superficial cheery conversation suddenly ceased from my end of the table, followed by several soft gasps. I lowered the goblet to see that no one else had drunk from theirs but were instead using them to daintily wash their hands at the conclusion of the meal.

I choked on the water and began coughing, my cheeks burning.

"Did you just drink the water from the finger bowl?" Princess Aveline asked in a scandalized whisper that carried several seats down to those who hadn't witnessed the spectacle. Their eyes—along with the sharp attention of the judging noblemen and unfortunately the king—snapped to me. My already warm face flamed.

Prince Liam acted immediately. He seized his own goblet and drank the entire thing in several gulps. "Finger bowl water is my favorite kind, particularly when flavored with just the right amount of lemon." He set it down with an exaggerated *clunk*. Princess Elodie pressed her napkin daintily over her lips to muffle her giggle while Princess Aveline gaped at him.

"Liam, you know perfectly well you're not supposed to—" But before she could give a proper scolding, Princess Rheanna took a tentative sip from her own goblet.

"That's the spirit, sister," Prince Liam said. She gave me a small, reassuring smile while Princess Aveline sniffed in disapproval.

Warm gratitude washed over me at their kindness, but the sweetness of their gesture melted away after a stolen glance at the frowning king and watching noblemen revealed their disapproving scowls; clearly they hadn't been fooled by Prince Liam and Princess Rheanna's attempts to help me cover up my mistake. My stomach knotted. When the final course of fruit was placed in front of me, my appetite—which had already begun vanishing several courses ago—left completely, replaced with churning nausea. Had my mistake been enough to expose this charade?

~

IT WAS a relief to finally return to the sanctity of my room. I collapsed in my vanity chair and pressed my forehead in my hands as I tried to suppress the memories from lunch. It had been going fairly well...until the end. Why had I made such a stupid mistake?

When I managed to emerge from my swirling thoughts, I noticed the note on my vanity. My heart fluttered when I glimpsed Aiden's signature.

Dearest Eileen, I promised last night to see you today, and I fully intend to keep that promise. I'm eager to hear how your decorum showcase went. If the idea pleases you, would you please accompany me on a stroll through the gardens after lunch? I'll wait all afternoon. Aiden

All my earlier annoyances that he hadn't braved court in order to wish me luck this morning melted away. I reread Aiden's note three times, each time my girlish grin growing wider. I tucked the note between the pages of my sketchbook and hurried through the corridors.

It was a beautiful afternoon in late spring. Aside from my attempts to get past the gate, I hadn't had an opportunity to spend time in the gardens. The aerial view of the royal grounds from my window had scarcely captured their splendor. Flowers in a myriad of colors and types were planted in ornate patterns, and the manicured shrubs and hedges were arranged in sophisticated artistry. I strolled the cobblestone pathways in awe, allowing the beauty and the blossoms' perfume to caress my senses. Beyond the gardens lay my beloved Forest. I stared at the majestic trees, my old friends. It seemed like forever since I'd last been cocooned within their familiar branches.

"I love the wonder filling your eyes. I knew you'd love the gardens." Aiden emerged from behind a hedge and my heart swelled to see him. I offered a shy smile before wrinkling my nose in confusion.

"Why were you hiding?"

"I have my reasons. But now that you're here, I have no need to do so any longer." He nodded to someone behind me and I turned around in time to see Alastar—who had as usual been trailing me—bow and stroll back the way we'd come.

Aiden offered his arm and I wound mine through his, clinging to his elbow more tightly than necessary. He smiled sweetly down at me before escorting me down a secluded path, as if he wanted us to remain out of sight. That tickled my suspicions and also reminded me of my earlier grievance.

"I was hoping to see you this morning."

Remorse twisted his expression, so sincere I felt my hurt fade away. "I'm deeply sorry I couldn't see you. I shall tell you my reasons why all in due time."

My hand fluttered to my neck, where his gift still resided. "You did send a token, so I knew I wasn't entirely forgotten. Thank you for the necklace. I've never owned anything so lovely."

"I'm so glad you like it. I'd promise to spoil you with many more lavish gifts in the future, but I know you wouldn't be swayed by such a gesture."

"That's true. I prefer fewer treasures so I can better cherish them."

He gently squeezed my hand. "It's one of the reasons you're special." He gently led me down a crocus-lined path and sat us down on the rim of a marble fountain. "Now please don't keep me in suspense a moment longer. How did your first task go?"

I reached my hand back to trail my fingers through the cool water. "I survived, but unfortunately it wasn't without several mishaps."

Aiden's lips twitched. "Define *mishaps*. Did you use the wrong fork?"

I studied the laughter already filling his eyes. "Why is that amusing?"

"Because formal dinners are rather dull affairs, and attending one with you and your charming errors would undoubtedly make them more interesting."

My smile escaped. "Prepare yourself, for it's rather ghastly: my careful posture frequently faltered, I used my roll to scoop up the gravy, a spoonful of sorbet fell into my lap… as you can see, I was plagued with all sorts of catastrophes."

Aiden's twitching lips broke into a full smile. "Come now, that's not that horrible. Please don't be distressed." He reached out and caressed my cheek. I instinctively leaned against his touch.

"I haven't told you the worst part."

His grin became wicked. "There's more?"

I buried my face in my hands. "I drank the finger-bowl water."

A stunned silence followed my confession before he burst into laughter. I snapped my head up to glare at him, but it was hard to put much force behind it with the way his eyes lit up and the sound of his warm laughter washed over me.

His laughter faded but his expression remained aglow. "My apologies for failing to mention the finger-bowl water. I didn't even think it necessary." He chuckled again.

"Stop laughing; it's not funny." I playfully splashed him with water from the fountain and he caught my wet hand to press a kiss to the back of it. All his amusement faded as his expression softened.

"I'm only laughing because your faux pas reminds me how delightful you are, one of many reasons I care for you. Please believe me that I hate the thought that you were

197

embarrassed." He ran his fingers through my hair and the gesture helped calm my skittering heart.

"My mistake wasn't charming, and it certainly didn't go unnoticed, even though the Dracerian royals tried to cover for me."

His caressing hand paused and he cocked an eyebrow. "Did they? How so?"

"Prince Liam made an exaggerated show of drinking the entire goblet, and even Princess Rheanna took a sip so I wasn't the only one to have done so."

"Princess Rheanna did that?" His brow furrowed. "Why would she…" He trailed off with a perplexed frown before his expression smoothed over and he resumed stroking my hair. "I'm so pleased you have people looking out for you when I can't. How are you feeling now that your ordeal is over?"

The embarrassment knotting my stomach was still acute. I shook my head and leaned against him, pleased when he wrapped his arms around me and held me close.

"You're trembling. What's wrong?"

"I made so many mistakes and the king kept watching me suspiciously. I'm going to get caught, I just know I am."

"Of course not. I promise. Please don't worry. I doubt you'll be discounted simply for bad table manners. And since you don't want the prince to pick you, losing any points in this silly competition shouldn't matter."

"I'm more concerned about a lifelong sojourn in the royal dungeons."

He enfolded my hands in his. "I promise I won't allow anything to happen to you. Please believe me."

"How can you be so sure?"

"I'm a member of the court with some influence. I'll use all the persuasion I have in order to protect the one who means the most to me."

I searched his dark eyes, so earnest as they seeped into mine. I wanted to trust him, but I still wasn't sure I was brave enough to allow myself to. Strangely, I felt more inclined to open my heart when Aiden began playing with my fingers.

"Have you been given your next task?" he asked as he attentively traced each of my knuckles. I shuddered at the sensation.

"It won't come until after dinner. Have you heard anything about it?"

He sighed. "Unfortunately not. I wish I knew so I could be better prepared on how to help you. I want you to do well."

I slowly pulled my hands from his, wary once more. "Are you really so eager for me to win?"

He cupped my cheek. "You believe I want to force you into an unwanted match?"

"I was under the impression you thought marrying a prince would be just what a common girl has always dreamed of."

"I admit I did, but I should have known you better than that."

"While Rosie has always dreamed of marrying a prince, I've never wanted such a thing," I said. "I love my life and don't need a title and wealth in order to be happy."

Tenderness filled his eyes. "Yet another of many reasons why you're so special. But"—his gaze became earnest—"do you think you could ever learn to be happy in such a life?"

I sighed. "Perhaps. It'd undoubtedly take some getting used to."

He frowned, as if my answer had disappointed him. He helped me to my feet and tucked my hand back in his arm. We resumed strolling, turning onto a path that twisted through plots of colorful primroses. "I know I possess the wealth and title you abhor, but if I weren't engaged, would you consider..."

My breath hooked and I froze. "What are you asking?"

He blushed, eyes shy. "I'm no longer betrothed. It took some doing, but I ended my engagement after our picnic at the waterfall, meaning I could now court you...if you'd have me. I wanted to tell you before now, but the right opportunity never presented itself."

"I—" I wasn't sure what to say. My heart pounded deafeningly, making it difficult to sort through the jumble of thoughts and emotions swirling through me.

"Is there a reason for your hesitation?" he asked gently. "Are you in love with someone else?"

I shook my head. "No, there's no one." And with the wounds still scabbing my heart, I could never allow there to be...while at the same time my scarred heart yearned for him. I'd forever regret it if I lost this opportunity because I allowed my fears to overcome me. Could I ever be brave enough to choose him?

"Then what's stopping you?"

"I—" I had no reason to give without admitting my greatest fears that choosing him would cause me to one day end up like Mother, abandoned and alone. "I just can't."

He took both my hands in his. "But you said you felt something for me." His tone was pleading, as if he desperately hoped my feelings hadn't changed.

I ached to deny the feelings I'd shared when under the truth cake's enchantment, but I couldn't—not with the adoring way he looked at me and the beautiful way he made me feel. Heat pulsed up my arms from his touch curling my fingertips.

The fears I'd been suppressing my entire life struggled to reach the surface again. I was so tired of this fight, of allowing my fears to rule me and dictate my choices. I wanted to choose Aiden. Couldn't I allow myself to have him, especially now that he was available?

"I'm afraid," I whispered. "A heart is too precious to risk, especially when a heart is so easy to break."

His expression softened into sweet concern as he searched my own. "You're afraid of having your heart broken? Is that why you've been resisting me?"

Mutely, I nodded. He sighed.

"My poor dear. What's happened to you, Eileen?"

My lip trembled and a single tear escaped to streak my cheek. Aiden gently wiped it away, a gesture so achingly sweet I nearly unraveled completely. He stepped forward, closing the distance between us and embracing me. He lightly traced around my eyes with his fingertip.

"There's pain in your eyes. Who hurt you?"

I squeezed my eyes shut and shook my head, not ready to share that heartache with him. Yet despite my best efforts, I couldn't prevent the process that was happening now, for my heart had been vulnerable and available to be stolen ever since I'd met Aiden. I feared he was now precariously close to possessing it completely.

Aiden drew me close to hold me once more. "It's alright if you can't tell me, and if you're not ready to move forward, we'll wait. We'll go as slowly as you need."

"What if I'm never ready?"

He began to rub my back in soothing circles. "I'll wait forever. So please don't be afraid. I won't hurt you. Please trust me."

I shook my head. "I want to, but I can't. That's something I cannot give."

He sighed, clearly disappointed. "Might I prove myself to you? Please, Eileen."

I tipped my head back and stared into his dark gaze boring into mine, pleading for me to give him a chance.

My hand curled around the note I'd written Mother before the luncheon. I toyed with the edges, considering, before I shakily pulled it from my sleeve. "Please find a way to send this to my mother in Arador," I said. "I can't bear the thought of her worry ever since my disappearance."

He hesitated before he took it. "I will."

He withdrew then, taking his warmth and security with him, and despite the sunshine, I shivered. Aiden tucked a strand of hair behind my ear. "I'll see you after you receive the second task."

He kissed my hand and started to pull away, but my fingers tightened around his, keeping him near me, needing him. While my fears prevented me from holding on to him, my feelings for him—which grew with each interaction— made it impossible to completely pull away.

CHAPTER 17

I paced the floor as I awaited Aiden's arrival, clutching the next task that I'd reread so many times I now had it memorized:

A princess possesses the knowledge necessary to rule—both a well-rounded education and an understanding of royal life, relationships, and expectations. A princess with wisdom is one who can better govern as queen.

This task felt far more daunting than the last, for appearances were far easier to feign than knowledge. How could I cram an entire lifetime of education into a single night? Even with Aiden's help it felt impossible...assuming he'd come. Not that I doubted he would, but the hour was growing late and he had yet to arrive.

Minutes dragged by. I practically wore holes in my satin slippers as I continued to pace, eying the door each time I passed. I frowned at the clock on the mantle. It was well after ten. What if he never came?

I nearly sobbed with relief when a knock sounded at the door. "Come in."

Aiden stepped inside with his usual warm smile and bow in greeting. I gaped at him. Despite my doubt, he'd come.

He tilted his head, brow puckered. "What's wrong?"

"You came." The words came out strangled.

He gave me my favorite crooked grin. "Of course I did. I promised I would."

I swallowed what would certainly become a spout of embarrassing tears. "You came." Even repeating the words didn't make them feel real.

His bewildered expression softened to understanding. "You were worried I wouldn't?"

I twisted a strand of my dark hair around my finger and avoided his eyes. Now that he was here I felt foolish for having doubted him. I lowered my eyes, saying nothing. He closed the distance between us and cupped my cheek, tilting my face so our eyes met. By the tenderness filling his expression, I could tell he read the words ingrained on my heart that I couldn't express.

He stroked my cheek. "I will always come. I promise."

I closed my eyes and allowed his words to wash over me. I ached to believe him. Little by little it was becoming easier.

Aiden's hand fell away, sliding down my arm until he reached the task still clutched in my hand. He frowned as he read it. "This is admittedly better than the last one, but it's strange that the king only seems concerned with finding a candidate for queen rather than a wife for the prince."

"Focusing on finding a queen seems logical considering the king's duty to prioritize the happiness of his kingdom."

"But couldn't both be achieved?" He shook his head. "I suppose it doesn't matter now; we can't change the test, we can only prepare you for it."

I sighed. "It's more impossible than the last. How can I gain all the required knowledge of a queen in a single night?"

"That would indeed be impossible," Aiden said. "But that's not going to be our approach. Instead, we'll discern what will likely be asked of you and give you enough knowledge that you can feign that you know more than you actually do."

While even that seemed overwhelming, for the first time all evening a flutter of hope filled me. "Do you really believe I can do this?"

"I have no doubts. I'll tutor you in all you need to know, even if it takes all night. I'll return shortly." He kissed my hand, but when he started to pull away I didn't let go.

"Where are you going?"

He enfolded my hand securely between his. "I need to get some books from the library. I promise I'll return soon."

I nodded, not trusting myself to speak, and when he dropped my hand I had to clench it to keep myself from reaching for him again. I didn't tear my gaze away from him as he backed slowly from the room. Even after the door closed behind him, I couldn't make myself stir. I stared at the door and waited.

He was gone nearly half an hour, but I refused to move. I'd have stood there all night; I'd waited far longer for Father.

Aiden's knock finally echoed through the room once more. I released my pent-up breath. "Come in."

Aiden stepped inside, his arms laden with books. He paused when he spotted me and furrowed his brow. "Have you moved from that spot the entire time I was gone?"

I bit my lip and didn't answer. Compassion filled his expression.

"I'm sorry I took so long to return." Aiden set the books on the desk and motioned me over. "Would you like to see what I've brought you?"

I managed to unthaw and slowly approach. He wrapped his arm around my waist and lifted the first book in the stack. "We'll only cover the basics in all the general areas I imagine you'll be tested in," he said. "First: the royal genealogies."

I frowned at the thick volume. "We're reading that entire book in a single night?"

He chuckled. "That would be dangerous, considering it's an excellent cure for insomnia—although sleeping is undoubtedly far more entertaining than reading this. We'll only go over the living royalty in Sortileya and the four surrounding kingdoms, along with notable historical royals within Sortileya's own royal history. From there we'll move on to other necessary subjects."

He picked up another book from the stack: *A Basic Guide to Diplomacy.*

I groaned. "I don't think I can do this."

"Of course you can. You're smart and perfectly capable."

Already a headache pulsed behind my eyes, making me feel anything but. I took a steadying breath in an attempt to quell my escalating panic. "It's not about being smart or capable; there's just so much knowledge expected of a queen. I doubt my own limited education covered subjects the Dark Prince desires his wife to know."

"I wouldn't be so sure," Aiden said. "An educated wife doesn't guarantee a happy marriage, for memorizing facts doesn't determine the kindness of one's heart, which you have in abundance."

I warmed at his words. "Really?"

He nodded. "Knowledge can always be acquired. I consider your sweet nature far more valuable. Remember: the Forest led you here, making your presence in this competition no accident. You can do this."

His dark eyes were so earnest and sincere, radiating his belief in me. I took a wavering breath and nodded. He stroked my cheek.

"It's a good thing you're not *trying* to win the competition. Imagine how much more anxious you'd be if your performance determined whether or not you could wed your true love."

He was right. I wasn't trying to win; I only needed to do well enough not to get caught. The anxious knots tightening my stomach gradually loosened. I managed a smile.

He tucked a loose strand of hair behind my ear. "Are you feeling better?"

"I will after this is all over."

"It will be soon. Now, shall we begin?" He took my hand and led me to the settee in front of the hearth, where we settled with our books.

Over the course of several hours, we went through the facts Aiden felt essential for a princess to know in all manner of subjects. Despite the cramming of so much information, the experience was still surprisingly pleasant. Although the subjects were extremely dry, Aiden was a fun study partner. He told dramatic stories to help me remember the names of both famous and infamous royals and the dates of important events. From there he summarized even the most daunting subjects in simple terms. Diplomacy in particular seemed extremely complex until Aiden broke it down.

"Diplomacy consists of flattering the one you're negotiating with in order for them to give you what you want, which is easiest to accomplish if you make it sound like it's in their best interest. It's also wise to ensure they appear to be in the right—even when they're clearly not—and to point out all the positives of the contract while skimming over the negatives, but never in a way that's dishonest. Simply... misdirection." His lips twitched as he eyed me. "You're smiling, Eileen. Why?"

I tried to mash my lips together in order to hide it but failed. "It sounds...conniving."

"Oh, it is," Aiden said. "But admittedly rather effective."

From diplomacy and royal history, we moved on to the geography of the surrounding kingdoms and the basics of foreign relations and trade—particularly in regards to Sortileya's economy—before finally ending the extended study session on rhetoric. As Aiden taught me, I marveled at his intellect and warmed at his praises when he complimented my own.

"And finally," Aiden concluded as we finally finished, "if you find you don't know something, it's better to admit it than make a guess and get it wrong. A ruler is praised more for humility than for a poor decision made in ignorance." He grinned and leaned back on his elbows, signifying the end of the lesson. "Congratulations, you've survived another tutoring session."

"I did." Amazing. I managed an exhausted giggle. "My head feels about to explode, but I feel much more confident about tomorrow. Thank you for your help."

His soft gaze penetrated mine, making me feel turned inside out. "As always, it was my pleasure."

We stared at one another for a reverent moment, the spell between us broken only by the chime of the clock. Aiden glanced at it with obvious reluctance. It was after three in the morning. "It's rather late. Shall we call it an evening?"

"Oh please, let's not." Despite the exhaustion pressing against my senses, I didn't want the evening to end. I'd never been with someone where hours melted away to form a single beautiful moment that, no matter how long it was, could never be long enough.

Aiden smiled and relit the candle on the side table that was nearly spent before twisting back towards me, sitting cross-legged so closely our knees nearly touched. The candle's flickering glow lit his handsome face.

"We shall stay up a little while longer, if that is your wish."

Aiden scooted closer, his touch going to my hair, where he pulled out my hairpins. My dark hair cascaded around my face.

He gently parted my curtain of hair. I held my breath as he traced his fingertip along the chain of my necklace and tugged it from beneath my collar. He stared at my locket before glancing back up at me, seeking permission. I slowly nodded.

Aiden opened the locket and held it in his palm, staring at Father's portrait. He traced the edge of its heart shape as he raised his questioning eyes to mine; it was the key that finally opened the stronghold protecting the secrets I couldn't keep any longer.

"Father gave me this necklace as a farewell gift," I began shakily. "He was only going to be gone for a few days, he said. He told me he loved me and promised he'd return." Tears burned my eyes. "But he lied. He never did."

Aiden's eyes softened as he reached out and wiped away the tears already staining my cheeks. "Oh, Eileen."

"He lied," I stuttered. "He left. He said he loved me, but they were only words. I trusted him and he—"

A shudder raked over me, but now that I'd started, I couldn't stop sharing the memory I'd kept buried deep for so many years.

"He broke Mother's heart. He broke mine. I don't want to experience that pain again. I can't. It's too agonizing." And finally my deep-rooted fear tumbled out, unable to be contained any longer. "Was there something wrong with me that caused him to leave?"

"No, Eileen, of course not."

"Then why did he? My own father didn't want me, and thus no one will ever—" My sobs escaped and Aiden enfolded me in a warm hug. I nestled close, burying my tear-streaked face against his chest. Aiden rubbed my back as he rocked me, whispering soothingly.

"I'm so sorry he left you, Eileen. But please believe me, there's nothing wrong with you." He paused. "I'm beginning to better understand your hesitancy in getting close to me."

I clung to him, hoping the gesture would keep him with me, for the longer I was with him, the more I realized how much I needed him. "What if you're wrong? What if you decide to leave me, too?"

"Impossible," Aiden murmured. "I could never leave you. Are you certain your father meant to stay away?"

"No. And not knowing for sure is the worst part."

"Then perhaps he didn't. Maybe something happened to him."

"It doesn't matter," I said. "All that matters is that he's gone."

Aiden nodded and nestled against my hair. "How many years ago was it?"

"Ten," I said. "He went to the capital to trade—or so he claimed—and never returned." I released a pent-up sigh, exhausted from all the emotions raging through me. Aiden's comforting hold tightened around me, enfolding me in a cocoon of security.

"I understand why you're hesitant to open your heart. When people leave—whether willingly or not—they leave a hole in our hearts that makes it difficult to trust anyone with something so precious again." Pain twisted his expression as he lowered his eyes.

"What is it, Aiden?"

He hesitated. "Mother died while giving birth to my sister, something I've never forgiven my sister for, nor my mother. Now that I'm older, I understand it wasn't Mother's fault, but at times I still feel angry towards them. Mother left me, and the hole in my heart from her leaving can never fully be healed."

My own heart broke for him. I rested my hand on top of his. "I'm so sorry, Aiden."

He stared at our touching hands before flipping his over to stroke my palm. "Nothing was ever the same after Mother died. I became hardened and withdrawn, pushing everyone away in my pain. I thought it easier to be alone than to face the heartbreak at losing someone so close to me again."

"You haven't pushed me away," I said softly.

He finally raised his gaze to mine. Whatever fortress protecting his secrets that used to guard his eyes now lay crumbled.

"I tried to at first, but the closer we became, the more I realized that there's something stronger than my fear of losing you—and that's loving you." He took both my hands and held them against his chest so I could feel his beating heart. "I'm finding that the more pieces of my heart I give away, the more it heals. I've never met anyone who makes me feel the way you make me feel." He dropped his gaze. "I'm hoping you feel the same way towards me…or have your feelings changed?"

I stared at the flickering candle, its dancing flame causing shadows to waltz across the walls. My feelings *had* changed, but instead of fading away, they'd only strengthened. I was tired of fighting against these emotions. I pressed my hand against my heart, as if the added pressure could somehow contain the swirling pain, a pain that became more acute the harder I fought against my heart's desire. This constant battle was too wearying. Could I allow myself to finally choose this path—to choose him?

I ached to tell him my deep feelings—that there was nothing I wanted more than him—but my fear still continued to hold me back. I hated how paralyzing it was, the power I'd allowed it to hold over me. How could I become brave enough to choose Aiden no matter the potential risks that came from a future together?

He cradled my face, so incredibly gently, a gesture that nearly undid me completely. "I know you're frightened. I am too, but my fears are nothing to the thought of living without you. Don't you need me as much as I need you?"

"I do need you," I whispered. "That's why I'm terrified of losing you."

"You won't if you let me in. I know the future is uncertain—everybody's is—but I promise to always be there for you. You're so brave, Eileen. Can't you trust this path?"

My lip trembled. "I've protected my heart far too long. What if I'm not strong enough to ever give it away completely?"

"You are," he said. "You must believe that."

"Can you help me be strong enough?" I whispered.

His gaze caressed my face as he thought for a moment until an idea lit his eyes. "May I have tonight's payment?"

The suddenness of his question shattered the mood. "What do you want?"

His hand released mine to trail up my arm and cradle my necklace in his palm. He stared at it long and hard before slowly looking up. "I want this necklace."

I gasped. No, he couldn't really be asking…I searched his eyes, trying to discern whether or not he was serious. He was. I yanked out of his arms. "You want the last gift my father ever gave me?"

"You don't have to give it," he said gently. "But I'm asking for it."

I clutched my locket protectively against my heart, so tightly it dug into my palm. He waited patiently, his dark eyes intense as he peeled back my secrets one by one, accepting each one, accepting *me*, just as I was. He now knew all of me—my brokenness, my fears, my lack of trust. He saw my raw, fiercely protected heart—one I was currently too afraid to give to him, unable to bear the agony should he break it—and yet he still looked at me with as much adoration as always.

He slowly held out his hand. I whimpered and clutched my locket even tighter, holding on to the symbol of Father's betrayal, of his broken trust and the pain his leaving had caused me.

But gradually my fingers loosened around the metal heart and I slowly unclasped the locket for the first time since receiving it. I searched Aiden's eyes, full of such sweet understanding.

"Can you let it go?" he whispered, and in that moment, I realized what he was really asking of me. He didn't want the locket but something far more difficult to relinquish.

I shakily dropped my locket in a coil in his palm. His fingers enclosed it before he tucked it away, taking it forever. Giving it to him somehow removed the burden I'd been carrying for years, leaving me feeling lighter and freer. My tears escaped, blurring his awed expression.

"You gave it to me."

I lowered my eyes, unable to speak. He pulled me close and held me. I snuggled deeper into his embrace, relishing in the feelings filling my now-free heart. When I'd initially resisted walking this path it was because I'd expected it to lead only to heartache, but after finally letting go of the past, I felt nothing but wonderful feelings. I'd never felt so safe, so warm, and so cherished. I never wanted Aiden to let me go.

But eventually he did, pulling away with obvious reluctance. "Thank you, Eileen. I know that was difficult for you, but I'm hoping that by letting go, you'll finally be able to heal." He pressed his lips to my tear-stained cheek. "I'll see you tomorrow."

He released me and left. I stared after him, my fingers stroking my now-empty throat where my locket had once resided before my touch lingered on Aiden's pearl necklace. It was as if a huge weight had been lifted from my heart, and for the first time since Father had left, I felt...hope.

CHAPTER 18

The stern noblemen—particularly the attending king—watched us through narrowed eyes, as if trying to discern whether or not any of us were suitable to become the wife of the Dark Prince and thus the future Queen of Sortileya. I fought to maintain the proper posture expected of a royal as I sat with the royalty of Draceria, a difficult task under the heated scrutiny. Prince Liam had informed us in a whisper that the watching noblemen were the king's most trusted advisors and were thus well-versed in royal knowledge.

They began the public interview, asking each of the two dozen princesses and noblewomen a question in turn, covering the topics Aiden had gone over in our late-night study session. I perched on the edge of my seat, clutching my hands in my lap, fighting not to fidget. Princess Elodie rested her hand on my bouncing knee.

"Do relax, Gemma."

I took a wavering breath, but it did little to still my pounding heart. I reminded myself once again that I only had to do well enough not to get caught as an imposter, for I had no desire to marry the Dark Prince, nor was there any danger of my being chosen.

"I'm surprised by the nature of these tasks," I said. "A proper, well-informed queen doesn't ensure a happy marriage." It had been Aiden's primary complaint as last night's studying had worn on.

"You know that marriage has little to do with love amongst the upper class," Princess Rheanna said. "It's all about alliances and power."

I glanced at Prince Liam, who'd been alternating between avoiding looking at his own intended and sending Princess Lavena skewering glares, which she eagerly returned. I studied Princess Rheanna sitting beside me, the embodiment of a princess trained from birth to be a future queen. It seemed unfathomable that the Dark Prince had rejected her...unless there was something more he was looking for.

"Then why did the Dark Prince break off his engagement with you?" I hesitantly asked. "It would appear he desires something more in a match than a proper royal."

Princess Rheanna's manner hardened. "He obviously found me lacking. He's quite particular."

"Obviously not *that* particular, else he'd have more involvement in the competition. The fact that he doesn't is undoubtedly strange..." Princess Elodie frowned thoughtfully before resting a gentle hand on her sister's arm. "Please don't think your broken engagement is through any fault of your own."

Princess Rheanna jerked away, the pain in her eyes intensifying. "We mustn't discuss it now. It's improper to whisper when we're expected to pay attention." She turned her rigid expression towards the questioning advisors.

Princess Elodie sighed as she leaned towards my ear. "Unfortunately, what's currently expected is completely boring."

Despite the nerves knotting my stomach, I managed a half smile before forcing myself to turn my own attention to the advisor currently questioning Princess Aveline on an aspect of Sortileya's government, which she answered smoothly.

I struggled to concentrate on her answer, a task made more difficult by the exhaustion pressing against my senses after my third night staying up late. I suppressed a yawn as Princess Rheanna was questioned next, followed by Princess Elodie, before the advisor finally turned the force of his stern gaze on me. I gulped.

"As you're well aware, Princess Gemma, the Kingdom of Sortileya has a vast and rich history full of many important events and prominent royals. When did Sortileya become its own kingdom, what were the circumstances under which it was born, and who is a significant ruler that descended from this royal line that you feel contributed to making Sortileya the beloved kingdom it is today?"

I slowly released my pent-up breath. Aiden had been certain a question of this nature would arise and thus had prepared me thoroughly.

"Sortileya was founded 741 years ago. It was initially part of the Kingdom of Draceria until a faction broke off, led by the king's younger brother—who became Sortileya's first ruler, Ferris the first—concerning the allocation of taxes. The portion of land taken from Draceria was part of the younger prince's inheritance, and over the years, Sortileya expanded through a series of treaties and invasions to become the prosperous kingdom it is today."

I took another deep breath, taking courage from the questioning advisor's nod of approval. So far I hadn't muddled my answer. Now for the final portion of the question.

"The members of the current royal family aren't direct

descendants of the first Sortileyan king. King Ferris the first's descendants only maintained power for a hundred years. The most notable ruler from his bloodline was the one responsible for changing the line of succession. When King Ferris the third fell ill with a mysterious illness, his heir, Prince Oscar, went on a quest to discover the antidote. Unbeknownst to him, the antidote had been created by an alchemist who was an enemy to the crown. Prince Oscar inadvertently poisoned the king and was executed for treason, causing the crown to pass to a distant cousin, whose family has ruled ever since."

Despite the dark nature of the story, I managed a smile as an interesting tidbit Aiden had shared came to mind.

"It's said that the antidote Prince Oscar acquired had been genuine but was replaced with poison by his sister, who was in love with the scheming cousin who inherited the throne. She exchanged the poison with the antidote in order to murder the king and frame her brother. The story serves as a lesson that if a ruler cannot discern his kingdom's enemies, he'll fall into their traps. This ensures only the shrewdest of rulers sit on the throne."

By the deafening silence following the conclusion of my answer, I knew I'd made a mistake. Aiden had told me the tale as a way to help me remember the doomed Prince Oscar whose folly had transferred the crown to the ancestors of the current Sortileyan monarchy. By the way the advisors' eyes widened and the other listeners guffawed, I realized too late that a future queen was expected to stick to straight facts rather than folklore.

"I see." The questioning advisor cleared his throat. "Where did you hear a story not found in the royal histories?"

I fidgeted beneath the scrutiny of the disapproving audience. "Knowledge comes from a variety of sources," I hedged.

"*Reliable* sources. It is beneath a royal to engage in rumors." And with a disapproving frown, the advisor turned to his next victim. I groaned quietly. Princess Elodie nudged me.

"Remember not to display emotion until you're alone," she said. "And goodness, where did you hear such a story?" She bit her lip to stifle her giggle as I obediently straightened and did my best to pretend to be a proper, emotionless human being.

"A nobleman told it to me."

Princess Elodie raised her eyebrows. "Did he want you to fail?"

"No, it was to help me remember Prince Oscar." Because for some strange reason, Aiden seemed to want me to make a good impression on the prince.

I forced myself not to think of Aiden or his motives as the interviews continued. While some of the princess candidates were more informed than others, all were as proper as expected, carefully keeping their personalities and any nerves hidden. I managed to do the same as I answered the next questions asked of me, my best response being the one concerning Sortileya's foreign alliances, one I managed to keep free of Aiden's humorous comments that had helped me stave off sleep and boredom the evening before. With each answer, the inquiring advisor seemed more satisfied with me —at least until I received my final question.

"A sustainable and thriving economy relies heavily on the efficiency and productivity of trade. Rulers must balance how many of the kingdom's natural resources should be kept for its own people and how many should be traded for resources the kingdom lacks. Outline all of Sortileya's natural resources and how they're used in trade with the surrounding kingdoms."

My mouth went dry, and by the interviewer's satisfied

smirk, I knew he'd asked me such a question on purpose, as if setting me up to fail. While Aiden had mentioned trade, he hadn't gone into great detail, believing that matters of trade wouldn't be the focus of the questioning due to the tradition that past queens weren't involved in such matters during their rule.

I frantically cast my gaze around, as if the answers I desperately sought would appear and save me from my own ignorance. From the astonishment I read in the watching audience and Princess Seren's smirk, I realized this question had been a trap. Who was responsible for springing it? It didn't matter; I was caught.

Hope fluttered within me as my gaze settled on Gavin, who I knew worked with Sortileya's trade. There were no rules against asking for advice...

"Sir Gavin, please inform me about the nature of Sortileya's trade."

He blinked in surprise before smoothly giving the information in quite a bit of dull detail. I did my best to remember all the main points, which I restated for the advisor. He gave me a long, searching look before nodding once.

"That's correct."

Murmurs erupted at that, and several of the other candidates sent me frowns and piercing glares.

"It's cheating to use information outside of one's own knowledge," Princess Lavena said. "Princess Gemma deserves to be disqualified."

The interviewing advisor held up a hand to silence the harsh whispers. "No queen, no matter how intelligent or educated, can know everything. A true ruler must be humble enough to accept help when needed and be well informed on whom to ask." He gave me another searching stare. "How did you know Sir Gavin could provide the answer?"

"I was informed he's involved in Sortileya's trade," I said.

The interviewer managed a wrinkly smile. "It's impressive that a stranger to our kingdom is so informed about Sortileya's court." He gave a satisfied nod before announcing that the second task had concluded.

The Dracerian royalty immediately congratulated me on what they considered a brilliant tactic, but their kind words did little to quell the unease now twisting my stomach. Princess Seren, Princess Lavena, and many noblewomen cast me dark, suspicious looks as they whispered behind their fans, the heat of their glares searching for my secrets. I may have survived the second task, but I felt in just as much danger of my true station being exposed than ever.

Dearest Eileen, There's somewhere on the palace grounds I'm eager to show you, a place I know will make you smile. Please spend the afternoon with me and allow me to take you there. Aiden

I beamed as I scampered ungracefully through the twisting corridors to the gardens outside, my heart fluttering in anticipation of the adventure to come.

I expected to find Aiden waiting at the front doors, but he was nowhere in sight. I paused on the front steps and nibbled my lip as I scanned the grounds. Aiden hadn't told me where to meet him, meaning he could be anywhere. After several minutes of waiting, I wandered through the gardens, avoiding any strolling nobility. I didn't find Aiden in any of the front or side gardens, so I searched the ones behind the palace that were devoid of guests, my heart tightening the longer I couldn't find him.

"Eileen!"

Aiden hovered behind the curved entrance to a hedge maze that stretched nearly the entire length of the back garden. I sighed in relief and hurried over. I pressed my hands on my hips and tried to look stern, despite the smile already emerging at seeing him again.

"I didn't anticipate a game of hide-and-seek."

His expression twisted in remorse. "I'm sorry. My plans to meet you at the front doors were thwarted when all of His Majesty's guests decided to take an afternoon stroll in the gardens."

I raised an eyebrow. "Why is that a problem?" Did he not want to be seen with me? Was it improper of me to be cavorting with a nobleman and he didn't want us to be caught?

"One of those prestigious guests happened to be the boring Duke of Rosewood, whose conversations are impossible to escape from. I decided to take cover until I could meet with you." He caressed my cheek. I shuddered at his touch and his smile widened at my response. "How did the second task go?"

"Well enough. There was only one answer I didn't know, and everyone seemed surprised I'd been asked it at all. Thankfully, Gavin informed me of the details. And then there was my faux pas of sharing your folklore about Prince Oscar."

Aiden grinned unrepentantly. "Did you really? Excellent."

"How is that excellent? I received a lot of titters for that mistake." I fought to make my tone stern, but it was impossible with the way Aiden's eyes crinkled from his smile.

"Because I'm sure it livened up what was likely the dullest afternoon. The nobility are far too serious. Are you concerned about your mistake? I'd think it'd please you, considering you're not interested in winning the prince's hand."

"I suppose you make a good point," I said.

"Then you have no need to worry." His brow furrowed, as if just realizing what I'd told him. "You sought help from

Gavin for your question? I didn't realize you two knew one another. Wait…does that mean you were asked about Sortileya's trade?"

"He's a distant relation of Rosie," I said. "And yes, I was. I thought it unusual."

"And did anyone else get asked such a question?"

I shook my head and his frown deepened. His concern only escalated the worry knotting my gut. "Perhaps I'm mistaken and more were asked such questions, but I confess I scarcely paid attention to the others."

As I'd hoped, Aiden's grave expression softened into a smile. "I can't blame you. It's quite the accomplishment you didn't fall asleep—or did you do that, too?"

I giggled and whacked his arm playfully. "I was certainly tired enough to do so, thanks to our late night."

At my mention of last night, Aiden's gaze lowered from mine to linger on my neck, where until yesterday Father's locket had resided. He raised his gaze to search mine, his now lined with concern. "Are you alright?"

I caressed my neck where only the pearl necklace from Aiden remained. It still felt strange to no longer feel the familiar metal against my skin or the locket's weight pressing against my heart. I hadn't noticed how heavy it had been until it was no longer there.

"You're worried I regret last night's payment?"

He ran a hand through his hair and nodded, the concern filling his dark eyes intensifying. "I confess I could scarcely sleep for fearing I'd hurt you. That wasn't my intention."

"I know it wasn't. That's why I gave you my locket."

He visibly relaxed, as if the worry that he'd hurt me had been his own heavy burden. He reached for my hand. "My brave girl."

Heat swirled through my cheeks. My blush deepened as he began rubbing his thumb along the back of my hand, sending pulses rippling up my arm and straight to my heart.

"You promised to show me an area of the gardens that would make me smile. Is it the maze?"

He glanced over his shoulder at its formidable presence. "Ah, so you've noticed the infamous hedge maze, an excellent place to hide should you ever need one. We'll explore it another day. I have another adventure in mind this afternoon."

He entwined our hands but after only a few steps I paused to look out over the Forest surrounding the palace, the rustling branches calling to me.

"You miss it, don't you?" Aiden asked gently.

"I've never gone so long without exploring the Forest."

"In time you will again." His voice was full of promise. He led me around the twisting outside hedge of the maze. Hidden behind it was a lovely blue-green pond full of cattails and speckled with lily pads, with golden koi swimming within.

As Aiden had predicted, I smiled widely. "What a lovely place."

"I knew you'd love it." We settled on the bank close enough that we were practically touching. My heart pattered faster at our proximity. "Most overlook this pond, considering it pales in comparison to the manicured beauty of the rest of the grounds, but you seem to appreciate a simpler, more natural beauty."

He knew me well. I yanked off my shoes and dipped my feet in the cool water, an un-princess-like act to be sure, but it earned me one of Aiden's endearing smiles, ones I coveted as much as he seemed to want to collect my own.

I leaned back on my elbows and gazed out over the pond and the dragonflies skimming its surface. "I wish I'd brought my sketchbook so I could preserve its image forever."

"We'll return another day if you promise to allow me to watch you sketch what is sure to be another masterpiece."

The blush already warming my cheeks deepened. He lightly traced it with his fingertip.

"Tell me, which picture do you have in mind for this scene: will you draw it from life or use the setting for a drawing inspired by your imagination?"

I pursed my lips in thought. "Perhaps both, as a tribute to such a lovely place."

The place became even lovelier when Aiden's arm wrapped around my waist to gently tug me against his side. It was both amazing how perfectly we fit together and rather startling the way my body responded—my heart flared to life as I melted against him, needing to be close to him. Despite these thrilling yet still terrifying sensations, I didn't pull away. Instead, I fought the impulse to lean my head against his shoulder.

Aiden began playing with the ends of my hair. "Have you forgiven me yet for entangling you in all this?"

"I have." It seemed like so long ago that I'd been determined to be angry with him.

"I'm so glad. Are you happy here?" He asked it so tentatively, as if afraid of my answer.

I considered. While staying at the Sortileyan palace was still stressful, strangely it now almost felt like home, especially during the moments I spent with Aiden, as if every path I'd ever walked had led to him. With Aiden I felt grounded, as if no matter where I was, as long as we were together I was exactly where I needed to be. It was both a frightening feeling and an incredibly comforting one.

"Although I do miss home, I am happy," I whispered. "You're here. I feel as if I belong with you."

His expression lit up and he scooted closer, his warmth enfolding me like an embrace. "I feel I belong with you, too.

You're remarkable, Eileen, and I don't need any princess test to show me that."

It suddenly became difficult to breathe. "You really do care for me." The thought was incredible.

"Very much." He caressed my cheek, and I leaned against his hand, even as my old fear pleaded for me to pull away before I got hurt.

But I couldn't. With each sweet moment I spent with Aiden, he not only broke down the defenses I'd built around my heart but stole another portion piece by piece.

How had this happened? How had he so effortlessly laid claim to that which I'd fought for so long to protect? And why did I no longer mind that my near-constant battle had ended with him as conquerer?

"I didn't know it was possible to care for anyone as deeply as I feel for you."

His low, husky murmur sent a tremor through me, causing me to instinctively lean closer while his sweet words prodded at the cracks in my heart, opening it further for him to steal, an act that I now realized was inevitable.

"I know your heart is protected," he said. "I used to protect mine as well. I feared losing it, but now I know that's not the worst thing that could happen."

"What could be worse?"

He cradled my face, stroking my cheeks with his thumbs. "Losing you."

In that moment, I knew I'd never push him away, not when he'd trusted me with his own heart. We'd travelled too far down this path, and there was no turning back.

Aiden's soft, cradling touch stroked my cheeks as he lightly pressed his lips to my brow. All the feelings I'd fought to suppress burst free, feelings which were far more beautiful than I could have ever imagined. I felt as if my heart were soaring, with no intention of ever being grounded again.

I caressed Aiden's face as I met his gaze. A new path was unfolding before me, one I'd hesitated exploring for so long but which I now felt brave enough to risk taking a tentative step down in order to discover what amazing destination lay ahead. If it led to my Aiden, then any obstacle would be worth overcoming.

I loved him, and that was all that mattered. Thus, I could choose him. I pressed my hand to Aiden's heart. It was mine, just as my own was his. It was time to put aside my fears and take a brave step forward.

He stroked my cheek, his movements incredibly careful, as if he knew how fragile my heart was and feared I might break. I leaned against his soft touch. With each gentle caress, I felt my heart opening further to him.

Aiden leaned down and as I lifted my face to meet him, his caressing fingers stilled as he once more searched my eyes, seeking permission for the next step on this beautiful journey.

"Please," I whispered in answer to his unspoken question. He smiled before bridging the remaining distance and kissing me softly.

For a moment time stood still before Aiden laced his fingers through my hair and kissed me fervently—not a quick kiss but a lingering one, one that was incredibly tender. I felt my heart blossom as healing warmth washed over me. My arms hooked around his neck, pulling him closer. His hand lowered to wind around my waist to mold me closer, his touch gentle, his lips soft on mine, perfect.

I realized I was crying as the salt of my tears stained the sweetness of our kiss, but despite my tears I wasn't at all unhappy. How could I be when my heart—which had been locked away for so long—was not only free but being treated so gently by this wonderful man? It was such an incredible feeling, far more beautiful than I could have ever imagined.

All too soon he broke the kiss, but thankfully he didn't pull away. My arms tightened around him as our gazes seeped into one another's. A heated blush crept across my cheeks as I smiled shyly at him. He returned it before leaning down to kiss me again, as gentle as a caress, and I kissed him back, needing to express the emotions I still didn't quite understand but which swarmed my heart. How could I have resisted him for so long?

A rustling in the hedge tore us apart. We turned just in time to see a shadow from within the maze withdraw from peeking through the leaves. Someone had been spying on us. For a moment we stared, clinging to one another. I could feel Aiden's pounding heart beating frantically against mine.

The lingering shadow of Aiden's kiss, once so beautiful, now caused my stomach to knot with worry. I wasn't sure whether it was forbidden for me to be with someone above my own station, but now that someone had caught us, I fervently hoped it wasn't unacceptable. The thought of being taken from Aiden after I'd finally allowed myself to choose him was torturous.

"Was someone spying on us?" I asked, my voice breathless. Aiden's hold tightened around me protectively.

"Yes, from inside the maze, and I have a hunch who it was." Disappointment filled his eyes as he looked at me. "I need to confront them."

He helped me to my feet. I picked up my discarded shoes and wove my arm through his, but he intertwined our hands instead, giving mine a reassuring squeeze.

"I don't want to leave you. I wouldn't if it weren't necessary."

I nodded. As much as I ached to stay with him, my mind was spinning. I needed time and distance to sort out my rushing thoughts.

Aiden led me around the outside of the maze and paused

at its entrance. He tucked my hair behind my ear. "Are you alright?"

Despite my disappointment from our interruption, the kiss itself still left me with tingly warmth. "That was wonderful. I didn't know it'd be like that."

He chuckled. "It did exceed my own expectations." He started to pull away but I clung to his hand, desperate to keep him near for a little bit longer. "Will I see you soon?"

"I'll make sure of it."

He leaned down and lightly kissed me again, squeezing my hand before pulling away and disappearing into the maze. I stared after him for a moment before slowly returning to the palace gardens to ponder. I lightly traced my lips as I not only relived our beautiful kiss but tried to figure out who'd been spying on us and why.

CHAPTER 19

The heat of Princess Seren's narrowed gaze had been on me throughout breakfast, scrutinizing my every move as if to gather evidence for her suspicions. I'd passed a restless night reliving my kiss with Aiden over and over, the sweetness of the memory marred by my worry over who'd been spying on us. With her frequent glowers, I didn't doubt it'd been the Dragon Princess. The question that remained was *why*.

"Are you alright, Gemma? You're looking a bit pale." Princess Elodie leaned close, eyes concerned. I took a steadying breath, fighting the urge to glance over at Princess Seren to see if she was still glaring at me. She undoubtedly was.

"I'm being watched."

Seeing my eyes flick in her direction, all four Dracerian royals glanced towards Princess Seren. Princess Rheanna's forehead furrowed. "Goodness, she's glaring at you. Did anything happen between you two?"

"No, I've never even spoken to her."

"You must have done something."

I frowned, considering. "Yesterday, someone saw me in a certain...situation. Perhaps it was her." My heart tightened in guilt. If Princess Seren had been the one spying from the hedge maze and had witnessed my stolen kiss with Aiden, she was likely affronted I'd kissed Aiden when I was supposedly competing for her brother's hand.

Prince Liam's eyes flashed mischievously. "What kind of situation? Do tell. I'm excellent at keeping secrets."

All three of his sisters snorted at that and I rolled my eyes; I'd already experienced his lack of ability to keep secrets and wasn't keen to do it again.

"You know it's true," Prince Liam said. "The closest I get to spilling any secrets I'm entrusted with is basing my intriguing tales on them, but since no one really believes a word I say, your secret would still be safe with me."

The thought of Prince Liam spreading my special memory with Aiden as the latest gossip caused my cheeks to burn. Princess Elodie noticed and gasped knowingly. "Ooh, did she see you with someone? Perhaps a man?"

I lowered my gaze to my eggs and bacon and didn't answer. Princess Elodie squealed.

"Are you involved with a member of the court? Well, no wonder you've been messing up during the tests on purpose; you want to marry the man you love, not the prince. If Seren caught you two together, perhaps she's jealous."

Hot envy burned through me at the thought that Princess Seren pined for Aiden. Could she have been his original fiancée? The grip on my knife tightened at the thought.

Prince Liam smirked down at my fist as he twirled his own knife between his fingers. "There's nothing that stirs women to violence quite like love, but considering this is Seren, you have no need to worry. I can't imagine her being in love with anyone. She's the Dragon Princess—prickly and unpleasant, with a heart made of stone. She's likely plotting something conniving and has chosen you as her victim. My congratulations."

My heart had no sooner begun to settle at the thought that the Dragon Princess wasn't interested in my Aiden when it flared to life at a new unpleasant possibility: was Princess Seren beginning to suspect I was posing as a royal? If she was, then one whispered suggestion to the Dark Prince or the king would be enough for her suspicion to be investigated, which wouldn't end well for me.

These worries haunted me the remainder of the morning. I wandered the gardens with my sketchbook tucked beneath my arm in search of the perfect scene to draw in order to distract myself. Despite the artistic beauty and storybook splendor of the grounds, no scene beckoned me to capture it with my pencils. Instead, other thoughts tugged at me— being in the gardens reminded me of yesterday's kiss. I could still feel the soft sweetness of my stolen kiss with Aiden.

As if my thoughts about him had drawn me to him, I heard his familiar voice drifting from the rose garden. My heart immediately fluttered. I crept closer and peered around a hedge.

Aiden paced the garden, Gavin watching with amusement. I tensed at Aiden's hardened expression. I hadn't seen such darkness in his eyes since the day we'd met in the Forest, and then briefly when we'd spoken of his mother near the musical lake.

"Goodness, I hate her," Aiden snapped. "If she ruins this for me out of spite, she'll pay dearly."

"Is she certain then?"

Aiden shrugged. "She drops constant hints and threats with that knowing smirk of hers." He continued pacing with long, agitated strides. As I watched, someone stepped up behind me. I nearly leapt when my permanent shadow whispered into my ear.

"Spying, Your Highness?" Alastar asked, his expression stoic as ever but his eyes lined with disapproval. I made a shushing motion and turned back towards the conversation.

"Can you blame her?" Gavin asked. Aiden glared at him, but Gavin didn't even flinch. "I hate to point this out, but you've never been nice to her. Can you be surprised she's seeking her revenge?"

Aiden's manner darkened further and his fists clenched. "I don't deny I deserve revenge, but so help me if she uses Eileen to accomplish it."

At hearing my name, I sidled closer.

"Princess Seren never has played fair," Gavin said. "I wouldn't be surprised if she follows through on her threats. Has anything happened recently that would compel her to act?"

Aiden sighed and rubbed his face with his palms. "She saw me kissing Eileen."

Gavin snorted. "You *kissed* her?"

Aiden glared at him once more. "Why do you sound so shocked? Would I have dragged her into such a ridiculous scheme if I didn't feel what I do for her?"

Gavin instantly became solemn. "No, you wouldn't."

"And now meddling Seren is going to attempt to ruin everything."

"It's your word against hers," Gavin said.

Aiden considered that before nodding firmly. "You're right, and I'd wager my word carries more weight than hers, but I refuse to stand idly by. I won't have anyone jeopardize the future I'm fighting for."

"Do you have a plan?"

Aiden nodded and motioned towards the opposite exit. "Walk with me and I'll share it with you." He left the garden, Gavin following close behind. Their voices drifted farther away until I could no longer hear them. Only when I was sure they were gone did I step from my hiding place and turn to a frowning Alastar.

"What do you think of that?"

"What do I think of what, Your Highness?"

I pressed my hands on my hips. "The conversation we just overheard, obviously."

"I didn't overhear anything, Your Highness. It's not a guard's place to eavesdrop."

"You may pretend you heard nothing, but you clearly did, whether you wanted to or not."

I furrowed my brow as I recalled the strange conversation I'd witnessed, my thoughts whirling. It appeared that Princess Seren *was* Aiden's ex-fiancée—although wouldn't I have heard about it if the princess had been betrothed all this time?—which meant Aiden's rank was higher than I'd initially supposed. I ached to ask Alastar for further details, but I doubted he'd be much help considering his usual stubborn refusal to share information with me.

But there was one primary concern I couldn't quench. "Does Aiden behave so harshly very often?"

Alastar said nothing. Did that mean he did? I sighed and sank onto a bench, slumping as I stared unseeing at the surrounding roses, their perfume doing little to calm my pounding heart.

"What of Princess Seren? Need I be worried about her?" The last thing I needed was a venomous, jealous ex hating me.

Once more, Alastar remained silent, and after a moment of restless waiting I was about to give up any hope of him saying anything when he hesitantly answered me.

"Princess Seren is undoubtedly a determined sort, but Aiden is even more so. As such, please don't worry."

That was easier said than done, but his assurances did slightly abate my concerns regarding the Dragon Princess, leaving only Aiden's conversation I'd overheard. I ached to confront him directly, but then he'd know I'd spied on him. Guilt twisted my gut that I'd done something so untrustworthy towards the man who had fought so hard to earn my own trust.

I resumed my wandering through the gardens without really seeing them, their beauty lost as my swirling thoughts insisted on reexamining the encounter I'd witnessed.

"Eileen!"

I spun around to find Aiden himself sitting by himself on a secluded bench, all traces of his earlier darkness absent. He straightened the stack of papers in his lap into a neat pile before bounding over to sweep me into a hug. My reservations melted the instant his arms enfolded me. I burrowed myself against his warmth. There was no doubt that this was where I belonged.

He pulled away just enough to dip down and kiss me, causing my entire being to become lost in his embrace. The memories from yesterday's kiss, which I'd been constantly reliving, hadn't done the experience justice.

Aiden broke away, only to immediately begin trailing soft kisses along my jaw. "That was so much better than I remembered."

I arched against him and his spoiling attentions. "I agree," I managed breathlessly. He nuzzled my neck and placed a quick peck against my throat before pulling away, happily keeping me in his arms, where I was more than content to remain.

"I've been thinking of you and had just gotten to the point where I couldn't bear to be apart from you any longer, so I've been writing you a note." He sorted through his papers and handed me a slip of parchment.

Dearest Eileen, It feels as if it's been far too long since I've seen you. How can one day feel like years? Can you please meet me at...

I peeked shyly up at him. "Where is this mysterious meeting place?"

"May I show you?" He rolled up his papers and hid them midst the fauna behind the bench where he'd been sitting. I watched curiously.

"What are those?"

He actually scowled at the now-hidden papers. "With a title comes all sorts of responsibility. To make it more bearable, I like to take my work outdoors—but I have no need to continue now that my favorite distraction is here." His hand trailed down my arm to intertwine our fingers. My hand tightened around his, finding comfort in his touch.

"What sort of work do you do?"

"Work far too dull to discuss when we're together."

I frowned at his obvious sidestepping of my question. "It's a secret, isn't it?"

He glanced down at me guiltily. I yanked my hand from his.

"I don't like secrets."

He reclaimed my hand and cradled it between his, black eyes wide and earnest. "There will soon be a time when there are no secrets between us, but until then, please forgive me for still keeping some from you. I wouldn't do it if it weren't absolutely necessary. Please, Eileen."

I searched his eyes and felt my reservations slip away at the sincerity filling them. I was tired of pushing him away in my insecurities. I wanted to trust him. I *did* trust him. I managed a smile in forgiveness, which he tentatively returned.

"Where are you taking me?" I asked as I rewound our hands.

"Unfortunately, I can't tell you, but rest assured a surprise is very different from a secret."

We resumed our stroll, which took us through the water

garden with its miniature waterfalls, enchanting brooks surrounded by colorful fauna, and elegant marble fountains. We exited right by the hedge maze where we'd met yesterday, a place he'd promised to take me.

I smiled up at him. "So we're to have an adventure in getting lost?"

"While that is one reason to explore the maze, I figured if we're hidden inside, it'll be more difficult for someone to spy on us again."

"Did you discover who was spying on us yesterday?"

He rolled his eyes. "It was Seren. She never rests from stirring up trouble."

"I wondered if it was her. She's been watching me closely —or rather glaring at me."

He gave my hand a reassuring squeeze. "I'm not surprised. She always sticks her nose in others' business. But please don't worry; I'll deal with her. In the meantime, just ignore her."

I slowed, tugging us to a stop. Now was not the time for Aiden's usual vagueness. "Why was she spying on us? How will you deal with her? Please tell me."

He sighed. "She was spying on us because she's angry with me. Fortunately for us, I have something over her that will ensure she remains silent."

A chill rippled up my spine at the fierce look filling his eyes. This was the Aiden that used to frighten me, and that in many ways still did. "Why do you hate her?"

He raised an eyebrow. "Who says I hate her?"

I traced around his eyes with my fingertip. "I can see that you do."

His jaw tightened. "I have my reasons."

"Tell me," I pleaded.

His expression darkened. "She took away something very precious to me."

"Is that why you broke off your engagement?"

Bewilderment filled his eyes before he actually laughed. "She's not my ex-fiancée. Even if she were, I broke off my engagement because I fell in love with you." He kissed me lightly. "Have I satisfied your curiosity? May we go exploring now?"

While his answers had only caused more questions, I offered him a tentative smile in agreement. We ducked inside the hedge maze and were immediately swallowed up by towering, leafy hedges surrounding us on all sides, with several narrow pathways twisting in all directions.

I nibbled my lip as I looked around. "Are you sure we won't get lost?"

"I know this maze well. I promise to guide you every step of the way."

His assurance eased some of the tension tightening my stomach. I leaned against him and allowed him to lead me down one seemingly random path after another, each twisting in sporadic directions. "It's so confusing. How will we ever find our way back out?"

"I've explored this maze for years. I'm rather close to the royal family and spent a lot of my time here at the palace while growing up. I always took great comfort in being in a place secluded from the world, surrounded by nature, where I could be alone with my thoughts or a book, or wander the maze for hours. It took many wrong turns to know it as well as I do, but now I'll never get lost again."

He led me down a particularly tight path that forced us to press ourselves closer in order to pass through. The heat of his body caused me to shudder. We continued walking whatever paths Aiden nudged us down. With every step, his confident navigating put me more at ease.

"Do you know the royal gardens as well as you know the maze?" I asked after several minutes of content silence.

"Quite well. Is there a reason for your curiosity?"

"Prince Liam speculates that there's a secret passageway that leads to the Forest. If you knew of it, I could escape."

Aiden's hold on my hand tightened. "Do you still want to leave so badly?"

I opened my mouth to say yes but paused. *Did* I still want to leave? I peeked up at Aiden, who stared down at me with undisguised yearning. He was a very compelling reason to stay.

"I don't know."

"Then perhaps I must work harder to convince you to stay with me." He gave my hand another squeeze before resuming walking.

Despite his earlier display of confidence, after several more turns he paused at a fork and frowned down each path, his forehead furrowed in concentration.

"Are we lost?" I asked.

"No..." But he didn't sound so sure. He managed a breathless laugh as he led me down one. "At least, I don't think so. I suppose we'll see." It took a few wrong turns before Aiden's confidence returned. "I know where we are now. The center of the maze is just up ahead."

The path opened up to a magnificent fountain. Roses grew in twisting patterns along the hedge walls, filling the air with their sweet perfume. I pressed my hand to my throat. "It's beautiful."

"I agree. Well worth the trip getting here." He pulled me gently down to sit beside him on the edge of the fountain. "This is my favorite place on the palace grounds. I often come here when I need to be alone."

He broke off a rose near its head and handed it to me. I cradled it in my palm as my reverent gaze took in my surroundings. I ran my fingers through the cool fountain water as I nodded towards the several paths that emerged from the encircling hedge.

"Are there multiple ways to get here?"

"Many. One day we'll explore all of them." His arm wrapped around my shoulders to pull me close. I rested my head on his shoulder. "I hope it's not just the maze we one day explore. I want a lifetime of experiences with you, Eileen."

He cupped my chin and caressed my lips with his own. At first I returned his kiss—until the implication of his words settled over me. I pushed him away.

"What do you mean?" I asked breathlessly.

His brow furrowed as he lightly stroked my cheek with his thumb. "I want to spend the rest of my life with you."

I embraced such sweet words, the most beautiful I'd ever heard. "I want the same." It's what had given me the courage to choose him. "But we're still from two different worlds."

He sighed. "And choosing my world would force you to give up the simple one you love so much. I just want to make you happy, Eileen. Do you think you could ever learn to be happy in my world if it meant we were together?"

"Of course, Aiden, but that doesn't mean we should do this now, not when I'm still entrapped in a competition to win the prince's hand."

Aiden burrowed against my throat and groaned. "I almost regret getting you involved. Are you suggesting I try to be patient?"

"It'll give us time to continue exploring this—*us.*"

"I love the sound of that." Aiden pressed a light kiss on my temple. "Although the competition really shouldn't matter; you don't want to marry the prince." Another kiss, this one on my brow, as if he was trying to appease me in order to convince me to change my mind. "Let's forget the competition and just be together." He dipped down to kiss my lips again, but I pressed my hands against his chest to keep him back.

"Please, we need to slow down." This was all too new and beautiful. I wanted to savor the experience.

"I know we *should,* but that doesn't mean I want to." He leaned down, undoubtedly to steal another kiss, but I kept him back.

"Aiden, please." Even with knowing all I felt for him, this was still too fast. While my fears had shifted from choosing him to being terrified of living a life without him, there was still so much I didn't know about him. While I no longer doubted he was the right path for me, I still wanted to walk it with caution.

At first he didn't move. Then with a sigh, he burrowed his face against my hair before he slowly pulled away, expression pained but still full of his usual sweet understanding. "I'm sorry, I'm not meaning to rush you. We'll slow down."

I gaped at him. "We will?"

"If that's what you want."

He scooted away and started to withdraw his arm, but I whimpered in protest. "I don't want you to slow down *that* much." I snuggled closer and sighed contentedly as his hold tightened. I laid my head back on his shoulder and smiled when he nestled his on top of mine.

"I'm sorry I pushed you away," I murmured.

"Don't be," he said. "I'm sorry I rushed you. It just feels so right to be with you. But thank you for being honest with me. I don't want to hurt you."

At this point, the only thing that could truly hurt me would be losing him. I didn't want that to happen. Perhaps the farther down this path we walked, the easier it'd become. No matter how long it took for me to trust not just him but the future together he promised me, I knew it would be well worth the journey.

CHAPTER 20

I nibbled my lip as I scanned the towering shelves of the vast palace library. Certainly such a grand library would contain the book I was seeking; the problem was I wasn't entirely sure *what* I was looking for. All I knew was I needed to uncover the mystery constantly gnawing at me; I had various pieces of a puzzle but lacked enough information to assemble it.

Something felt...*off*. It had from the moment the Forest had gone so uncannily still when I'd first gotten lost in the storm, only for it to lead me miles away from home to the palace. Its motive for my presence here had never been adequately explained, and with each passing day I felt more unease with the situation, especially when I remained uncaught. It seemed a bit too lucky to be coincidence.

"Feeling bookish, Princess Gemma?" I turned to find Prince Liam leaning casually against a shelf with his usual cheeky grin. "Or perhaps you're still on the quest to uncover the secret passageways. Maybe pulling on the correct book will open a hidden panel." He began to yank books off the shelf at random.

"Goodness, Liam, what are you doing?" His three sisters had arrived, Princess Aveline wearing her usual frown of disapproval.

"Causing mischief."

She wrinkled her nose. "Do you ever do anything else?"

"I've been known to be charming should the need arise."

All three of his sisters scoffed, but Prince Liam ignored their reaction and continued tugging out books.

"What are you doing here, Gemma?" Princess Elodie asked.

"She's searching for the secret passageways," Prince Liam said. My face heated with a blush.

"I haven't been looking for them for a while." As unnerving as my presence at the palace had been at the beginning, the longer I stayed, the less inclined I was to leave.

"If it's not the secret passageways, then what are you searching for?"

"I'm not entirely sure…" As I spoke my gaze settled on a volume blending into the shelf: *The Noble Families of Sortileya*. My heart gave an excited leap. For as close as we'd become, Aiden still remained as much a mystery as everything else around me, a mystery I most wanted to solve, considering I'd chosen a future with him. Perhaps learning more about his lineage would provide some of the answers I sought.

I tugged the book free and eased it open. Prince Liam leaned over my shoulder. "Aristocratic genealogies, huh? If it's a noble you're interested in learning more about, you'll glean more truth from gossip than from that tedious beast. That's how I gather all my own information." He wriggled his eyebrows.

That certainly explained a lot. "Perhaps I find dry history more interesting than rumors."

He leaned further over my shoulder, squinting at a prestigious family tree taking up two full pages. "Looks *fascinating*. Well, to each their own."

"I didn't invite you to read over my shoulder, Your Highness."

"Your Highness?" He made a show of looking affronted. "What did I do to deserve such an offensive address?"

A cold voice interrupted our conversation. "My question exactly. Someone as ridiculous as you certainly doesn't deserve such a title."

We all turned to see who had spoken. Princess Lavena stood regally at the end of the row with her look-alike handmaiden in tow, her nose upturned and a sneer directed towards Prince Liam.

"Oh, it's *you*." He swore bitterly, ignoring Princess Aveline's scandalized retribution for his language.

Princess Lavena tossed her hair elegantly over her shoulder before gliding over. "What an unpleasant surprise to see you too, Liam."

"Now that you've done so, we've both filled our quota for the rest of our lives, so be so good as to leave me alone." He turned his back to her. She rolled her eyes before turning a smirk to me. "Why, if it isn't the incompetent princess."

My chest tightened. With the sneer she was giving me... did she suspect?

"You know," she continued, "I heard the most interesting story about a commoner pretending to be a noble. Have you heard it before, *Princess* Gemma? It's a fascinating tale."

My heart pounded in my ears. I ached to escape her suspicions, but my knees had locked.

"Since when has anything you had to say been *fascinating*?" Prince Liam said coldly. "Is that the word for your usual scorn and biting comments?"

Princess Lavena shifted her coldness from me to glare at

him. Princess Elodie took the opportunity to shuffle to my side.

"I've seen that calculating look of hers before," she whispered. "She's going to rile him. It's best we take cover now." She took my elbow and guided me down the row. I gratefully followed. We'd no sooner turned the corner than their raised voices echoed from behind us. Princess Elodie sighed. "And there they go."

It took a moment for the fear to unclench my throat so I could find my voice. "Is she always like that?"

"Often worse. Poor Liam can't stand her. I'm not sure how those two will survive their match. Rhea and I are convinced they'll murder one another not even a day in."

"And Prince Liam truly can't get out of it?"

Princess Elodie shook her head. "He's searched for every loophole. The contract is set. It was originally arranged between our late brother and Lavena, but after our brother's sudden death, Liam inherited not only the crown but our brother's betrothed. As I'm sure you've gathered, he's rather unhappy about both." She sighed. "Poor Liam. It was rather startling to not only become the heir but to be forced into an engagement with someone he's never gotten along with." She shook her head sympathetically.

Behind us, the raised voices had turned into shouts. Princess Elodie released my arm and turned around with a worried frown.

"Oh dear. If you'll excuse me, I should go make sure the two don't kill one another." She hurried gracefully away. I headed in the opposite direction, trying to put as much space between me and the suspicious Princess Lavena as possible.

Once I'd gotten a safe distance away, I settled into a seat to peruse the volume of lineages, but only a few pages in, I grew bored and abandoned it. Perhaps Prince Liam was right: there were more interesting ways to gather information. I searched the many shelves for something new to read.

"What are you looking for?"

I spun around with a startled gasp and came face-to-face with Princess Seren. She was gorgeous, as was typical for a royal, but hers was more of a hard, cold beauty. Her dark hair was pinned in an elegant style woven with sapphires matching her lavish silver-trimmed gown, both of which emphasized her startling grey eyes, narrowed at me as if she meant to skewer me.

It was clear why she was called the Dragon Princess. Not only did her voice hold an air of constant displeasure, but her expression was twisted into a fierce scowl and fire filled her light eyes. With the way she was glaring at me, she clearly had plans to unleash it.

My nerves were still heightened after my conversation with Princess Lavena, a conversation I now fiercely hoped Princess Seren hadn't overheard. The tension from that encounter returned full force. I took a deep breath in an attempt to calm myself.

"I'm searching for reading material," I said, fighting to keep my voice from shaking, but despite my efforts, it sounded strained to my ears.

She smirked. "I see. You spend an abhorrent amount of time in the library, as if you're relying on it just to survive this experience."

So she suspected, too, which was likely why she'd been watching me so closely. I fought to remain calm, a difficult feat when my heart threatened to leap out of my chest. "And you spend a lot of time spying on me."

She laughed coldly. "You believe I'm spying on you? What a rash claim, one unwise to make from one of your station."

My breath caught. Oh no, she knew; she *had* to. Princess Seren was the last person I wanted to discover my secret, for she could easily turn me in to the king or her brother, the Dark Prince.

But then I noticed the calculating way she studied my reaction, as if she were still seeking evidence to support her claim. I swallowed and forced myself to keep my expression impassive, all while fighting the urge to escape this interrogation before it became even more damning.

"It sickens me that one of your background is mingling with those of superior birth," she continued.

I raised an eyebrow. "You're referring to my royal background?"

Her eyes narrowed further. "You claim to be a true princess?"

Mouth dry, I forced myself to maintain a confidence I didn't at all feel. "Isn't that what this competition of Prince Deidric's is meant to prove?"

Princess Seren's smirk returned, as if it were a permanent feature on her face. "I must admit you're doing remarkably well considering your inferiority—a bit *too* well. You've obviously been receiving assistance. But from whom?" Her forehead furrowed in thought as she considered the puzzle before understanding settled over her. "I see. *Aiden's* been helping you. I saw you two together the other day. You've obviously gotten quite...*close*." She rolled her eyes. "The fool. He'll regret his interference."

My heartbeat escalated. Would Aiden be punished for his involvement? The thought twisted my stomach in nauseous knots. "He has nothing to do with it," I stuttered, my heart pounding so loudly I was certain she could hear it.

"He has everything to do with your situation. He's trying to keep his assistance a secret, but I suspect the truth even if I don't yet have definite proof. But I will, and then I'll delight in watching your secret exposed. I'll ensure you get just what you deserve from this competition."

With a final smirk, she spun around and flounced away. I stared after her for a moment, fighting to control my panting, hyperventilating breaths as the walls of towering bookcases closed in around me, suffocating.

Escape—I needed to escape.

I stumbled blindly from the library and through the corridors, unsure where I was going, only knowing I needed to get away. I'd rather face the guards flanking the outside gates that prevented my exit into the Forest than experience whatever harm Princess Seren's suspicions could do to me, or worse, to Aiden.

I spun around a corner and ran right into him, as if my panic and need to see him had drawn him to me. The papers he'd been carrying flew everywhere. Alastar slipped out from trailing me in the shadows and promptly began picking them up. Aiden didn't even give him a second glance, his worried attention focused solely on me.

"Eileen! I'm sorry, I wasn't watching where I was…Eileen, love? What's wrong? Are you alright?"

For a moment I gaped at him, faintly registering that this was the first time I'd seen him in the halls of the palace. He was here. I flung myself at him with a sob. His arms wound around me, holding me close.

"What is it? What's wrong?"

"I need to leave," I stuttered. "I can't stay here any longer."

"Calm down and tell me what happened."

"I'm being found out. First Princess Lavena's comments and then Princess Seren's…what's worse, she knows you've been helping me."

"Seren?" He muttered a curse and stroked my hair. "Don't worry, she can't hurt you."

"You don't understand. She will. She'll hurt both of us." I tried to tug out of his arms—never mind the thought of separating myself from his warm and soothing embrace felt as suicidal as remaining in the palace—but his hold was firm.

"No consequence is so dire as for me to regret helping you," he said, brushing a kiss along my brow. "Now please tell me what happened."

I shook my head as my embarrassing tears escaped. I wiped them away, but he'd already seen them.

"Please, Eileen." His voice broke.

My ache to return home—which had been temporarily masked by the contentment I'd been experiencing—returned. I'd allowed the elegance of the palace and the joy I'd felt with Aiden to distract me from my worries concerning Mother and the danger of my situation, but my conversations with Princess Lavena and Princess Seren had shattered the façade that I could be safe here. I couldn't stay any longer.

"I want to go home."

"I know you do. Tell me what happened first. Please."

I shook my head again. "Not here." We were too exposed in this corridor. Aiden scanned the opulent hallway, lined with many doors that could open at any time and have someone stumble upon us. He nodded curtly.

"I understand. Come."

He took my hand and led me briskly through the corridors, casting me frequent concerned glances as we walked. Even though the panic from my encounter with Princess Seren still pounded through my bloodstream, Aiden's presence calmed me with each step.

Aiden's intended destination turned out to be the palace roof, which we reached by ascending a winding back staircase. At the top, Aiden pushed against the ceiling and it opened to reveal the settling dusk. He hoisted himself up before turning around and helping me through.

Outside, the sky blazed with the golden rose of the setting sun. A calming breeze caressed my skin and tangled my hair. Still kneeling, Aiden pulled me into another embrace and held me close, an act which immediately broke the dam of tears I'd been struggling to suppress. I buried my face against his chest and cried.

He stroked my hair and murmured sweet words into my ear. It was amazing how soothing his attentions were; with each touch I melted further into his comfort.

Eventually, my sobs stilled until I was only sniffling against him and occasionally hiccuping. He nestled against my head. "What happened?"

"I can't do this anymore," I stuttered. "First Princess Lavena confronted me in the library, then Princess Seren. She knows, Aiden, and if she tells..." Cold fear rippled over me, suffocating me just like the noose would should this charade end in the disastrous way I so feared. "I'm frightened."

His arms tightened around me in a protective embrace. "Oh Eileen, this is all my fault. My selfishness got you into this mess. When you first arrived at the palace, all I could think about was how happy I was to see you again, how this was an opportunity for us to be together. I'll never forgive myself for forcing you into a situation that's brought you nothing but pain."

It was startling how the thought of his distress was more painful than my own. I caressed his face. "Please don't blame yourself."

"But it's all my fault. I've hurt you."

"It's not your fault Princess Lavena and Princess Seren discovered who I truly am, and it's not your fault I'm frightened now. You mean so much to me, Aiden." I nestled deeper into his tender embrace.

"Does this mean you'll choose us?" Hope filled his voice. "Please do. I've never met anyone who not only makes me so happy but who's so noble in character. How could the prince not pick you?"

I groaned and pressed my forehead against his heart, which beat as frantically as my own. "I don't want a prince, I only want you."

He hooked his fingers beneath my chin to raise my gaze to meet his, his own searching and pleading. "I want you, too. No matter the outcome of this competition, I want you to choose me."

"Would I be allowed to?" For I felt certain that no one could say no to royalty, no matter how much they wanted to.

"No matter how lost one is, there's always another path," he said. "Can't I be yours?"

I ached to say yes, for no path had ever felt as right as the one that led to him. But even though I'd already chosen him, my fear still lingered, not completely releasing me from the bars of my self-made prison, making me still unable to tell him I chose him.

Aiden waited a patient moment for my answer and sighed sadly when I remained silent. Guilt prickled my heart at the pain my limiting fears were causing him. I needed to overcome them, not just for myself but for him, for *us*.

He caressed my hair, his yearning-filled gaze seeping into mine. "You're not ready, are you?"

"Not quite," I said. "I've been thinking about when you spoke of a future together in the hedge maze. I want one with you, but I just need some more time."

"Of course, Eileen. I'll give you all the time you need. But can I really be so selfish to claim you when doing so would make you unhappy?"

I stroked his cheek. "You're afraid you'll make me unhappy?"

"I'm afraid of hurting you again." He took a wavering breath. "There's something I need to tell you."

I peered up at him, curious. He searched my expression, opened his mouth to speak…but remained silent.

"What is it, Aiden?"

He leaned against my touch. "I don't know how to tell you. What if you leave me?"

"Why would I leave you?"

He pulled me into another hug, clinging to me as if afraid I'd slip away if he let me go. "Because I know you miss your old life, the life I took you away from when I entangled you in this competition. I need to make it up to you. Do you still want to leave?"

It was the invitation I'd been seeking since arriving at the castle. Did Aiden know of a way out of this that up until now he hadn't shared with me? Was escape really within my grasp?

I searched his expression for his sincerity. After all his efforts in keeping me here, would he really help me escape? With the fear from the princesses' suspicions I considered it, but one look in Aiden's eyes changed my mind. I couldn't turn my back on the opportunity of being with the man I loved, no matter how frightened I still was.

I cared for him and I knew he cared for me in return. I relished the way he looked at me, as if after years of searching he'd found exactly who he'd been looking for. As I stared into his eyes, I realized I felt the same way about him. With this thought, the terror tightening my chest slowly eased.

"No, I don't want to leave, not anymore." And I snuggled closer, sealing the decision my heart had made.

CHAPTER 21

*M*y hands shook as I stared at the final task:

For all the decorum and knowledge a princess possesses, she must still win the heart of the prince in order to be of his choosing. Prepare to present yourself at tomorrow night's ball, where each will dance with His Royal Highness before he chooses the queen who will rule by his side.

It wasn't the task itself that frightened me. After I'd managed to fumble my way through proper etiquette and royal knowledge, I could surely learn to dance in a single evening; I'd seen Rosie dance on several occasions, so it wouldn't be completely new to me. No, it was the fact that I'd be forced to dance with the Dark Prince. It would be my ultimate test in this deception. Why hadn't I seized Aiden's invitation to escape when I'd the chance?

I didn't hear Aiden's knock until it became louder and more insistent. I walked numbly to the door to yank it open.

Aiden's eyes widened as he took in my expression. "What is it? What's wrong?" He closed the door behind him and rubbed my arms soothingly. I pressed my forehead against his chest and allowed him to hold me.

"I don't know if I can do this," I whispered. He wrapped his arm around me and gently led me to the settee in front of the crackling fire, where he lowered us.

"Is it the final task?"

I nodded and wordlessly handed it to him. He read it. "Why are you so worried? This is the easiest one." He rubbed my back as he nestled against my hair.

I tipped my head up. "I'm afraid to dance with the prince."

Aiden's brow furrowed. "Are you afraid he'll pick you?"

"I'm afraid of being found out, of being seen for who I truly am. I'm a fraud."

"You're not a fraud," Aiden said. "You're the most genuine person I know. As such, you'll be fine. You're strong and will get through this. Will it ease your heart to know I'll also be at the ball?"

"You will?" This both pleased me and horrified me. "That means you'll see me dance with the prince." My cheeks burned deeper at that thought.

He tilted his head. "Perhaps I could pull faces at you during your dance in order to get you to smile."

"Oh, don't do that; what if it makes him like me? I don't want to encourage him at all."

His lips twitched. "You're right; you're bound to be chosen even without my interference."

Horror filled my heart at the thought. "He mustn't choose me. I can't pretend to be something I'm not the rest of my life; eventually my deception will be revealed." But that was nothing to the thought of living the remainder of my life without Aiden.

"No matter what happens, I promise you'll be alright. Don't worry if you mess up; you'll still outshine every princess there."

I knew he was trying to ease my worries, but they only escalated. "Why are you so certain I'll be picked?"

He caressed my cheek, his gaze adoring. "Because you're wonderful."

"Then let's hope he's too blind to see whatever it is you do."

He reached for my hand and rubbed his thumb along the back of it. "You really don't want to be chosen by him, do you?"

"That's what I've been trying to tell you."

He frowned. "Does the thought of being royal still upset you?"

My stomach knotted. "It does, but it's more than that."

I caressed his cheek. He rested his hand on top of mine and leaned against my touch. "Do you want to be chosen by someone else instead?"

His look was hopeful and smoldering, one that ignited my insides. I stared at him in return, hoping he could read the words from my heart in my eyes, ones I couldn't express. I wanted him, *needed* him. I ached to confess my feelings; I'd regret it forever if I didn't. I had to summon my bravery tonight, somehow.

I forced myself to pull away from his warm embrace, needing space to think. "Can you really dance adequately enough to teach me?"

"I'll have you know I'm an excellent dancer and an even better teacher." He helped me to my feet before bending over my hand to kiss it. "Princess Eileen—"

"Please don't call me that."

His lips quirked up. "My darling Eileen, may I have the honor of this dance?"

Mouth dry, I nodded. Aiden wrapped his hand around my waist to pull me closer. I melted against him with a contented sigh, marveling once more at how right it felt to be with him.

"Our first dance," he murmured into my hair. "I hope you save one for me at the ball."

I couldn't speak. I pressed myself closer to him, allowing all of him to envelop me.

"Rest your left hand on my shoulder and gently place your right hand in mine. There, see how easy this is so far?"

"Until we start to move." I was beginning to regret refusing Rosie's multiple attempts to teach me how to dance.

"We're only doing a simple waltz, so you'll be fine." He squeezed my hand assuringly. "Each of your steps is a mirror image to mine. We'll start by making a square with our feet. I'll step forward with my left foot while you step back with your right."

I did and managed a choked laugh of relief when I succeeded. He held me closer, his heated touch enveloping my waist.

"Now, I'm going to step to the right with my right foot in an upside-down 'L' shape while you move your left foot back to the left so we still face one another."

I narrowly missed stepping on his foot. "Oh no, I almost maimed you."

He chuckled. "You can step on my feet all you want if it means we're dancing together."

"I doubt the prince will be so accommodating."

"I thought you'd welcome such a mishap, considering you don't want to be picked," he teased. "Don't worry, you'll be fine. Now, the next step…"

The waltz continued step by step, each performed several times until I could dance without prompting. Although I was unmistakably rough and lacking in natural grace, I wasn't as terrible as I'd feared. Rosie would be proud.

Aiden hummed the familiar waltz tune I'd heard performed during the village dances as he twirled us effortlessly around the bedroom, leaving me to savor not only the dance itself but the dance with *him*. An intense, warm emotion filled my heart to be wrapped securely in his arms.

With each spin Aiden pulled me closer, as if he meant to keep me near him always. His hand resting at my waist moved up to massage the base of my back, sending pleasant tingles rippling up and down my spine. Each touch from him only ignited the feelings burning within me, the need to remain in this moment with him forever.

I rested my head on his shoulder and snuggled close, sighing contentedly as he rested his head on top of mine. In my need to be even closer to him, I stood on tiptoe and brushed a soft kiss against his lips, a kiss that melted into a long, lingering one. My arms hooked around his neck and my fingers burrowed in his chestnut hair.

Eventually we not only broke the kiss but slowed our waltz to a stop.

"Eileen?" Aiden's soft voice penetrated the reverent stillness and drew my gaze to him once more. "Have you had a chance to think about our future?"

I nodded as I unwound my arms from around his neck and intertwined our hands. "I can't imagine any future without you."

He cradled my face and pressed a soft kiss on my brow. "Neither can I. As such, there's nothing I've ever wanted more than what I'm about to ask you for." He pressed his free hand against my pounding chest. "I want your heart. I know you've been through a lot of pain," he continued gently. "I know your heart has been protected and will take time to completely relinquish to me, but I also know that as soon as you do—as soon as you allow faith to be stronger than your fears—you'll finally be able to heal. Trust me, I know. I love you, Eileen, more than I've ever loved anyone, and if you trust your heart to me, I promise to cherish it forever."

He loved me. I found myself completely unprepared for the

effect those beautiful words would have on me. Warmth enveloped me, as if I'd been dipped in the sun, and my heart soared.

Mother had told me that love was worth experiencing even at the risk of losing it, that she'd choose Father again even after knowing the outcome of that choice. I hadn't understood her then. I understood her now. I was no longer afraid of choosing love, only of losing my opportunity to embrace it.

Aiden shifted uneasily at my extended silence. "Please, Eileen…" He held both my hands and pulled them to his chest.

"I can't give you what you already have," I whispered. "My heart is already yours." It had been for a long time.

I would never forget the joy that lit his expression at my words. "Oh Eileen, really?"

"It's always been yours, even before I realized it."

"And mine is yours." He embraced me, holding me tightly, as if he never intended to let me go. I snuggled closer, marveling at how simple it had been to choose him, how right this felt. "Tomorrow at the ball I'll claim you," he murmured into my ear. "Everyone will know we belong together. Will you save me a dance?"

"I'll save you every dance." I kissed him lightly, sealing the promise. As magical as dancing with Aiden at a ball was sure to be, I knew that it wouldn't hold a candle to our dance tonight, the one that had allowed me to finally tell him I'd chosen him and would continue choosing him forever.

CHAPTER 22

J'd scarcely slept. How could I with all that had transpired between Aiden and me? Whenever I'd tried to sleep, the beautiful memory of our dance would fill my mind, causing me to grin as my toes curled in delight. My heart felt lighter than it ever had, on the brink of soaring away.

The sky had been a swirl of grey all morning, a sign of approaching rain. I ignored the sky's threats and ventured outside anyway, unaffected by the biting chill and too restless to remain cooped up in the palace. I strolled the cobblestone pathways weaving through the manicured gardens, so unlike the wild beauty of the Forest, whose dark, majestic trees surrounded the Sortileyan Palace, taunting me with their presence.

Despite its bout of mischief in leading me to the palace, I still longed for the sanctuary of the woods—its minty, pine-scented air and dappled green light as the sun danced through its canopy of leaves. I missed the whispers of the trees, the air that was thick with mystery and possibility, and especially the thrill that came from taking whichever path it had in mind and seeing where it led.

The decision to follow the Forest's constantly shifting pathways had led me here, and now I was facing another path I never imagined I'd one day walk. How freeing it was to finally embrace what my heart had been leading me to all along.

I found myself at the maze, where Aiden had invited me to explore a future with him. I ran my hand along the hedge wall as I walked the outside, not daring to venture inside without Aiden's sure guidance to keep me from getting lost.

Aiden, the man I'd chosen. I smiled and pressed my hand to my heart.

I began searching for him. As if the Forest also had control of the garden pathways, I felt it guide me in a specific direction, one I followed, trusting it would lead me to where I needed to be.

I slowed when I heard loud, antagonistic voices coming from up ahead, one of them as familiar as my own. Dread knotted my stomach as I crept towards the water garden. Inside, Aiden stood with his back facing the entrance, his attention riveted to Princess Seren, who glared at him.

"Your threats won't keep me silent," she said. "I know all about your scheme, and I won't let you get away with it. His Majesty will never allow it."

"You can't stop me." Desperation filled Aiden's voice. "I refuse to be swayed from my decision by anyone, least of all you. I've chosen my path and nobody will prevent me from taking it."

Princess Seren's glare sharpened. "You're a fool. One day you'll realize that."

Thunder rumbled through the sky, as if affirming her words, before the threatening rain escaped. She covered her head and scowled up at the sky.

"Even arguing with you isn't worth the rain soiling my gown."

Aiden rolled his eyes. "Appearances are all you seem to care about. But I'm not like you; I only want someone who makes me happy."

"And you truly think that imposter will give you that? You're of noble birth. If you choose that commoner, you'll regret it forever. Perhaps not immediately, but one day you'll realize all you gave up for her. Then you'll toss her aside. Why wait? Just do it now."

My heart lurched as she voiced the very fears I'd worked so hard to overcome, ones that waited in the wings to revisit me at any vulnerable moment.

Princess Seren smirked. "Or perhaps she'll be the one to leave you when she discovers everything you've kept from her. Some secrets require too high a price, even for her." The rain picked up and Princess Seren shivered. "If you insist on continuing our fight, let's at least do it inside." She turned towards the exit and spotted me, watching with a pounding heart, a heart that felt on the brink of breaking all over again.

"We're not finished, Seren." Aiden seized her firmly by the arm as his gaze fell on me. His mouth fell open and his hardened manner immediately softened. But it was too late. I'd already seen and heard too much.

I didn't realize I was crying until Princess Seren smirked. "Looks like I won't be ruining anything for you after all; you did it yourself by showing your sweetheart what you're really like."

What he was really like.... Once more, witnessing Aiden's hardened persona put a chink in my resolve. I knew without a doubt that I loved him and wanted a future with him, but was he truly right for me? I ached to move forward, but there was still so much I didn't know. Was love enough? Had I been so afraid of losing the opportunity to embrace love that I'd chosen him too quickly?

Aiden released Princess Seren and stepped forward, eyes pleading. "Eileen?"

I couldn't face him now, not when I was so confused by what I'd just overheard. Distance—I needed distance.

I turned and bolted. Aiden immediately ran after me. I wove through the gardens, slipping and sliding on the wet cobblestones, my wet hair dripping down my back and onto my already tear-stained cheeks. My breath came in sharp bursts but I didn't slow. The palace's front doors loomed ahead and I ran harder.

"Eileen! Please wait."

Aiden caught up and seized my wrist with surprising gentleness and tugged me to a stop. I glared at him as I feebly tried to wriggle free, but as before it was futile. Even if he hadn't been holding me, the emotion in his eyes rooted me to the spot; the pain filling his pleading gaze was more acute than my own.

"Please, Eileen, I need to talk with you."

I finally gave up the fight. "About what?"

A shiver rippled over me. Aiden tugged off his cloak and draped it over my shoulders. I drew it around me and waited for him to speak, getting more soaked the longer we lingered in the rain.

"Did you overhear my conversation with Seren?"

I flinched at the memory. I didn't want to think about that encounter, didn't want to dwell on Princess Seren's words and all they'd revealed: was the darkness I'd once again witnessed the true Aiden rather than the one who'd stolen my heart away? If what she said was true, I had a greater need to protect my heart. But how could I protect something that wasn't in my possession any longer, but in his?

Aiden's eyebrows drew together as he searched my teary expression. He reached out a hesitant hand to brush away my tears. "How much did you hear?"

"Enough." I gave another tug on his hold, and although he released me his eyes pleaded for me to stay and listen. I still cared enough that I obeyed.

"Seren is angry with me and is using you to hurt me," he said. "But nothing she said is true. Please don't believe it."

I pressed my hands to my hips. "Oh, really? None of it is true?"

He lowered his eyes. His silence confirmed my fears.

"You promised me I could trust you," I whispered.

"And you can." He reached for my hand and despite my reservations I let him, needing him to touch me, even now.

"How? I want to, but you keep giving me reasons not to." I took a deep, steadying breath. "What are you keeping from me? Can't you tell me?"

He opened his mouth—as if he meant to do just that—before he snapped it shut with a remorseful sigh. Avoiding my eyes, he shook his head. "I can't tell you now."

I yanked my hand away. "Please Aiden, don't do this. Our relationship is still too new." I could already feel it slipping away. We'd barely lasted a few days. Was this path doomed even before we had a chance to walk it together? My voice choked on my sob. "Please, Aiden. It took me so long to trust you."

He took my hand again, squeezing it desperately. "I promise I'll tell you everything, but now isn't the right time."

"Then when *will* it be?"

He groaned and buried his face in his hands. "This is such a mess. Please, Eileen. You must trust me a little while longer."

He stepped closer, cradling my cheek. Against all sense I leaned against his touch, relishing the gentleness of it, a tenderness that couldn't be faked, which made me want to believe that this path was still one worth pursuing, despite the potential risks.

"I can't promise I'll never hurt you," he continued. "Despite how much I care, I still have many weaknesses. But I will promise to not only do my best to never hurt you but to always love you. I'll protect your heart and cherish it forever…if I can still have it."

He didn't even need to ask. Love was illogical…yet somehow still achingly beautiful. Thus I needed to be brave.

Aiden's fingertips caressed my cheeks and my pulse quickened. With a deep breath I stepped closer, allowing Aiden's warmth to enfold me, blocking out the chill from the rain. His arms tenderly wound around me to hold me close, a gesture which reaffirmed my decision to trust him once more.

I took his cloak and wrapped it around both of us so we were sharing it before I nestled back against his chest. As I did so, I caught sight of a corner of folded parchment sticking out from the inside pocket of his cloak, the hand-writing peeking out familiar.

My stomach jolted. "What's that?"

He stiffened, guilt twisting his expression, confirmation of my horrific realization. I snatched the parchment. My heart sunk as my eyes confirmed my suspicion.

"My letter to Mother, the one I gave you days ago." I raised my stunned gaze to his dark, remorseful one. "You never sent it."

He avoided my eyes. "No, I didn't."

I gaped at him as this newest betrayal burned through me. "But you promised you would." The thought of Mother's pain and worry over this past week sickened me.

"And I will…eventually."

"*Eventually*?!" I crumpled the letter in my fist. "How could you not send it after I told you how much my father's disappearance hurt me and Mother? Don't you realize how important it is that my mother knows where I am? That I'm safe? I've been gone a week. She likely thinks me dead because *you* didn't send my letter."

Aiden winced, revealing his anguish. "I'm so sorry, Eileen, I—"

"You're *sorry*? Is that all you have to say?" The tears burning my eyes finally escaped. "How could you? You told me you would send my letter. I believed you."

"And I will send it," he said, eyes pleading. "I just need to wait for the best moment."

"The best moment for who? For *you*?"

He flinched. "No...I mean, I know it looks bad, but please trust me. I promise I—"

"*No!*" Tears trickled down my cheeks, fast and furious, but I made no attempt to wipe them away, and when he stepped forward to do it for me, I slapped his hand away. "You broke your promise. I can't trust you. I can't trust anyone."

"But Eileen—"

"*No!* Why should I give you yet another chance? You entangle me in a mess that risks my life and don't even have the decency to deliver a letter to ease my frantic mother's heart. I'm all she has left, and you're not only keeping me from her but causing her to believe the worst fate has befallen me. This isn't love; this is selfishness."

Aiden moaned and buried his face in his hands. "I'm so sorry, Eileen."

I threw the letter in his face and spun around to stomp up the front steps. This time he didn't come after me.

I'd been right all along. Love wasn't worth all of this.

CHAPTER 23

*T*he clock on the mantle inched ever closer to the time of tonight's ball, where I'd not only be forced to dance with Prince Deidric but see Aiden again, neither of which I wanted to do. Alaina had been knocking on my locked door for the past hour, persistently ignoring my order for her to leave.

"Please open the door, Princess. I must prepare you for the ball."

"I'm not going to the ball," I told her for the dozenth time.

"But His Majesty has ordered it," she protested. "Forgive me for refusing your orders, Your Highness, but I must obey the Sortileyan royal family."

I gritted my teeth at her formal address. "Please stop addressing me in such a way."

I couldn't bear to be called princess one more time. I desperately wanted this nightmare to end so I could return to my old life and especially to Mother. The thought of her frantic worrying escalated my anger towards the man who'd broken my trust by failing to deliver my letter.

Alaina ceased knocking for a blissful moment before exclaiming, "Your Highness!"

Unsurprisingly, she continued to ignore my request. I groaned and collapsed backwards onto my bed, where I pressed my pillow over my face to smother her repeated knocking. Still, as annoying as her persistence was, its endurance was a price I'd gladly pay in order to avoid not only the elegance and glamor of the ball but especially the Dark Prince and Aiden.

More knocking. I unburied myself to glare at the door. "Go away."

"Eileen?"

My breath hooked. That voice…. "Aiden?"

"Yes, it's me. Please open the door."

"No, I don't want to see you." I reburied my head, this time to protect myself from the effects of his honey-smooth voice, already doing strange things to my insides. My legs tingled, defying me by their wish to go open the door to my betrayer. I fought to resist this ridiculous impulse.

"Please, Eileen, I want to talk to you."

"I refuse to hear anything you have to say."

"Please listen." His tone was pleading. "I'm so sorry about this afternoon."

I tried to ignore him, a difficult feat when the pillow did little to tune out his words. I fought to ignore the part of me that was relieved about that.

"Please open up, Eileen. If you do, I promise I'll—"

I bolted upright and glared at the door, never mind he couldn't see it. "Oh, you *promise*. Such empty words from one who's broken previous promises made to me. As such, I never want to see you again. Now go away."

"Eileen, *please*, I just want—"

"Go away!" I threw my pillow very satisfyingly against the door, with plenty more piled on this bed to use should the need arise; I'd likely use all of them with how stubborn Aiden was proving to be.

His knocking paused. "Did you just throw a pillow at me?" Amusement filled his tone and my own lips twitched. Thank goodness he couldn't see my bad mood faltering.

"I did, and so help me, if you force that door open, the next one will hit your face, with many more to follow; this bed is drowning in pillows."

He chuckled and the warm sound seeped over me, weakening my defenses. "Oh, my Eileen." His laughter faltered and he returned to knocking. "I'll happily risk any attack from you if you just open up and let me talk to you."

"Why should I grant your request when I'm determined never to see you again?"

"Because I want to help you escape."

I'd just seized another pillow and taken aim but froze at his words. "What?"

"I'm going to help you escape before the ball."

I blinked at the door, still stunned. "Why?"

"For one thing, I have it on good authority that the prince has chosen you as his wife—"

"*What*!?" Panic clawed my throat. Impossible. That wasn't supposed to happen; it *couldn't* happen. "I'm a failure at being a fake royal. How can a stranger who doesn't even know me really be so insane as to—"

"Eileen, please." He kept knocking, and the aggravating sound was causing the beginnings of a headache to throb against my temples. "I know you don't want this, and I feel horrible for the pain I've caused you. You're right that I've been terribly selfish. I wanted your heart so badly that I put my desires above yours. But no longer. I need you to be happy, so I'll take you back home so your mother will no longer worry. I'm so sorry I didn't send your letter. I know I've messed up and thus don't deserve your trust, but I need to do this for you so I can somehow make it up to you. *Please.*"

His knocking ceased as he waited for my answer. I blinked back my tears as I gaped at the closed door. I knew his speech had been nothing but words and thus I had no reason to trust them...but I did, even after everything. Regardless of how fragile my trust currently was, he still possessed my heart, a heart that urged me to take a leap of faith one last time.

I scrambled from the bed and yanked the door open. My breath caught as I took him in, in all his finery. He wore a ceremonial dress uniform and looked incredibly regal.

"Are you armed?" he asked.

The pillow I'd brought to hit him with slipped from my fingers. My cheeks warmed as I gaped at him. "You're... dressed up," I managed. His own gaze had been hungrily caressing my face. He grinned crookedly.

"I mentioned last evening I'll be attending the ball, which I believe is starting in an hour."

"So my maid has told me countless times." I searched the hallways for her, but she was nowhere in sight. "How did you get her to leave me alone?"

"A bit of persuasion." He hesitantly took my hand and rubbed the back of it with his thumb, all while his remorseful gaze seeped into mine. "I'm so sorry about betraying your trust, my Eileen, especially after I promised I wouldn't."

I bit my lip to keep it from trembling. "Why didn't you send my note?"

His fingers tightened around mine. "Because I was afraid if your mother knew where you were, she'd come take you away from me. I didn't even think of the pain she must be experiencing at your disappearance or how much my actions would hurt you. I thought of no one but myself. It was inexcusable."

I didn't trust myself to speak, not with the sudden lump in my throat, so I only nodded. "You're going to take me home?"

"Yes. Now is the best time to leave, when everyone is distracted by the ball."

"A ball you're expected to attend."

"You're much more important to me than duty. Now, shall we make your escape, my dear?"

He offered his arm. I retrieved my sketchbook before I returned and slowly wound my arm through his, curling my fingers at his elbow. Despite everything that had transpired between us, being with him felt so *right*. I nestled closer with each step as he led me through the corridors, down a back staircase, and out a side door into the water garden. The air was brisk and smelled fresh and earthy from the recent rain. The sun hung low in the sky, dappling its golden light across the rain-splotched fauna.

"How will we manage to escape when this past week you've told me it's impossible?"

He gnawed his lip guiltily. "I have more to apologize for: I could have helped you escape from the beginning. But I was afraid if I did I'd never see you again. Once more I must beg your forgiveness."

I sighed. Even though I was still angry, I was tired of turning away from him, for I loved him. That would never change. He hadn't intended to hurt me; he only feared losing me, a fear I understood because I desperately didn't want to lose him either.

"You did say you weren't perfect. I'm immensely disappointed that you were correct."

"But despite my imperfections I do love you, Eileen, and will strive never to hurt you in such a way again." Agony hardened his expression, and he looked away to stare unblinkingly ahead. "Considering we likely won't see one another after today due to my betrayal, I can at least keep that promise."

My hold tightened on him to keep him from slipping away. I couldn't lose him, a fact that only became more clear the closer our separation became, and in that moment I finally better understood what Mother had been telling me about love: sometimes it hurt, but the beauty of it made it not only worth the risk but a journey worth taking.

Aiden paused in front of a marble fountain in the shape of a majestic dragon, water spewing from its mouth. "Alastar has told me you've been searching for secret passageways. You yourself once asked me if I knew of the one that leads to the Forest."

"Are you about to share the secret?"

"I trust you won't tell." He winked before releasing me and hopping onto the rim of the fountain, where he pressed the dragon's eye. The fountain rumbled before shifting a few feet to reveal a staircase descending belowground. I gaped at it.

"Amazing. There really are secret passageways."

"I'd once hoped we could explore them together, but..." Sadness filled his voice, reminding me that it wasn't just passageways we wouldn't explore; our separation would also prevent a lifetime of wonderful memories. My already abused heart twisted at the thought.

Aiden rested his hand on my lower back to guide me down into the dark passageway. As we reached the bottom step, the fountain above us shifted and slowly slid back into place. It closed with a resonating *thud*, swallowing us up in darkness.

I shivered and Aiden soothingly rubbed my arms. "Come, let's take you home, where you'll be safe."

Calm enveloped me. Unlike when he'd first spoken those words earlier, this time I believed them.

Despite the smothering darkness surrounding us, Aiden found his way easily, as if he'd traversed this route many times. I clung to his hand and trusted in each step he took. The passage wasn't long, and soon the ground began to slope upward. At the top, Aiden pushed a hidden knob embedded into the stone wall. The ceiling shifted and opened up to the sunset-shrouded sky and the familiar trees of the Forest towering over us, my old friends.

Stepping into the Forest again felt like being granted breath; it bathed my senses in the scent of pine and earth, the sound of the swaying branches, and the feeling of coming home. The trees opened in invitation for us to step inside, where a single path awaited us.

Aiden led me down this twisting path. I glanced behind me and watched the trees rearrange themselves to not only swallow it up but mask the palace from view. A strange sense of loss filled me to no longer see it.

The last time I'd been in the woods, I'd been wandering lost in the storm before the pathways finally guided me to the palace. Now that I was leaving it behind, I realized that the Forest had taken me to a destination far different than I'd imagined: not to the palace, not to the Princess Competition, but to Aiden, and with him the experiences that had forever changed me. It was only by trusting the Forest's ever-changing paths, despite not knowing where they were leading me, that I'd experienced such a remarkable journey.

We walked deeper through the trees, but I no longer noticed the gorgeous colors and scenery, conscious only of Aiden's presence beside me. He was here. No matter how many times I pushed him away, he kept returning. I knew he always would. Despite the moments he'd hurt me, I could no longer imagine being without him.

He helped me over a log, the heat of his touch lingering around my waist. I rested my hands on his shoulders and stared into his dark eyes, full of sweet concern. "Will you be happy, my Eileen?"

How could I? Now that I'd met Aiden nothing would ever be the same. I could never return to the way things were, especially after experiencing the feelings I felt for him. I could never forget them, forget him. I loved him, I'd found him, and if I allowed my old fears to overcome me once more and push him away, I'd always regret losing him.

Aiden cradled my cheek, his riveted gaze full of fierce adoration. "Will you be happy, Eileen?" he repeated.

His expression was so earnest. I leaned against his hand, basking in all I felt for him. I loved him; I loved being with him; he made me happy. My life would never be the same without him, not after he'd broken down all my defenses and stolen every piece of my heart.

"Will you?" I asked him.

"I can be content if you're happy. You couldn't find it with me, so I'm hoping that letting you go will allow you to find what you're looking for."

How could he not understand that *he* was what I'd been searching for? My heart had known it, but I'd repeatedly ignored its gentle urgings with every bump in our journey together. No longer. My path was not to return to my life in Arador, but to move forward with Aiden, wherever that would lead us.

I took a deep, wavering breath and stepped closer, bridging the distance between us. I cradled his face.

"I love you, Aiden. I gave you my heart, and no matter what happens, it can never be taken back. It's always been yours and it always will be. I now realize I don't want to go back home, I only want to be with you. I just need Mother to know I'm alright before we can begin our new life together."

He wrapped his arms around me to hold me close. "Oh Eileen, there's nothing I've ever wanted more than you."

I smiled and stood on tiptoe to kiss him, but to my surprise he pulled away, his expression pained.

"Wait, Eileen. There's something I need to tell you before we can finally be together, those secrets I've been hiding from you that I can't keep any longer. I hope you'll still want me after I tell them to you."

I clung to him, needing to keep him near. "I'll always want you." After the long, exhausting journey to come to that realization, it was one I'd never forget.

"First I have a riddle for you."

I gave a half laugh, half sob. "Another riddle?"

"The last one, I promise." He cradled my face, his expression grave.

The sound of pounding footsteps and crashing branches pierced the reverent moment. Aiden's brow furrowed as he glanced behind me. He stiffened and in one move he'd drawn his sword and yanked me behind him, just as an entourage of royal soldiers stepped into view, surrounding us with raised swords, their piercing gazes focused intently on me.

Fear seized me in a tight grip. It had finally happened: I'd been caught.

CHAPTER 24

My heart pounded as I stared at the surrounding soldiers, encircling us like a noose with their sharp swords. I pressed myself closer to Aiden, his warmth the only thing keeping my escalating panic from completely overcoming me. Why hadn't the Forest protected us? I suppose even its love for us couldn't override its allegiance to the king.

"Lower your swords." Aiden's words were clipped and full of authority.

The soldiers obeyed him, lowering their weapons but not sheathing them. I blinked, surprised at the ease with which Aiden had been obeyed.

"What's the meaning of this, General Duncan?" Aiden demanded, his expression hardened.

A dark-haired soldier stepped forward and bowed. "Forgive us, Your Highness, but we're under orders from His Majesty."

"*Your Highness*!?" Shock pierced my suffocating fear. The soldiers and swords faded from my awareness as this emotion eclipsed me. I could only focus on Aiden. I gaped at him in utter disbelief, searching his black eyes. He couldn't be...he was just a nobleman. He would have told me...*why* hadn't he told me? "You're a prince? Of which kingdom?"

Aiden's face twisted with guilt as he met my gaze. "I'm so sorry," he whispered, his hold tightening around my hand. "I tried to tell you so many times."

His attention snapped back to the soldiers, a problem more pressing than the shock and confusion raging within me at this revelation that Aiden was a prince.

"I order you not to touch Eileen," Aiden said.

"Apologies, Your Highness, but His Majesty's command overrules even yours."

Aiden scooted farther in front of me, placing himself as a protective shield between General Duncan and me. "I don't care. I refuse to stand aside and let you take her."

General Duncan's stance didn't falter as he took in Aiden's defense and our intertwined hands. "I'm sorry, Your Highness, but I'm under orders to bring her before His Majesty."

The regality cloaking Aiden melted away as he crumpled, his eyes full of so many apologies when he turned and cupped my face, pressing his forehead against mine. "Eileen."

My whimper escaped as I pressed myself closer, needing to feel the security and assurance that only came from him. "What's going to happen to me?" I stuttered.

Aiden pulled me aside to give us a small bit of privacy. "Nothing, darling. Everything will be alright. Trust me."

Despite the promise of his words, fear filled his voice. His gaze caressed my face, as if committing my features to memory in case this was the last time we saw one another.

I clung to him more tightly, desperate for him to remain with me. I'd fought too long and hard for him, for us, only to lose him now. How ironic that the Forest that had brought us together would now become the place where we were torn apart.

"Don't leave me," I pleaded.

"I'm so sorry, I have no choice. I need to go ahead and explain everything, but first there's something I need to tell you." His gaze penetrated mine. "I'm not just a prince; I'm the Dark Prince Deidric."

My breath hitched at this second startling revelation. "What?" But his name was *Aiden*, not Deidric.

"I should have told you before now; I tried to before but it just never seemed to be the right time. This wasn't how I wanted to do it." He ran his fingers through my hair. "I promise to explain everything, but first I need to talk to my father. I'm so sorry for the mess I've entangled you in, but I promise I'll get you out of it."

There were so many questions I had, but now wasn't the time. I stroked his face and he melted against my touch, relieved at my acceptance.

He leaned down to kiss me but hesitated, as if afraid that my learning his true identity would change everything between us. And perhaps it would have if the old Eileen had discovered the truth. But I was not that Eileen anymore. I no longer feared falling in love, but of losing it—of losing him.

I stood on tiptoe to meet his kiss. Light, soft, and full of tenderness. I kissed not the Dark Prince but Aiden, the man I'd fallen in love with, and in that kiss I realized I trusted him completely. No matter what happened, we'd always remain together.

Aiden stared longingly at me after we broke apart before he turned to the surrounding soldiers. The hardness I used to fear filled Aiden's expression as his regality returned.

His sharp glare took in every soldier. "No harm is to befall Eileen. She is your future queen and will be treated with respect. Do I make myself clear?"

Future queen? Me? The panic filling my chest escalated.

General Duncan bowed. "Understood, Your Highness. Our instructions were only to bring her to the king. Rest assured no harm will come to her. You have my word."

Aiden stroked my cheek with his thumb before reluctantly releasing me and stepping back, pain filling his eyes as if he'd just severed himself from his heart.

I scrambled for his hand, the panic his presence had managed to quell rising again as he pulled away. "Don't leave me."

He gave my hand a reassuring squeeze. "It'll be alright. I'll go ahead to explain everything to my father. I promise to protect you."

I searched his dark eyes and slowly managed to loosen my vise-like grip. "I trust you."

He turned to Duncan. "Remember my orders. You're not to touch her." He kissed my cheek before he disappeared down a path that had opened up, a shortcut that the Forest immediately sealed off behind him.

The fear clenching my heart tightened as General Duncan and his accompanying soldiers, swords now sheathed, escorted me down another trail that twisted towards the palace I'd just escaped from.

With each step, I struggled to process all I'd learned about Aiden's true identity. This entire time, he'd been the Dark Prince Deidric? All the unexplained riddles fell into place— why Aiden had enrolled me in the competition for Prince Deidric's hand, why Aiden had never been present at court during the tasks, why Aiden had been assisting me so I would win...these thoughts and more swirled through my mind as we entered the palace.

Inside, the marble hallways were abandoned except for an occasional footman. Murmurs and music drifted from the ballroom down the corridor where the final task was taking place. I ached to escape back to the Forest or even to the ball —anywhere rather than confronting the formidable king.

The sound of laughter and music faded as General Duncan led me down an opposite hallway. My pulse palpitated with each step and skittered to a stop when he paused outside a guarded door.

"General Duncan to see His Majesty," he informed the guards. One opened the door enough for him to slip through. I wiped my sweaty palms on my gown as we waited. After a tense moment—during which my nerves flared to life all over again—he returned.

"His Majesty will see you."

General Duncan escorted me into the vast, gilded throne room. Inside, the stern king sat on a gold-and-jewel-encrusted throne, surrounded by guards and his closest advisors, all watching me with sharp intensity. Princess Seren stood beside him, smirking, while on his other side...sweet relief washed over me to see my Aiden. Worry twisted his expression, but his eyes were adoring as always. He strode towards me and wrapped me in the security of his tender embrace.

"Eileen," he murmured, pulling me close. I clutched his uniform as I burrowed against him. His breath caressed my skin as he leaned down to my ear. "Don't worry, I'm explaining everything to Father."

I peeked out. One glimpse of the king's hardened countenance revealed that Aiden's explanation wasn't going well. Aiden wound his arm around my waist and turned us to face the king.

"Your Majesty, may I present Princess Eileen, my chosen bride."

I shakily curtsied.

The king cocked an eyebrow. "Princess *Eileen*? Not Princess Gemma of Malvagaria? It appears there's been some deception going on." He gave Aiden an accusing look. "She's not even a princess, is she? I've suspected something amiss about her. It appears my instincts were correct."

I remained silent. My chest tightened; each hitching breath became a struggle.

The king's frown deepened as he surveyed us. "So it's true? You're nothing more than a peasant?"

I swallowed and struggled to force words past my parched throat. "Yes, Your Majesty, but I swear it was never my intention…" I trailed off, fear silencing me. Aiden jumped in.

"As I've been explaining, Father, I'm the one who—"

The king's hand snapped up in silent command and Aiden stilled. The king continued to stare at me, the force of his accusing eyes causing my heartbeat to escalate.

"If you're not a princess, then you're obviously a spy sent to infiltrate my kingdom."

I frantically shook my head. "No, Your Majesty." But my protests came out as only a squeak.

"Then how do you explain the presence of a common girl competing for the hand of the crown prince?"

I pressed myself closer to Aiden. He rubbed my back soothingly. "She knew nothing about the competition until she stumbled upon the palace."

The king frowned and shook his head. "Too coincidental."

"You're correct; it's no mere coincidence," Aiden said. "I told the Forest to lead her here so she could compete for my hand."

My head jerked towards him in astonishment. He'd given the Forest such instructions? My heart fluttered at this realization.

"Eileen knew nothing about the competition until after her arrival, when I told the guards and servants she was a princess," Aiden continued. "She didn't even know my true identity. I had to hide it from her because she never wanted to marry a prince. But I love her and want no one but her to be my queen. I'm just hoping she'll still have me now that she knows I'm the crown prince."

The king's expression darkened as he slowly rose, tall and foreboding arrayed in his royal regalia. He took an imposing step closer. "Yes, you're the crown prince, while she's nothing more than a commoner." He slowly raked his gaze over me. Despite my elegant appearance, he sneered in disgust. "Dressing her up can't change her inferiority. She'll never do."

I stiffened and Aiden's hold tightened. "But she passed all your tests," he protested.

"She barely scraped by, undoubtedly due to your efforts, making her unqualified to rule. I only agreed to allow you to break your engagement if you found someone just as eligible as Princess Rheanna to marry." He glared at me and I withered beneath it. "You agreed to choose a *true* princess, which this girl clearly is not."

"She's just as eligible as the other candidates," Aiden said. "If the terms of our agreement were that my chosen bride were of noble or royal birth, then you'd be correct, but instead you merely dictated I marry someone shown to be eligible within the confines of the contest *you* designed, something her participation in the contest has proven. There's no law forbidding the crown prince from marrying a commoner."

The king's jaw tightened. "Maybe not, but there's *tradition*, and it's a tradition that we'll maintain, especially when your choice is a peasant." He advanced another step further, eyes flashing, like a tiger on the prowl who meant to devour me. My blood chilled. "You tell me you're not a spy and you don't want to be a princess. What other possible motivation do you have to infiltrate the palace at the risk of your life should you be caught?"

I looked up at Aiden. "I love him."

The king snorted. "What does love have to do with his duties and obligations as the crown prince? His responsibility is to find a suitable wife to be Queen of Sortileya. And you, as a commoner, are not suited."

I clutched Aiden's hand more tightly. "Your Majesty, I swear, I never wanted to be a princess; I only wanted Aiden." The thought of being queen caused my stomach to churn.

"You cannot have him," the king said. "I'll hear no more of this. Deidric, you'll proceed to the ball at once and choose your wife from among the many eligible women in attendance."

"Father, you can't force me into an unwanted marriage," Aiden said. "If I'm not allowed to marry Eileen, then I'll not marry at all. Your royal line will die with me, and the throne will pass to Oscar."

The king's eye twitched. "My inept nephew will bring the kingdom to ruin."

"Furthermore," Aiden continued, "having a queen with Eileen's common background will not only provide the monarchy with a unique and invaluable perspective on how to better rule our people, but it will also appease our subjects. Her natural compassion will make her a benevolent and beloved ruler."

The king frowned, considering. "There has been some restlessness amongst some of the poorer villages...perhaps your marriage to her will help defuse the situation." For an entire minute, the two stared one another down before the king softened at Aiden's pleading expression. "You love her?"

"More than anything," Aiden said fiercely.

The king nodded. "Very well." He straightened back into

his regal posture. "I refuse to allow my royal line to die or my kingdom to suffer from an inept rule. You've left me no choice. Against my better judgement, for the good of the kingdom, I grant my permission for you to marry this commoner."

My heart lifted and Aiden's arm around me tightened with his own relief as his face broke into a boyish grin. "Thank you, Father."

A timid knock at the door announced the arrival of a footman. "Forgive the interruption, Your Majesty, but many of the guests are questioning your absence, as well as the absence of the crown prince."

The king sighed. "Undoubtedly, rumors are already spreading as to why my son hasn't yet shown up to fulfill his duty for the final task."

"I couldn't say, Your Majesty," the servant stuttered.

"Inform our guests that we'll be there shortly." The king waved him out. The footman departed with a bow, and Aiden glanced back at the king.

"There's no more purpose for this ball; I've already chosen my bride."

"Regardless of your choice, you'll fulfill your duty as crown prince and see this competition through till the end."

Aiden bowed. "I understand. Thank you, Your Majesty."

Muttering darkly to himself, the king strode from the room, followed closely by his entourage of advisors and guards, leaving behind Princess Seren, whose initial gleeful smirk had twisted into a glower. Aiden's hardened persona returned as he glared at his sister.

"You've gone too far this time, Seren," he said. "I warned you not to interfere, especially when you know I've been your only ally against the arranged betrothal you detest so much."

I rested my hand on his arm, a warning not to allow his

dark persona to overcome him. He took a deep, calming breath before turning back to his sister.

"Treat Eileen with respect; otherwise I'd suggest you prepare for your voyage."

Princess Seren's haughty disdain melted away and her face paled. Without another word, Aiden escorted me from the room. I followed in a daze. My head was spinning with all that had transpired. Aiden was the Dark Prince. His father, the king, was allowing us to be married. All the fears and worries of the past week melted away. Despite my fears of being caught coming to pass, I'd somehow escaped the consequences. Aiden had protected me, just as he'd promised.

I knew that it would only be one of many promises he'd keep throughout our life together, and our path—despite the obstacles we'd faced since we'd first met—now lay open before us.

CHAPTER 25

hen we were several paces away from the throne room, I released my pent-up breath. Aiden tugged me into an alcove and held my hands against his heart, his gaze earnest. "Are you alright, Eileen?"

I nodded as I nestled close, right against his settling heartbeat. "You kept your promise."

"I'd never let anything happen to you. I can't lose you." He pressed a soft kiss on the back of each hand.

"Unfortunately, I'm not out of danger yet. I may have survived the gallows, but I may not live through the ball."

"Is there any doubt you won't after the detailed tutelage from your skilled dancing instructor?"

I giggled breathlessly, feeling slightly giddy with the feelings of relief coursing through me. For the first time since arriving at the palace, the constant cloud of worry over being discovered for who I truly was had vanished along with all my fears and reservations, leaving only the sweet feelings I felt for Aiden.

"Will you save a dance for your prized pupil?"

"I'll save you every one I'm not obligated to give to the

other participants." He played with my fingers, his gaze fixated to mine. "There's so much I need to say to you, so many apologies and explanations, but there isn't time now. I promise I'll explain everything soon."

I nodded, believing him. How wonderful it felt to trust him.

He kissed me, smiling against my lips. "Then, my dear, you should quickly prepare for the ball, where the crown prince will at last reveal his choice to the court."

I grinned slyly. "Does this mean I won the competition?"

He laughed and embraced me. "You won before it even started. It was never a contest, merely a formality to appease my father."

"You did more than that—you somehow convinced him we should be allowed to marry." I hooked my arms around his neck and beamed up at him. "What payment do I owe you for that triumph?"

"Hmm, I haven't actually thought about it." He considered before grinning mischievously. "How about your firstborn child?"

I laughed. "You only want my firstborn? It seems fitting I share them all with you."

"Deal." He gave me an affectionate squeeze before releasing me and escorting me to my room.

"So, Deidric, is it?" I asked with a teasing smile. His cheeks blushed crimson and he rolled his eyes.

"No, please, I hate that name. It was my father's choice, and my middle name, Aiden, was my mother's. All my close friends call me Aiden." He paused outside my door and raised my hand to kiss it softly. "I'll see you soon. Don't keep your prince waiting."

"I won't," I whispered breathlessly. After giving my fingers a reassuring squeeze, he departed. I watched him disappear down the hallway before I slipped inside my room, where Alaina awaited me, expression frantic.

"Oh, thank goodness," she tittered. "I've been so worried about you. The ball has been going on for ages. We have to get you ready."

She bustled over to tug off my dress and replace it with a violet satin ballgown with silver trim. "I hope you're not too late," she said as she plopped me in front of the vanity to fuss with my hair. "I daresay the crown prince has danced with every eligible lady by now and has made his choice."

My lips twitched. He *had* made his choice, and it was me. I pressed my hand to my heart as if the gesture could keep my happiness from swelling to bursting.

Alaina had me readied in record time. Alastar awaited me outside the door. He gave me a shy half-smile that revealed he knew everything had worked out between me and Aiden. I returned it, mine full of giddy relief. How everything had changed. My bubbling joy along with the absence of worry felt wonderful.

He offered me his arm. "May I escort you, Princess Eileen?"

For the first time, the title no longer felt wrong, but a part of me. I accepted his arm and allowed him to lead me down to the gilded ballroom, swarming with crowds of nobility dressed in their finery, swaying to the soft, twirling music of a waltz.

I slipped inside and took in the glistening chandeliers casting golden patterns that danced across the marble floor. The flowers' perfume tickled my senses as I searched the room for Aiden. I didn't find him, but my gaze caught those of the king and Princess Seren sitting on a raised platform, glaring pointedly. I hastily looked away.

"There you are, Gemma." The Dracerian royalty bombarded me. Princess Elodie immediately looped her arm through mine. "Where have you been? We've been looking everywhere for you."

"Fashionably late, a genius tactic in this quest for the Dark Prince's hand," Prince Liam said with a wink. Princess Aveline frowned.

"She's far too late to be fashionable. Why, she arrived after Prince Deidric."

I wrinkled my nose at his formal name, even as my heart fluttered at her reference to my Aiden. "Where is the prince?" I returned to scanning the dance floor, crowded with waltzing couples.

"There." Princess Rheanna pointed towards Aiden, who was dancing with a noblewoman with gliding movements and the most proper of expressions, no emotion in his eyes—until he twirled his partner around and his gaze settled on me. He lit up and I smiled in return. We stared at one another for a beautiful moment before Aiden reluctantly tore his gaze away.

"Well, that was interesting." Prince Liam gave me a knowing look. "Do you two know each other?"

I smiled shyly. "Certainly. Prince Aiden and I are good friends."

"Prince *Aiden*?" Princess Elodie giggled. "He rarely gives anyone permission to use his middle name; he didn't even grant it to Rhea, and they were engaged for years."

Princess Rheanna blushed and lowered her eyes.

Prince Liam leaned in close with a cheeky grin. "It appears you've been cheating by meeting with the Dark Prince in secret. Another brilliant tactic."

Princess Elodie beamed. "Ooh, have you captured the Dark Prince's heart? I suppose that means he actually has a heart, doesn't it?"

Prince Liam rolled his eyes. "I don't understand all the rumors surrounding him. Am I right, Gemma?"

Gemma...now that the competition was over, at last I could tell them the truth. "I'm actually not Princess Gemma of Malvagaria. My name is Eileen. I'm a common girl from a tiny village. Aiden and I met and..." I shrugged.

They all stared at me in disbelief. Prince Liam reacted first, his face breaking into a wide grin. "Brilliant, absolutely brilliant. Sneaking into the Princess Competition to nab a prince for your husband? Genius." He winked and the tension that had been tightening my chest slowly eased.

Princess Aveline's nose wrinkled at me as if she now deemed me unworthy to stand in her presence, but Princess Rheanna offered a shy smile, and Princess Elodie once more looped her arm through mine. "How romantic. This entire competition makes more sense now." She bounced on her heels. "Look, the dance is ending. Perhaps Deidric will claim you for the next one?"

Aiden escorted his partner off the dance floor and immediately headed in our direction. Before he reached us, Princess Lavena intercepted him with an exaggerated curtsy. Disappointment and annoyance flashed across Aiden's expression before he reined his emotions back behind his rigid, polite mask. He bowed to Princess Lavena and led her onto the dance floor.

"Excellent." Prince Liam rubbed his hands together. "If I'm lucky enough, Lavena's *delightful* charm will win Aiden over."

Even though I didn't doubt his devotion, jealousy still flared in my heart, sharp and prickling, as I watched Princess Lavena's exaggerated smiles and coy expressions throughout their dance. Aiden's polite expression tightened in annoyance.

Throughout the dance, Prince Liam quietly chanted beside me. "Please pick her, please pick her, please pick her..."

As if he heard Prince Liam's pleas from across the room, Aiden glanced over with a raised eyebrow. Prince Liam clasped his hands together imploringly. Aiden smirked and subtly shook his head before his gaze slid to me, smoldering, causing my heart to flip-flop.

Princess Elodie sighed. "He's looking at you as if you're his other half. His choice has obviously been made; it appears the contest is over."

I grinned girlishly.

"As wonderful as Eileen is, I'm convinced it's Princess Lavena he wants," Prince Liam said, sounding pathetically desperate.

"Why would he want her when *you* don't?" Princess Aveline asked.

"While her only suitable match is a fellow ogre, I'm hoping Aiden has recently suffered a blow to the head that renders him temporarily insane."

"He's chosen Eileen. Isn't it obvious?" Princess Elodie's smile brightened as she leaned in close. "Do tell us how it happened."

"We met before the competition. We fell in love, but in order to be together, first he had to break off…" I warily eyed Princess Rheanna, whose eyes had lowered once more. I gently took her hands. "I'm so sorry I'm the cause of your broken engagement. I didn't mean to hurt you."

She took a long, wavering breath as she looked up. "I'm not mourning him, for I've never been in love with him. It's just…" She stared unseeing at Aiden dancing with Princess Lavena. "It's rather humiliating that I wasn't good enough for him."

Princess Elodie wrapped her arm around her sister just as the waltz came to an end. Aiden escorted Princess Lavena towards us.

"Liam, Princess Lavena was just telling me how eager she

is to dance with you next." His expression remained stoic while laughter filled his eyes.

Princess Lavena blanched and Prince Liam glared at him. "Unfortunately, I've already promised the next three dances to my dear sisters. Haven't I?" He gave each of them a pleading look. Princess Elodie giggled as she accepted his arm.

"Certainly, Liam." She stood on tiptoe towards his ear. "But you'll owe me a week's worth of desserts."

"For this rescue, make it a year's worth."

Princess Lavena—looking just as relieved as Prince Liam to have wriggled out of a dance with her intended—slipped away.

Aiden smiled warmly at me as he held his hand out. "You look beautiful, my dear. May I have this dance, Princess Eileen?" His grin broadened. "I could call you that forever."

I rested my hand in his and he pulled me towards him, wrapping his arms around me to hold me close, far closer than he'd held his previous partners, a gesture that announced I was his choice. I sensed everyone's gazes fixated on us and felt my face heat.

"Aiden, everyone is staring."

"Let them stare. They'll know by the end of the ball you're to be my queen, hence I see no reason to resist my affections for you just to keep it a secret for a bit longer." He pressed the tenderest kiss on my brow.

"Confident I won't change my mind, are you?"

He jerked back, eyes worried. "Have you?"

I immediately regretted my teasing. "Never, but I wouldn't object to you trying to persuade me during our dance. Perhaps you can pull faces to get me to smile."

He chuckled in relief and offered his arm. I took it and happily allowed him to escort me onto the dance floor. The stares of the crowd intensified, but my attention was only on

Aiden. The music began and we spun into a waltz. I immediately looked down at my feet, fearing I'd step on him.

"Keep your head raised," he whispered in my ear. "Trust your fiancé to lead you."

My heart warmed at the word, a word I had never thought would apply to me. I met his soft gaze. "We're really to be married, aren't we?"

"We are. Despite my frequent fears that our union would be impossible now there's nothing keeping us from being together forever."

With these beautiful words we melted into our dance, one that was magical and far too short. I noticed every touch and tender look from Aiden, the sensation of him playing with our clasped hands, and the adoration filling his eyes. I was aware of no one but him, even after the last notes of the music faded and our waltz slowed. Each spin on the dance floor reassured me that he was the correct path.

Aiden gave me an affectionate squeeze. "Are you ready?"

I nodded and allowed him to lead me to the two empty thrones on the raised platform. Aiden lifted my hand as he turned us to face the watching crowd. A hush settled over the nobility as they watched us with wide eyes. Aiden wordlessly helped me sit in the empty throne on the right while he took the one on the left.

As I settled against the soft cushions, my nerves melted away, replaced with a sense of calm, and I straightened with a confidence I'd never known. As much as I'd resisted the idea of being a princess, settling into the throne felt so...*right*, undoubtedly because of the man sitting beside me. How strange that I'd gone from a girl terrified of a future of romance to one who'd found it and now knew I couldn't live without it.

The king rose from his throne and cast me a long look before he forced a smile for the watching crowd. "My son,

His Royal Highness Crown Prince Deidric, has selected his bride. May I present the future crown princess of Sortileya, Princess Eileen."

My stomach fluttered as everyone bowed and curtsied. Aiden took my hand and gave it an assuring squeeze. I returned it. We smiled at one another and I basked in the love and adoration filling Aiden's eyes.

I was exactly where I belonged.

IT WAS a long time before we could slip away from the ball and its crowds of curious well-wishers. Our natural destination was the Forest, where we walked hand in hand, swinging our arms back and forth. It was hard to imagine that the last time we'd walked this road, only hours earlier, it was towards goodbyes and separation; now it only led to the promise of a bright future.

The canopy of branches had parted above to bathe us in silvery moonlight that illuminated the path, which opened up to the pink-blossomed clearing of the musical lake, Aiden's special place, now ours. The lake was aglow in the night and its soft, melodic tunes filled the perfume-shrouded air.

We settled on the bank, facing one another knee-to-knee. Aiden took my hands and held them securely between his. "It's time for my promised explanation, the one I should have given you long ago."

"About why you kept your identity a secret?"

He nodded and began playing with my fingers. "I felt no need to tell you who I really was when we first met in the Forest, though I had a strong compulsion to know who you were. After I realized I was falling in love with you during our picnic by the waterfall, I planned on waiting until I knew for certain that I could court you, since at the time I was still engaged."

He took a wavering breath and continued.

"The first night I visited you after you'd arrived at the palace, I fully intended to tell you everything—about who I was and why I'd enrolled you in the princess competition—but my plans shattered when you informed me you had no interest in being a princess."

He winced at the memory, as if the pain of that rejection was still fresh. I bit my lip guiltily.

"After I realized your feelings concerning the matter, I decided to wait a few days until you got used to the royal life in hopes you'd change your mind." He frowned. "Only you never seemed to."

I stroked his cheek in apology. "It would have been easier to accept if I knew you were the prince whose hand I was trying to win."

He smiled wryly. "I considered that, but I was afraid that if you knew, you'd think I was foisting my title on you and that you'd be afraid of denying my affections, making it diffi-cult for you to say no to a prince who was in love with you. I also feared that knowing who I truly was would make it harder for you to be yourself; I didn't want you to change around me or pull away. What if you thought you didn't deserve me due to our vastly different stations and decided that the noble thing would be to step aside so I could choose a real princess?"

As I searched the vulnerability filling his eyes, any lingering wounded feelings for his keeping his secret for so long faded away. He'd only done it to protect me and our relationship, especially while it was still a fragile bud, not yet blossomed, as it was now.

Aiden's hold on my hands tightened. "I didn't consider any of these thoughts when I first broke off my engagement and asked the Forest to bring you to the competition; I just saw it as the path for us to be together. I thought I was doing the right thing keeping it from you...until I saw how distressed you were in my world, how much my secrecy was hurting you, which caused me to believe you'd be happier returning to your simple life and remaining outside my world of royalty."

Understanding filled me. "That's why you decided to take me home. You didn't want me to feel intimated or choose you out of obligation."

He nodded. "I thought I was being noble and sacrificing, but now I realize I wasn't motivated by what I thought was best for you, but rather my own fears that you wouldn't want the true me. By my refusing to tell you who I was, I wasn't protecting you like I'd convinced myself; I was deceiving you and taking away your opportunity to decide for yourself what life you wanted. For that I'm sorry."

I searched his eyes, full of sweet sincerity and love, and smiled in forgiveness. "You were only trying to do what you thought was best. I can't fault you for your choices, especially considering they're in the past. We're together now."

"We are. I love you, Eileen. I want to spend the rest of my life with you."

I closed my eyes and basked in his words. He loved me, truly loved me, and nothing could sway me from our chosen course...except for one final fear, a new one that had emerged after learning his true identity.

I lowered my eyes to our intertwined hands. "But you're right about one thing: you're a prince and I'm nothing but a mere commoner."

He ran his knuckles along my cheekbone, his eyes full of such incredible tenderness when I peeked back up at him. "There's nothing common about you, my Eileen."

"But you've had to help me through every single task to prove myself worthy to be your bride. If it weren't for you—"

"Eileen dear, please listen to me." His expression became very serious. "Those tasks weren't my criteria for the woman I want as my wife but were dictated by my father. I don't care whether my wife has proper decorum, knows the royal histories, or can dance at a ball. None of that matters. I had my own process of selecting the woman to entrust my heart to."

"You did?"

He nodded and continued stroking my cheek with such gentleness I was certain I'd melt. "I found everything I was looking for in you. During the first task, you possessed the grace to extend forgiveness after I'd involved you in this competition; this grace of spirit and tenderness of heart means more to me than whether or not you walk with any. And when you drew your portrait, it showed me you look beyond the surface to see people for who they truly are, a trait that will be invaluable as my future queen."

Tears trickled down my cheeks, but I made no move to wipe them away, so Aiden did, an act which only made me cry harder.

"The second task showed me not only your intelligence but your resilience and determination to work hard. Even when you feel lost and overwhelmed you push forward, no matter the difficulties, and always remain true to yourself."

As I continued to cry, Aiden leaned forward to kiss away my tears, and my heart cracked open further.

"In the third task, I learned just how fragile your heart is and how much I'll need to take care of it. But I will. I promise, Eileen." As he spoke, he withdrew my locket I'd given him as the second payment. "When you gave me this, you began to let go of your past. It gave me hope that together we can move forward into the future."

He carefully clasped the locket around my neck, but unlike when I'd worn it before, it was no longer heavy. I opened it and cradled the heart-shaped pendant in my palm; I smiled to see that not only did it contain Father's portrait, but now Aiden's as well.

I raised my gaze to his before leaning over and pressing a soft kiss to his cheek. "Thank you, Aiden."

"Have I assured you of your precious worth?" he asked.

"You have, but I'm still uncertain about our future." I nibbled my lip. "Marrying you will make me Sortileya's future queen." My stomach knotted. "Aiden, I can't be queen."

"I know you feel intimidated now," he said gently. "But that won't happen for many years. You'll have plenty of time to grow into the role."

I took a wavering breath. "I'll require many more late nights of your helping me to make me queen material."

He pressed several soft kisses along my knuckles. "You're already equal to the task. You possess the essential character-istics of a future queen. You're a true princess in spirit, and thus everything else will come." He flashed a mischievous smirk. "But be that as it may, I'll still gladly help you all you like...for a price."

I giggled. "What sort of price do you have in mind?"

"While you have everything to offer me, including a life-time of happiness, I wouldn't say no to another kiss."

I laughed and he joined in as he helped me to my feet. He hooked his arms around my waist and nestled me close. I stood on tiptoe. "That's a price I'll gladly pay anytime."

His hands wove through my hair as he leaned down to kiss me, far more earnestly than his others had been, yet the kiss was still so soft, so gentle, so many beautiful things. When we broke away, I saw reflected in his adoring eyes so many promises, promises I now allowed myself to believe, another confirmation that the path chosen by my heart was the right one for me.

We entwined our hands and he led me down a path that opened up at his silent command. Even though we walked away from the rosy glow of the lake into the darkness of the night, I trusted Aiden and the Forest to take us where we needed to be.

Which reminded me.... "You really asked the Forest to lead me to the palace for the Princess Competition?"

He gave me a guilty smile. "I couldn't very well have the woman I loved absent from the quest for my hand."

"Why does the Forest obey you?"

He affectionately patted a maple as we passed. "They're loyal to their prince. But despite their allegiance to me, they love you the most."

We approached the edge of the trees, which opened enough to show a glimpse of the palace, its windows lit with glowing lanterns. The single path wriggled before us before splitting into two, one leading to the palace and the other snaking deeper into the Forest in the opposite direction.

Aiden squeezed my hand. "Which shall we take?"

I didn't even need to study the two diverting pathways to know the answer. While the Forest had initially forcibly led me to the Sortileyan Palace and the competition that illuminated my true feelings for Aiden, the choice to return was up to me, and that decision had already been made.

I tugged Aiden down the path leading to the palace. "This one."

Together we walked it to an unknown but undoubtedly beautiful future.

EPILOGUE

I stood in front of the tall, gilded mirror, staring in awe at my reflection. I scarcely recognized myself dressed in my white gown of silk and lace, my dark hair arranged in an elegant updo woven with pearls that matched the jewelry adorning my ears and neck. I looked exactly like a princess. Alaina fussed with my appearance, making sure my dress was just right.

Mother came up behind me to rest her chin on my shoulder, which she gave an affectionate squeeze. "You look beautiful, dear."

"I never imagined I'd ever find myself dressed in a wedding gown, mere minutes away from marrying the love of my life."

"I kept telling you over and over that one day you would." Rosie appeared in the mirror behind me to help hook my lacy veil in my hair. "Everyone has a happy ending, including you. To think yours includes an actual prince..." She sighed contently. "It's the most magical ending imaginable."

I smiled. "I don't care that he's a prince, just that he's *my* prince." The words sounded foreign on my lips, for they were ones the old Eileen never would have spoken. But that was the wonderful thing about journeys: they had a way of changing oneself.

Rosie stood back to survey her handiwork and gave a nod of approval. "Stunning. You deserve nothing less on the first day of your happily ever after."

Mother's beam grew as she took in my appearance, admiration shining in her eyes. "This is what I've always wanted. I'm so happy for you, dear. Your father would be so proud of you."

I took a deep, wavering breath, allowing the ache his absence in my life had caused to fill me again. Aiden had informed me only a few days previous that he'd finally received the results of an investigation into Father's fate that he'd been conducting ever since the night I'd given him my necklace: while on his way home, Father had succumbed to a terrible illness that had swept through the capital, which meant he'd been on the road to return to us at the time of his death.

While the knowledge was healing for both me and Mother, it still left an ache in my heart, one that would likely always be there, but the pain was different now. I knew my love for Aiden and for my family and friends would help heal not only that hole but those I didn't even know I had.

"I miss him," I told her. How he would have loved the adventure I found myself in.

"I miss him, too. But he loved us. And Aiden loves you."

"And he won't ever leave." I'd said the words countless times since choosing to trust my heart to him. Making the decision hadn't made all my fears, insecurities, or pains go away completely, but it had brought new emotions I'd never expected in the years I'd fought against this future—peace, contentment, fierce joy, and love—always love.

A knock on the door pierced my reminiscing. Before Alaina could move to open it, I rushed over to fling it open myself, ignoring her usual mutterings about not allowing myself to be waited upon properly. I could do without the royal nonsense of servants and protocol, but I couldn't live without my prince, who stood outside the door dressed in his own regal finery.

His black eyes widened and his mouth fell agape. For a moment he merely stared before he stepped into the room and put his arms around my waist.

"My princess." He leaned down and kissed my brow. The moment he pulled away I stood on tiptoe to place my own kiss on the tip of his nose.

"My prince."

My favorite crooked grin lit up his face. "I still can't believe my good fortune." He pressed the tenderest kiss on my lips, leaving me no doubts as to his affections.

Aiden pulled away and stared into my eyes with such an affectionate look that I felt incredibly adored. "It's bad luck to see your bride before the wedding," I said. He chuckled.

"I simply couldn't wait to hold you in my arms once more." After another kiss—this one on the top of my head—he looped my arm through his. "Shall I escort you to our wedding, my dear?"

I gave his arm an affectionate squeeze before turning to Mother and Rosie, both watching me with tears of happiness and wide smiles. I hadn't seen Mother so happy since our tearful reunion after Aiden arranged for her to come to the palace to find me safe and sound. My happily ever after truly seemed like the most beautiful of fairy tales, just like Rosie and the stories we'd read together had always promised it would be.

They followed as Aiden escorted me to the grand ballroom, where we became husband and wife. As we gave our vows and sealed our union with another kiss, I knew that whatever obstacles lay in our future, we'd overcome them together, for Aiden was not only the right path for me but the one I'd continue to choose forever.

THANK YOU

Thank you for allowing me to share one of my beloved stories with you! If you'd like to be informed of new releases, please visit me at my website www.camillepeters.com to sign up for my newsletter, see my release plans, and read deleted scenes—as well as a scene written from Aiden's POV.

I love to connect with readers! You can find me on Goodreads or on my Facebook Page.

If you loved my story, I'd be honored if you'd share your thoughts with me and others by leaving a review on Amazon or Goodreads. Your support is invaluable. Thank you.

Coming Soon: Rosie's story, *Spelled*, inspired by *The Frog Prince*.

ACKNOWLEDGMENTS

I'm so incredibly grateful for all the wonderful people who've supported me throughout my writing adventures.

First, to my incredible mother, who's worn many hats over the years: from teaching me to read as a toddler; to recognizing my love and talent for writing and supporting it through boundless encouragement and hours of driving me back and forth to classes to help nourish my budding skills; to now being my muse, brainstorm buddy, beta-reader, editor, and my biggest cheerleader and believer of my dreams. I truly wouldn't be where I am without her and am so grateful for God's tender mercy in giving me such a mother.

Second, to my family: my father, twin brother Cliff, and darling sister Stephanie. Your love, belief in me, and your eager willingness to read my rough drafts and help me develop my stories has been invaluable. Words cannot express how much your support has meant to me.

Third, to my publishing team: my incredible editor, Jana Miller, whose talent, insights, and edits have helped my stories blossom into their potential; Karri Klawiter, whose talent designed the most beautiful book cover I could have ever dreamed of; and Kathy Habel, who helped me market so I could share my story with readers.

Fourth, to my wonderful beta readers: my dear Grandma, Charla Stewart, Alesha Adamson, Emma Miller, and Jessica Anderson. I'm so grateful for your wonderful insights and suggestions that gave my story the last bit of polish in order to make it the best it can be. In addition, I'd like to thank all my ARC readers, who were so willing to give my book a chance and share their impressions. Thank you.

Fifth, to my Grandparents, whose invaluable support over the years has helped my dreams become a reality.

Last but not least, I'd like to thank my beloved Heavenly Father, who has not only given me my dreams, talent, and the opportunities to achieve them, but who loves me unconditionally, always provides inspiration whenever I turn to Him for help, gives me strength to push through whatever obstacles I face, and has sanctified all my efforts to make them better than my own.

ABOUT THE AUTHOR

Camille Peters was born and raised in Salt Lake City, Utah where she grew up surrounded by books. As a child, she spent every spare moment reading and writing her own stories on every scrap of paper she could find. Becoming an author was always more than a childhood dream; it was a certainty.

Her love of writing grew alongside her as she took local writing classes in her teens, spent a year studying Creative Writing at the English University of Northampton, and graduated from the University of Utah with a degree in English and History. She's now blessed to be a full-time author.

When she's not writing she's thinking about writing, and when's she's not thinking about writing she's...alright, she's always thinking about writing, but she can also be found reading, playing board games with her family and friends, or taking long, bare-foot walks as she lives inside her imagination and brainstorms more tales.

Made in the USA
San Bernardino, CA
11 March 2019